KA'ALA

ENCHANTED HAWAI'I COLLECTION
BOOK THREE

LEIALOHA HUMPHERYS

HŌKŪLANI
PRESS

This book is a work of fiction. Any references to historical events, real
people, or real places are used fictitiously. Other names, characters, places,
and events are products of the author's imagination, and any resemblances to
actual events or places or persons, living or dead, is entirely coincidental.

First paperback edition October 2022

ISBN (paperback) 978-1-7378074-9-0

ISBN (ebook) 978-1-959157-00-7

Published by Hokulani Press

Santaquin, Utah

United States of America

www.naturallyaloha.com

 Created with Vellum

This book is dedicated to those who protect the innocent and fight for God's truth in their communities. Please keep doing what you do. The world needs brave souls like you.

HAWAIIAN

KAUAI

NIʻIHAU

OʻAHU

LANAI

Shipwreck Beach

Polihua Beach

Keahiakawelo

Lanaʻihale

Kaumalapaau Harbor

Waiakeakua

Lopa

Naha

Spouting Cave

Manele Bay

Kaunolu Town

Puʻu Pehe (Sweetheart Rock)

Hulopoʻe Bay

PREFACE

He la koa, he la heʻe.
A day to be brave, a day to flee.
A Hawaiian proverb that means there is triumph and
defeat, winning and losing, and ups and downs in life.

CHAPTER ONE

*M*ailou, the old bounty hunter who stalked my shadow, was back... and with him, the possibility that I could get crushed in his arms. It wasn't the crushing that scared me though. It was the fact that if he tried to hurt me, I could hurt *him* in self defense.

After all, I was not trained to kill. I was trained to protect.

And that included myself.

It was a hot day when I spotted Mailou amongst the people arriving in large canoes. He was easy to see, being the tallest of everyone on board the canoe. His graying hairs and hardened facial features were distinct from others too, as he was a descendant of the Nawao, the ancient race of giants.

Fishermen from Lahaina in Maui, merchants from Oʻahu, and other wayfarers came to the shores, keeping the Lanai boat inspectors busy this morning.

I shuddered, wondering if Mailou accomplished his quest. Not long ago, a thief stole goods from the local chief of Lanai. Mailou and Akamu, his young apprentice of sorts, took on the task of pursuing the thief.

Akamu wanted nothing but acceptance into the creed, an ancient group of secrecy on Lanai, now since dispersed.

Meanwhile, Mailou wanted me.

The Lanai chief asked my father, Oponui, for permission, and, much to my dismay, my father agreed.

As if sensing someone watching him, Mailou looked straight at me. His dark eyes held nothing but evil. I stepped back into the shadows of the palms, then turned and hurried away. I had only a few minutes to make my escape and avoid Mailou, though I didn't doubt he'd follow my every move, just as he did before he left. Where his obsession and stalking of me came from, I didn't know. All I knew was that I needed to watch my back at all times.

Everyone suspected Mailou to be a brute and murderer, but nobody could truly confirm it. He had two previous wives, but they mysteriously disappeared. The bounty hunter claimed they ran away from him, but rumors circulated that Mailou crushed them in his arms and cast their bones into the sea. The fishermen swore they saw the sharks feeding on the debris.

My stomach tightened.

Was Mailou holding anything in his hands? Not that I saw. Was there a chance that Mailou failed his quest? And where was Akamu?

I'll find out soon enough. Gossip spread like wildfire on our small island of Lanai. No visitor, stranger, or local went by unnoticed around here. Everyone was into everyone else's business. And though I tried to keep myself and my operations undercover, some people still knew what I actually did in secret.

I hurried along the shores of Hulopo'e bay, hoping to trade some kapa, a homemade cloth made from the wauke plant, for fresh catch from the fishermen. They usually stood along the reefs, casting their nets into the ocean.

But as I walked along the shore, scanning the shallow reefs, I frowned. The fishermen were not there, as they must have gone to greet the strangers and visitors on the canoes that morning. It wasn't uncommon, but I sighed impatiently.

I had too much work to do today. The *Makahiki,* a time of peace and celebration, had just ended, so people were returning to their normal trade routes and voyages. And soon, people would return to Hana, the place where King Hua gathered his armies to wage a bloody war against Kohala of the Big Island.

The reason I'm doing all of this... Yes, the wars were the reason I was out here, looking for the fishermen, and trying to gather food to provide meals for the next couple of days.

My older brother, Kona, would arrive today. But he wouldn't come alone... and I needed to be prepared.

Maybe I'll just look for limu or 'opihi, I thought, knowing that I needed to get some kind of food. I figured that by the time I finished looking, the fishermen would return.

As I stepped along the reef carefully, so as to avoid stepping on any *wana* (sea urchin), the sticky, salty air brushed my skin. The waves breaking along the reefs caused warm, humid mist.

The sound of splashes caught my attention and I paused.

I learned to respect the ocean, and the creatures within. If there was a *manō,* shark, nearby or some other ocean life,

I wanted to give it some space. Sometimes large ocean creatures got snagged in the fishermen's nets, and I didn't want to encounter something that might attack me.

As I stepped closer to the splashing, I blinked hard.

It was no dolphin, no shark, not even a fish. Bright, teal-colored scales cast blinding reflections all around. I squinted, wondering if I was dreaming.

It's no dream...

Long, sun-kissed hair, the most flawless tanned skin, and a body with a multi-colored tail on the end bashed against the reef.

"Let me help you!" I said, pulling a knife from my bag.

The mermaid stopped moving and glared up at me, her teal eyes piercing, yet full of mystery, like the sea.

"Are you the fisher who put this net here?" she asked, her voice deep and confident as the ocean.

"No, but I'm so sorry this happened to you." I truly was. The fishermen were rumored to occasionally find mermaids around the island. When they did, they killed the mermaids and tossed them to the sharks.

"Mermaids are dangerous creatures," the fishermen warned the rest of us islanders.

I stepped closer to her, cautious as ever, in case she grabbed and tossed me into the ocean. Though I took people's skepticism with little worries, now all the rumors of mermaids came to life in my head: *they drag people to the depths and drown them. Their voices lure people to the deep, where they never return.* The list went on and on.

But I never hesitated to help someone in danger, and I wouldn't stop now.

"The fishermen don't usually put their nets on this side," I said, now crouching and cutting the nets entangled around her body.

"That's what I thought too," the mermaid said, then rolled her eyes. "Maybe it was a new fisherman or something."

"Maybe." I glanced at her, finding that cuts lined her arms and gashes covered her scale covered body. "Are you alright?" I asked.

"I'm fine. Just annoyed that this happened. This never happens."

I nodded. "We'll get you out of here, don't worry."

The mermaid let out a grunting noise, like a sound of disdain. "You're not going to kill me?" she asked. "I know the people of Lanai. I know these fishermen. I've listened to them. All they can talk about is killing a mermaid"

She wasn't wrong. In fact, many of the fishermen had mouths that ran wild, with nothing to restrain them. I pursed my lips, the ocean water now drenching my feet, hands, and arms.

"Well I'm not like them."

"You're all the same, you Lanai people."

"I wasn't trained to kill," I said, feeling stern as I looked at the mermaid. "I was trained to protect."

Her eyes narrowed at me. "You must be Ka'ala."

I returned my attention to the net. Most everyone on the island knew me (or knew *of* me), so it wasn't surprising that the mermaid heard gossip about me... though there wasn't much to gossip about. The people who knew my true secret kept it a secret.

"I'm Moana," said the mermaid. I pulled the rest of the net loose and hung it on the reef. Whoever cast the net here was in for a surprise. A ripped or broken net would take time to fix.

Moana pushed against the rocks and stretched her long

tail. "You really are brave," she added, then bowed her head. "I am indebted to you."

"No, it's fine."

"If you ever find yourself in a dire situation, you can call my name. I will hear it, because the ocean will tell me you are calling."

I tipped my head. "There is no payment—"

"Keep up the great work," Moana said, now smiling, the first I saw on her face. "The people of Lanai—and the people of Maui and Kohala—need you more than you know."

Before I could say something or ask any questions about how she knew of my underground operations, she leaped into the air. Her teal-scaled body reflected rainbows on the water's surface, then she dove into the water, disappearing forever.

AFTER THE STRANGE encounter with the mermaid, I scoured the reef for limu and opihi. I found a good amount, enough to feed a family or more. Much to my annoyance, however, the fishermen didn't return to their nets before I finished.

Keeping a close eye on the shadows, in case Mailou stalked me, I then made my way back to the canoes. I planned on trading with the fishermen then hurrying back to my home to make additional preparations.

I never knew who my brother would bring by.

With no Mailou in sight, I hurried to the canoes. Many were large enough to ferry passengers and goods from other islands. But one canoe caught my eye. It had bright red sails, and was much smaller than the other canoes. It made me suspicious.

Red was the color of *ali'i*, royalty. Was King Hua of

Hana here? Or perhaps he sent someone to do his dirty work, like collect taxes, demand volunteers for war, or some other ridiculous task to aid in his endless wars against Kohala on the Big Island.

I spotted the group of Lanai fishermen ahead, their laughter and chatter filling the air as they conversed with visitors and strangers.

I have to hurry. My little sister, Melika, and I still had to get the beds ready, prepare the meal, and make sure everything was in order before Kona's arrival.

"I'll take that."

The voice startled me and I turned to see a young man standing to the side of the royal canoe, a long leiomano, shark tooth knife, in his hand. A servant, or what looked like a servant because of his young age, passed the weapon to the person who spoke.

The speaker was taller than me, with a royal yellow kihei across his chest. His dark, wavy hair was pulled back, but strands fell out on all sides, giving him an annoyingly effortless look. White scars ran all across his body, not something uncommon to see nowadays, as many men were wounded and scarred from the bloody war.

There was something weird about one side of his face, as though it had been wounded and since healed. I didn't want to stare to identify what happened. Many men who returned from the war came home with deformities, including my own father, who limped wherever he went, and my older brother, who walked with a crutch because of the loss of a leg.

Because I was startled as I passed his canoe, the young man glanced at me. It was just a glance, but, as if everything went in slow motion, he did a double take.

Our eyes met, and he gaped. I looked away, feeling a

blush start up my cheeks, shyness overcoming me. I could feel him studying me, and I made sure to avoid any eye contact. But avoiding eye contact did nothing to remove the curious look he gave me, one I was too afraid to explore.

Once I passed him and his canoe, I couldn't resist a peek back.

He smiled wide at me, like I said something that made him happy. My heart skipped a beat and my blood pumped faster.

He smiled at me. A smile crawled up my own lips and I turned before it spread across my cheeks.

I still couldn't figure out what happened to the man's face, but he was quite handsome, regardless.

He works for the king. Don't pay him any attention, I cautioned myself.

I looked ahead, vowing not to bother with the young man. Anyone associated with or working for King Hua I secretly considered to be an enemy.

After all, King Hua was to blame for everything, including all the people I kept hidden in my home: the refugees and sacrifices fleeing from the king and the war. It was said that King Hua of Hana waged wars against Kohala because the priests prophesied it was his to claim and rule. He had a hundred hula dancers and monthly feasts with limitless amounts of kava and nights of debauchery. Rumors spread that no woman was safe around him, and would be seized for him or his favorite captains, royals, and priests.

My stomach tightened at the thought of the king, and an opportunity, a few years ago, that slipped through my fingers.

I could have ended these wars.

I realized that the young man was still watching me. I

blushed at the recollection of his double take and the way it made my heart skip. It was quite charming. I shook my head, as if shaking away the thoughts. The only reason the double take made me smile was because no man had ever done that to me before.

CHAPTER TWO

*A*fter trading with some fishermen, I hurried up the path to my hut. I lived deep in Waiakeakua, surrounded by lush ferns and tall trees. It was the perfect, secluded place to keep people hidden and safe.

A soft breeze blew through the palm trees, keeping the island cool and comfortable. My feet barely made any noise on the dirt path. I learned to walk in silence, and trained myself to always be alert. Every suspicious shadow, creaking of a tree, or bird call made me check my surroundings.

The people of Lanai never bothered to climb the steep hill to my home, but with Mailou back, I couldn't be certain of anything. Who knew if he'd come to my home to hurt me? He'd never tried it before, but I was on high alert now. Because what if he succeeded? He'd probably come to carry me off as his wife this very day.

My stomach knotted at this. I'd have to wait and see.

"There you are!" Melika rushed down the hill to help me carry things. "The beds are ready and the *imu* should be just about done," she said. Melika, my younger sister, was fifteen years old. Though we were sisters, I took on all the strangest features from my parents, while she had a natural beauty and grace.

Everything about her was stunningly dark: rich brown skin smoother than a coconut shell, dark brown eyes, straight hair black as midnight, and dark lips.

I was the opposite: freckles covering my entire light brown skin, sunrise colored eyes, wavy hair a brown color that bordered on *ehu* (a reddish color caused by the sun), and coral lips.

Not to mention I was quite short, so Melika stood a little taller than me.

"Ua left about an hour ago," Melika said, chatty as ever. Ua was my best friend since childhood, and another help in running my sanctuary. "Did you see anyone interesting at the shores this morning?"

The double take of the young man flashed through my mind. I ignored it.

"Mailou is back."

Melika gasped. "No!" She almost dropped the bundle in her hands.

"Careful with those–"

"Don't tell me he had the thief–don't say it! Ka'ala, we have to hide you... now!"

We were about as different in our appearances as we were in personality: Melika was loud, young, and outgoing. I was quiet, preferred to be alone, and shy. But despite our differences, I loved my sister. Dearly. She and Ua were my best friends, and they trusted me–sometimes more than I trusted myself.

I was completely in charge of all the rescue operations. I told Melika, Ua, and Kona where to go, what to do, and, so far, my secret remained a secret.

The memory of the mermaid resurfaced and I pursed

my lips. Moana knew about my operations too, meaning rumors spread to even the mermaids. But she, like many others, kept quiet about it.... Because I was doing a good deed, and if word about it got out, the king of Hana would definitely come after me.

"I didn't see Mailou carrying anything though."

"Kona will visit father tonight and ask," Melika said. "But we'll keep you far away from father and that bounty hunter, understand?"

I gave her a side look, both annoyed and grateful for her help. She giggled, knowing what my look meant.

Don't tell me what to do.

"Sorry." She nudged me with her elbow. "I'm just worried, alright?"

"I know." I gave her a reassuring nod and we reached the hut by then. It was unlike any other hut on the island. In fact, I paid Mailou's apprentice (or whatever he was), Akamu, to build it when he wasn't employed in his bounty hunter duties.

Akamu was incredibly tall, strong, and good with his hands. He didn't mind getting paid with some delicious, hot meals, something he probably didn't get often. Ua was a wondrous cook, and Akamu got the hut and fence built in less than a week. What he didn't know, however, was that I added my own devices later: barriers of protection, warning sounds, and more.

Melika held open the gate and I glanced at the 'ohi'a fence that surrounded the hut. It was the first barrier of protection. Only a fool would dare climb over the 'ohi'a, because if one looked closely, there were small, carved wood spikes placed all along the top of the fence.

"Mahalo," I said and stepped past Melika, walking up

the few steps that led to the porch. The creaking sound on the first step was loud, just as I intended it to be.

The second step bent a little under my weight, and it pulled a string under it. The string, though hidden, was connected to bamboo chimes, hanging nearby. The string caused the bamboo chimes to clash against each other, making yet another loud, distinct noise. I nodded, always pleased that my devices worked as they should.

The porch floor squeaked under each of my footsteps until I walked into the hut. Passing the door frame of the hut, however, I moved aside coral and shell stringed hangings. They made clicking sounds against one another.

Melika stepped directly behind me, as there were certain places in the main living area of the hut that had traps. Yes. Wood traps that snapped or clamped down on one's ankles. We always directed our guests where they could and couldn't step, and, so far, nobody had gotten hurt.

People who broke in, however rare that was long ago, got hurt in the traps, and never returned.

Melika and I placed the food on some banana leaves in the corner of the living room and then I brushed my skirt off before making my way to the back room, directly behind the living room. No huts had been built like mine before–it was genius of its own. Akamu had been skillful and carried out every one of my requests.

One of the requests was that the bedroom have a large sliding door.

"Nobody has doors," he had said, giving me a weird look. But I insisted on it, so he did it. I now slid the door to the side, and it made a low, growling noise. Of course I intended the door to be that way, as it was yet another warning noise.

"It's perfect, thank you for setting these up," I said to Melika, now looking at all the fresh kapa beds spread around the room. There had to be at least ten of them, though we usually had no more than four or five people here at a time.

Melika smiled, pleased with her efforts. I lived here for several years, alone, until she moved in with me. It was refreshing to have her here, and, mostly, I was grateful she had distance from our sickly mother and controlling father.

After our mother got sick, my father, Oponui, wanted to send me to Lahaina to live with distant relatives. I didn't want to be far from Melika, worried that something might happen to her (father marrying her off too young, bounty hunters going after her, or something else). So I asked if I could live, secluded in the highest part of Lanai. My father granted my wish.

I paid the local chief for the land with my lei and kapa making skills. Meanwhile, I stayed with Ua at her home, gifted by her late grandfather, until I had the means to pay Akamu to build the largest, most unique hut on Lanai.

"Did the brush grow back?" I asked, stepping towards the large back window. Windows were another thing huts didn't normally have, but, with Akamu's skill and my ideas, we made it possible.

"Most of it." Melika stood next to me and we glanced at the thick ferns growing outside the window. The ferns and brush were grown there on purpose, in case someone needed to hide outside the hut in a hurry, or if we had to clear the room and stow things away. A heavy windstorm smashed most of the brush, but it looked normal and thick now.

"Anyway, we should get working on that imu," Melika said, heading out the front door. I followed and we got to work removing the hot, heavy stones from the fire pit in the ground.

We had barely uncovered the food when Ua raced up the hill, fresh kapa in her hands, and gourds of water hanging from strings around her shoulders.

The smoky smell of burnt banana leaves, combined with the salty pork, earthy laulau, and taro, filled the air.

"Smells amazing!" Ua said, dropping the gourds by the porch and approaching us. People said Ua and I looked like twins. We both had the same build, same skin color, and almost the same eyes... except I was covered in freckles, and she was not.

Ua and I weren't related but had been best friends since childhood. Her grandfather, Lile, taught us both the art of *lua*, the art of fighting and war. And, of course, it wasn't for the purpose of killing, but to protect ourselves and others.

Many people did not know I possessed the skills I did, and I hoped nobody would ever have to know.

"I have news!" Ua said, out of breath.

"About Mailou?" Melika asked, pausing to listen. I gave her a look and we continued pulling the food out of the pit while Ua spoke.

"'Ae." She let out a big breath. "Ka'ala, you're safe!"

"What?" At this, I stopped what I was doing. "What do you mean?"

"He failed." Ua and Melika burst out in laughter and cheers. Ua looked like she would explode. "Ka'ala, he didn't get the thief. He didn't get any of the chief's treasures either." Ua clapped her hands.

I sat back, stunned. *The gods are watching over me.* Looking at the sky, I thanked them. I thanked my ancestors. And I thanked whoever else had stopped Mailou from bringing back the thief or the treasures. Did Akamu have something to do with it? I was spared this time.

"Nobody knows *how* Mailou failed. And nobody knows what happened to Akamu." Ua shrugged. "I'm sure we'll hear all sorts of rumors in the next weeks." She continued, "But the main thing is that you aren't forced to marry that cruel man!" Ua and Melika celebrated while I remained in place.

Spared. I was lucky this time. And so was Mailou. I wouldn't be forced to hurt him in my own self defense.

"No emotions, as always," Melika said, nudging me. She continued pulling food from the pit and Ua jumped in to help. "What else Ua?"

"We need to be careful because a king's man is here."

I almost piped in that I saw him, but I remembered the young man's double take and thought better of it. I didn't need Melika to tease me about it.

"Do we know who he is?" I asked instead.

"He's one of King Hua's captains. He hasn't told anyone for sure why he's here, but he has made it clear that he is doing an inspection of everyone and everything here on Lanai."

"Why?" Melika asked.

"Beats me. I'm sure we'll hear all the rumors about it soon enough." Ua let out a yelp as she dropped a wrapped bundle of laulau. "That's hot! I don't know how you ladies do it."

"Says the best cook around," Melika said with a grin. Ua rolled her eyes. Though she had a special touch to all the food she made, she did not have tough hands like Melika and I.

"Do we know his name?" I asked, motioning for the girls to follow me and bring the food into the hut. The kalua pig and laulau, wrapped in thick banana leaves, were ready to serve, but we'd have to pound the taro into poi. And since Kona tried to dock onto the shore late at night, long after the commotion died, we had to keep the food warm.

Ua shook her head. "Didn't hear it, but I'm sure we will soon."

"Any other gossip?" Melika asked. She was the only one that didn't go often to the shores. It was better for me, as I didn't have to worry about her being around the fishermen or creed members (when they were here). Melika kept the hut tidy, washing the kapa bedding in the nearby river, making food, weaving lauhala, making kapa, and keeping the house.

Meanwhile, Ua and I moved about, keeping an eye on the canoes for Kona, my brother, or Nai'a, another young woman part of our rescue efforts. We traded and bartered for goods that would serve our refugees.

"There were some girls on the shore looking forward to Kona's return," Ua said, and frowned at this. "It seems that everyone has been interested in him since he came back from war."

"Because he's the only eligible bachelor around," Melika said, placing hot taro on a large stone slab sitting at the side of the hut. It was true. My older brother, Kona, was back from war because he lost a leg. Luckily he survived, but he used a crutch to get around, and so was not fit to go to battle again. And because all the other young, eligible men were not eligible until the war ended, Kona was quite the catch.

"I suppose." Ua still frowned, but when she met my eyes, she shook her head, as if clearing her thoughts. "Anyway, we need to keep an eye out for him. If he doesn't get here late enough, there may be a group of young women eagerly waiting to greet him."

"There are always young women eagerly waiting to greet him," Melika said. "You two." It was supposed to be funny, but Ua sighed and I bit my lower lip.

"Oh you're no fun. Come on, let's do this," Melika said, and we joined her in pounding the taro into thick, purple poi. All the while, my thoughts went to the king's man, the "inspector." What was he doing? What was he "inspecting?"

I glanced at Ua, who had gone unusually quiet. And what was she thinking about?

CHAPTER THREE

arkness covered the sky over Lanai. Ua huddled in a bush a distance away from me, keeping watch for anyone who might sneak up behind us. Meanwhile, I crouched close to the shore, my feet planted in the sand as I scanned the horizon for Kona's canoe. A lauhala bag hung from my side, with a few fruits (in case anyone on Kona's boat needed food now), kapa wrappings for wounds, and an extra knife, for safety.

Quiet as ever, Ua approached. "Coast is clear as far as I can see."

"No women eagerly waiting for his arrival?" I teased and she rolled her eyes.

"Not that I saw."

The moonlight sparkled on the water of Hulopo'e bay. The smell of salt and brine filled the air. The gentle waves lapped on the shore.

I glanced at the canoes lined up along the shoreline, noticing that the canoe of the king's inspector remained. It meant that the young man who did a double take earlier that day was probably sticking around for a little while.

I told myself I'd worry about it later, because he knew nothing of me, and I didn't need to draw unnecessary attention to myself. King Hua and all of his men were bad news. The king was the reason I was here, hiding with Ua, and waiting for Kona to show up.

"There he is," Ua whispered, pointing to a speck in the distance. Kona had always been an expert wayfinder, learning from a grandmaster, Nai'a's grandfather. How he navigated in the night was beyond me, but I appreciated his skill.

Even more so, I appreciated his willingness to help me with my plot. When he came home from the war, nearly bleeding to death, I told him everything. I wanted to be honest with him before he died. But he survived, and he vowed to help me rescue as many people as possible from King Hua's wicked clutches.

Ua and I waited with extreme patience, our eyes focused on the canoe silently drifting to the shore. I kept glancing around, in case someone else rushed out to greet Kona. My heart pounded in my ears. Who would Kona bring this time? Wounded warriors from Kohala? Endangered citizens from Hana? People brought to the king's high priest for human sacrifices?

"Let's go," Ua said, once the canoe hit the sand. We hurried from the hiding place, our feet making no noise, until we stepped into the water. As we pulled the ropes of the canoe, docking it on the shore, Kona jumped off the boat, a bundle in his hand.

"Kona," I breathed, grateful to see my older brother safe, once more. He was taller than me, like Melika, with a wide nose, soft brown skin, and freckles. Kona didn't have nearly as many freckles as myself, but just enough to soften his hard Hawaiian features. His black hair was pulled into a bun on top of his head, and he leaned his shoulder against the canoe for balance.

This was risky business, all of it. We stood in the water and I reached out to hug him, but he held out the bundle to me.

"No time, Kaʻala. You take this first. Ua and I will bring the rest of the refugees."

I didn't fight but, instead, took the bundle, shocked to find that it was not food. Not a treasure. It was... a baby.

"Kona..." I began to say, my eyes wide. Ua suppressed a gasp.

"The king wouldn't kill a baby..." she started to whisper.

"I'll explain everything later," Kona said. "But you need to take her, in case she wakes up again. I barely got her to sleep just now. It's part of the reason I took so long. She's hungry, and needs a woman's arms."

"Are there more?" Ua asked, standing behind me and placing her hand on my shoulder.

Kona nodded. "'Ae, children." He then gave me a look. "I'm serious. You need to go now."

I agreed, knowing that if the baby awoke, and I didn't have food or a place to settle her down, she would alarm every place I passed of our plight.

"See you soon," Ua said, squeezing my arm and following Kona onto the canoe.

I peeked at the baby's face in the moonlight, and my heart welled up in sadness.

A baby.

This was the youngest of all the refugees and people I'd taken into my sanctuary. Was the king of Hana and his high priest so disgusting and evil that they would sacrifice a *baby* for the bloody war?

She was a cute baby, so small, with brown skin and long

black eyelashes. How old was she? Probably not even a year old yet.

I took a shaky breath, got out of the water, my skirt sopping wet, and ran. Keeping the baby close to my chest, so it wouldn't be affected too much by the bumpiness of the ride, I followed the path back to my hut.

If I could get there before the baby awoke, that would be ideal. Already my mind raced with questions: *Could the baby eat poi?*

Did it need milk of some sort?

Could I take care of it and keep it happy?

What if it was colicky? Would that alert passerbyers?

Would Nai'a be able to take this baby to safety? Would she find someone who could care for it?

I snapped out of it when I felt a shift in the energy around me.

Someone's here.

I veered off the path and ducked behind a thick koa tree.

Is it Mailou? My heart pounded, and the baby shifted.

Oh no. Please don't wake up. I gently rocked her, while glancing behind the tree. A breeze made the leaves and branches rustle against one another. Cold sweat broke out on my forehead, and my hands clammed up. I checked the baby's face, finding her letting out a big yawn.

Don't wake up... not now...

Much to my relief, she wiggled a bit and continued to breathe steadily.

Something moved in the trees on the other side of the path. I swallowed hard. Someone was definitely following me.

I was close to the hut, and, once there, I could hand the baby to Melika and confront the stalker, if necessary. But I couldn't face the stalker now, not while holding the little one. And I certainly didn't want to wake up the baby. Her cries would wake up the entire island at this hour.

Feeling for the knife hidden under the belt of my skirt, mostly for comfort, I took a shaky breath.

It was now or never.

I darted back onto the path, sprinting. Immediately, the person, whoever it was that hid in the brush, followed. The leaves and branches rustled, and I realized two things: this was someone skilled in stealth, and it was too light and nimble to be Mailou.

A little part of relief went through me that it wasn't Mailou, but then more panic rushed in. If it wasn't Mailou, then who was it?

The figure ran alongside me, but in the shadows of the trees and bushes. I couldn't make out who it might be in the darkness. And I didn't want to lead them straight to my home. Feeling that I had no other options, I pulled a mango from my side bag. I was still running, but so was the figure in the bushes. With all the aim I could get while running, and with my left hand (my non-dominant hand), I hurled the mango.

A surprised "oof" from the bushes made the figure stop, giving me enough time to get ahead and away. I tried to make out the sound of the "oof." It was definitely a man, but not Mailou. I went through all the voices of the fishermen and people of Lanai. But it was too indistinct to make out.

Focus Ka'ala. All I had to do was get this baby to the hut while the stalker was distracted. For now.

The baby wiggled again from the bounciness of my sprint but just as it started making fussy noises, I burst through the gate. As I bounded up the porch stairs, the creaks and groans made noises, the bamboo chimes brushed against one another, and the coral strings clicked. Melika, who had been keeping watch on the porch, rushed to me.

She didn't ask questions until I ran into the bedroom and rocked the baby side to side.

"Poi," I said to Melika, and she fetched a bowl of it that we made earlier.

"Ka'ala..." she said, nothing but shock in her voice as she dipped her finger in and fed the baby.

"I don't even know if she's old enough to eat that," I said, still rocking the baby. She stopped fussing when the poi touched her lips.

"Maybe some coconut milk?" I asked and Melika nodded, coming back with a small coconut bowl. "I was followed..." I panted between words. "I'll keep watch at the front. Kona and Ua will be here soon with others."

I handed Melika the baby, not even sure if I'd ever seen my younger sister hold a baby. "Keep her head supported," I said, showing Melika how to hold her. "Do your best. I need to keep watch." I patted Melika's arm and hurried back to the porch.

I sucked in a slow, deep breath, studying the path and trees beyond the gate. Everything looked and sounded normal, but what if that man, who I couldn't identify, was out there? Watching? Someone had definitely followed me... but who? The brief image of the king's man passed my mind, his double take that morning.

Can't be. He would have to be trained very well to be so stealthy.

Instead of keeping an eye for Kona and Ua, with whatever people they'd bring, I put out the lights around the hut, pulled my knife from under my skirt belt, and hid in the shadows of the porch, waiting.

I could wait all night for whoever stalked me.

Instead, Ua appeared at the gate, crouched down, someone in her arms, with three small figures surrounding her. My stomach tightened as she urged them to the porch.

They're just children...

I greeted the children with a smile and kept my finger over my lips, a reminder to keep silent.

"Come in," I said, leading them into the hut.

"'Ake is coming with three more," Ua said, letting down a little girl from her arms. 'Ake was Kona's code name, as we didn't use our real names in front of the refugees.

"Three...." I gave her a questioning look and she nodded.

"Three children."

I grimaced. Ua brought four little ones. That meant we had seven children and one baby. What had happened? Did King Hua really intend to kill children? What kind of monster was he?

A horrible one... one that will burn in the afterlife, I thought, putting on my smile again to calm the children. Their nervous energy filled the air.

"You must be hungry," I said, once the children were inside. "'Elepaio will help you get some food." Ua, Melika, Kona, and I never used our real names in front of our refugees. It was the safest way to stay unidentified and out of sight from the ali'i. We each used bird names: I was 'Iwa, Ua was 'Apapane, Melika was 'Elepaio, and Kona was 'Akeke'e ('Ake for short). Another young woman, named 'Eleu, who took the refugees to freedom from the island, was nicknamed Nai'a, after the dolphins she loved.

I returned to the porch, keeping watch, knowing that our code names were just another part of the operations. But even more important was that nobody *saw* what we did.

I scanned the trees, looking for the person who followed me. Perhaps I hit my stalker straight in the head.

I wouldn't be surprised. Even using my left hand, I had a killer aim.

Kona hobbled up the gate, a child on his back, and two more trailing behind him. "Come in. Come eat," I whispered to the children, giving them hugs before ushering them inside. Many of them were visibly shaking.

Poor things.

I now faced my older brother, and we hugged. "Were you followed?" I kept my voice low, keeping an eye on the trees and bushes beyond the gate.

"Not that I could tell."

"Good." Before pushing my brother into the hut to eat with the children, I squeezed his arm. "What happened Kona? They're just children."

My brother never cried. He was not a sensitive type at all, but his whole look softened. "They were going to be put on the altar for sacrifice," he said. "Hua has been losing the war. 'Io got them out."

'Io. 'Io was the code name for Prince Kekoa, King Hua's son. We met a few years ago, and he was the first to help me in my underground operations.

But I had no time to think of my gratitude towards the prince. I wanted to puke. King Hua and his high priest were the vilest of creatures. Too bad Ua and I didn't kill the king when we had the chance those years ago. We couldn't...

I refocused, not wanting to dwell on the unpleasant memory, the one where I'd failed... everyone.

"The baby too?"

"It was left at Hua's hut." Kona turned to help me study the forest for anyone who might have followed. "Apparently the baby's mother was... forced on by Hua." He shook his head. "Instead of taking responsibility for his actions, Hua was going to have the baby killed with the other sacrifices."

I held my stomach and gave Kona a look. "You're not serious..."

"It's sickening, I know. 'Io somehow got them all out."

"Why doesn't 'Io just stab the king in the heart?" I asked, my fists clenching. Perhaps the king's reasons for invincibility worked against Ua and I, but maybe it didn't work against his kin.

"You can't control everything," Kona said, letting out a soft sigh. "But you need to do what you can and start in your own community, just like you're doing." He placed his hand on my shoulder. "You're already doing enough, 'Iwa. And so is 'Io. Don't take on the world when you're already doing what you can to make it better."

I frowned. "But the king..."

Kona squeezed my shoulder. "We'll talk more later. Thanks for keeping watch."

"Of course. Eat something and get some rest," I said, and gently pushed him inside, but my resentment for the king grew only stronger with each passing day.

CHAPTER FOUR

The night wore on, and I remained on the porch, keeping my eyes peeled for any movements in the bushes. The nights Kona arrived always filled me with anxiety and questions.

What if someone saw what we were doing?

Is that stalker out there now, watching?

"I'll take watch now," Ua said, stepping onto the porch, avoiding the creaky boards, and making her way next to me. She sat cross legged and yawned. Her hair, pulled up into a messy bun, like my own, had begun to fall out.

"I can do it," I said. "You should rest."

"*You* should rest. You've been up before sunrise this morning." She wasn't wrong. I awoke early, too nervous to sleep. The day flew by, and I'd been so anxious about Kona's arrival that I didn't even tell Melika and Ua about the mermaid, though I was sure they would've loved to hear it. My thoughts were also distracted by the children, the return of Mailou, and the mysterious captain-inspector.

"Really," Ua said and squeezed my arm.

"Thanks Ua."

"Of course." She smiled, but it looked tired. "None of this would be possible without you, Ka'ala."

I didn't want to think about it, because, again, Ua was right. As I stepped into the hut, I almost bumped into Kona.

"Where are you going?"

"To keep watch."

"Ua's got it."

Kona shrugged. "I'm as antsy as you are." I understood his meaning, and I didn't want to force him to sleep if he couldn't. But he'd been navigating and bringing these children to safety all day. Furthermore, he'd taken care of the baby, probably a task even bigger than navigating the canoe or keeping the children hidden.

"See you in the morning then," I said, then headed towards the back bedroom. But instead of entering, I paused and peeked out the front door. Kona never used to refuse a chance to nap. Sure enough, as I snuck a look out the door, he sat next to Ua, an awkward silence stretching between them.

I'd never thought of Ua, my best friend, and Kona, my older brother, as a match. And, for whatever reason, seeing them there made me wonder if it was a possibility.

I shook my head, knowing it wasn't my business.

It is my business. Because if they decided to get together romantically, it could ruin our operations. Ua was needed here, while Kona was needed back in Hana, transporting the refugees out.

If they got together, Ua would always want to be with him, no doubt about it. I suppressed a sigh, knowing I couldn't worry about that now.

Besides, there had never been anything between Ua and Kona. Other island girls seemed to surround and flirt with Kona as we grew up, while Ua and I did our own thing. For now, though, I needed rest.

I stood at the door of the bedroom, observing the children. The youngest, of course, was the baby in Melika's arms. The oldest child had to be around ten years old.

My stomach knotted once more.

How could King Hua do this to the children? How could he *ever* feel ok about killing innocent people, *especially* children?

I took the baby from Melika's arms, noticing that my younger sister began to doze off.

"Oh, sorry Ka'ala," she said, waking, and looking at me wide-eyed.

"Shh, it's alright. Get some sleep." She didn't refuse, and crawled into her own kapa bed to rest.

I sat on my bed, leaning my back against the side of the hut, and looked at the baby. My heart wept in anger and sadness.

This was unfair. The war was unfair. And all of it was caused by one evil, cruel king. What more could I do though? Here I was, providing a safe place for refugees, including those of our so-called enemies, prisoners of war from Kohala.

Rest, my mind told me. But even as I tried to close my eyes, my thoughts drifted to feelings of failure, to the night Ua and I tried to kill the king... and, no matter how hard we tried, something prevented our attempts.

King Hua of Hana was invincible... or was he?

THE MORNING LANAI sun beat on the island, and I made my usual morning walk along the shore, greeting the fishermen, trading for food, and keeping an eye out for any suspicious activity or for Mailou.

As I walked by the canoes, I sensed excitement. The people of Lanai thronged to the small canoe with red sails. My interest peaked.

The king's man. The so-called "inspector" delivered a speech to the crowd, but I was too far to hear it. I checked my surroundings for Mailou, and, once clear, joined the group.

I picked out bits and pieces of the man's speech, and mostly had to glean the rest from the group.

"He is here on assignment from Hua," said a local woman to me. "Says that the king needs him to uncover a mystery. This captain here will be inspecting everyone's homes… at unpredictable times."

I tried to conceal a frown, because I couldn't stand the word "unpredictable." Though my life revolved around the unpredictable, I didn't want this captain to be dropping in at a most inconvenient time.

With the baby, any time was inconvenient and unpredictable.

"Because of his rank, he can do anything he wants," the woman continued, rolling her eyes. Another woman, eavesdropping on our conversation, pitched in.

"We'll keep him distracted long as we can, Ka'ala."

Though not all the residents of Lanai knew my secret, the ones who did respected me and would never tell a soul. That's just how we locals worked.

I nodded to her in gratitude. Though I didn't know *why* the captain was inspecting, I had two theories.

The first was that he heard about my operations, and that a place on Lanai offered refuge to anyone, including the enemy.

The second theory was that he was here to investigate the night Ua and I mocked the king. I didn't like to think of the memory, because of the feelings it conjured, but I knew, for a fact, that nobody knew it was Ua and I... except Prince Kekoa. He, like us, wanted to make sure the king didn't hurt any of the Lanai residents. But he saw everything that we did. And, not long after the king and armies left, he returned to meet us specifically.

It was the beginning of our undercover operations, the one that saved many lives from the cruelty of King Hua.

That troubling night occurred years ago, but I had no doubt Hua was still embarrassed as ever about it.

I relived the entire thing in my mind: When a storm threatened the seas, Hua and his armies camped on the shores of Lanai. That night, King Hua, drunk as a dog, went looking for trouble.

Ua and I took our chance, acting as dumb, drunk girls, leading him deep into the forest. We gave him more kava to drink, prepared in its strength to knock the king out.

And once he was drunk with sleep, I tried to stab his heart. But as my knife went to his chest, something stopped me. It felt like invisible hands pulled me back.

I got desperate. I tried choking him, strangling him, but nothing worked. That was when Ua and I realized... he had something on him, maybe even a spell or ward of protection.

We tied and gagged him up, disappointed.

"I promise it won't take long."

I snapped back from the memory, hearing the captain's voice as he answered questions from the crowd. I snuck out of the crowd by taking steps back.

But, as if sensing I was there, the captain turned and looked at me. He wasn't close enough to hold a conversation, and people surrounded him, but our eyes met.

My heart skipped a beat, and I hurried away.

I want nothing to do with the captain. He works for Hua, and therefore he is wicked. And, since he was a captain, I had no doubt he joined the king in his disgusting revelries: drinking, promiscuity, bloody warfare, and who knew what else...

I hurried towards Manele bay, eager to trade for some fresh fish. No doubt Ua and Melika had their hands full with the children. Meanwhile, Kona left early that morning to pay his respect to our sick mother, Kalani, and uncaring father, Oponui.

In the distance, the fishermen pulled fish from their nets and I picked up the pace, grateful I got here at the right time.

But as I walked straight for the fishermen, a figure appeared from the shadows of the trees, making his way towards me.

Oh no...

The tall, giant body walked with purpose, and I had no doubt he would crush me now. He didn't get the chance last time, so why wouldn't he do it of his own accord?

The fishermen were too far to call out for help. I had no other option but to turn and head the other way.

I whirled around towards the direction I just left. I turned around so fast, I didn't realize that someone had run to catch up to me.

My eye caught hold of the yellow cape hanging from the man's neck and my insides rolled.

The captain. He grabbed my arms and my first instinct was to defend myself, especially because he invaded my personal space. I relied on my reflexes, whipping my knife from the hidden place at my belt and holding at the captain's face.

"Don't touch me or get any closer," I warned, but guilt panged my chest as he stood closer than I thought. The knife nicked his chin, and I stepped back, still keeping the knife pointed at him.

He put his hands up. "Whoa, calm down, I won't hurt you."

I glanced behind me, seeing that Mailou moved back into the shadows, disappearing from view.

The captain smiled, his teeth white and straight, his brown skin kissed by the sun. I became aware of my freckled skin and messy hair pulled into a bun.

"Hey there," he said, bowing his head, "I didn't mean to startle you." He glanced at the knife, then my face, and felt his chin. A sliver of blood had begun to trickle and I grimaced that I had hurt him.

I put the knife away, noticing how he looked from me, again, to the knife, as if he had figured something out.

"Sorry, you startled me," I said, but my insides kept turning. "Are you alright?" I asked, already reaching into my bag for a clean, spare kapa to wipe the blood.

He saw me use my knife. Nobody on the island had ever seen me use my knife in self defense, except Ua and Melika, of course, who I occasionally practiced with.

I didn't realize my heart had pounded in my ears at just the thought of passing Mailou. But he was gone, and I was spared this time.

Thanks to the captain, I suppose.

Because my heart beat so loudly, I didn't register that the captain had answered my question and asked me something. He waited, expectantly.

"Excuse me?" A blush spread up my cheeks as I looked up at him. He had to be as tall as Melika and Kona. His toned physique stared at me, as well as all the scars lining his body.

The corner of his lip turned up, and now I could see what happened to his face. The captain had probably been wounded in battle, like a leiomano had slashed across the right side of his face. The gash started at his forehead, went through his eye (and luckily his eye was unharmed), and reached his chin. But it had since healed. The area of the scar looked rough and textured in comparison to the rest of his skin.

He had dark brown eyes, a clean beard and mustache, and his wavy hair looked, once again, effortless.

Though the scar on his face should have possibly ruined his looks, it made him look more... masculine.

"I asked what your name is," he said and tried to conceal a smile as he studied me.

"Oh." The sun beat down on us, and I usually liked the warmth from it. But now I just felt hot all over. "Only if you share your name," I said, and immediately regretted it. Was I... *flirting* with him? I'd never flirted with anyone before, and his smile was an easy and immediate reward that made my head spin.

I just attacked and flirted with him...

"Are you alright?" I asked once more, knowing that I hadn't heard his answer earlier. He studied me again, then nodded.

"Of course, it just scratched the surface." He paused before adding, "You're very skilled with the knife."

"I was startled, otherwise I would have never brought it out."

He nodded, then held out his hand. "I'm Kaaiali'i. You can call me Ali'i though."

"Captain Ali'i–" I shook his hand, and it felt warm, rough, and hardened from the battles he fought.

"Just Ali'i, please."

I frowned. "But we aren't friends, and your status demands I use your title."

He held the leiomano hanging from the belt around his waist and shrugged. "Well then let's become friends." He flashed his charming smile once more. "I prefer if you use my name only." Ali'i then shifted, as if unsure of what to say next. "So... what's your name?"

"Oh." I cleared my throat. "Ka'ala. I'm Ka'ala." Now I sounded like a little child, stumbling over my words.

He stared at me, and all sorts of feelings rushed through my body. What should I say? I felt awkward as ever.

And he says let's become friends?

I grabbed the strap of my bag. Friends? He really thought I'd become friends with one of King Hua's captains? The king's captains were his most prized warriors. He cared more for his captains, the men leading his armies to war, than he ever would for his own people.

No. Ali'i and I would not be friends.

I tipped my head. "Well, it was nice meeting you. Good day." I turned around, *again,* to head towards the fishermen. No doubt Mailou was gone by now, and I could get my fish before hurrying back to the hut. I could only hope the baby was doing alright and not crying.

"Wait!" Ali'i caught up to me, walking in step with me. He was tall, and it took no effort, even though I took the longest strides I could. "Who was that man earlier? The tall one?"

"Mailou," I said, trying to pick up the pace, but Ali'i stayed with me.

"Was he bothering you?"

"No." I didn't need to tell Ali'i any information. The less he knew about me, the better.

"Well, you were about to run away from him."

I glanced at him. "I was not."

"It seemed like you knew him." He held the handle of his leiomano. "He isn't your husband, by chance, is he?"

"No, he's not." I said it almost too quickly.

"Are you married?"

"No."

"Been married before?"

"No."

"Courting?"

"No." At this, I realized that Ali'i was asking about my relationship status, and heat spread up my cheeks again.

"Do you intend to court anyone?" he asked.

I'd never thought of it before, as I'd been so wrapped up in running my safe haven. Only last night, when I saw Kona sit by Ua did I realize we were of age to court and marry.

I shrugged. "It never crossed my mind." Before he could ask anymore questions, as I had a feeling what his next question might be, I cut in, "You ask a lot of questions, don't you?"

"Only to people I'm interested in," he said.

"And I'm a person of interest?"

"'Ae, of course." The ease with which he said things made my stomach do all sorts of flips.

"A person of interest for your inspections or personal reasons?" I eyed him.

He chuckled, and the sound of it made my hair stand on end. But why? I dared to look at him, finding the smile on his face again.

What a lovely smile... I remembered thinking about it

the first time I saw him, and even now, it had a charm to it. He looked not only friendly, but...

Attractive. I blushed at the very thought. No. He was not attractive. He was a captain to the king, and, therefore, a dishonest, dishonorable sort.

A breeze blew by and moved loose pieces of hair into my face. I brushed them aside.

"Both," he said, then added, "Look, I just wanted to meet you."

"And you have." I slowed down, losing my breath. Why were the fishermen so far today? "What have you learned from your inspection of me?" I asked now, and tried to look as bored as possible. "Am I the girl you're looking for?"

Ali'i stared at me, again, and I couldn't help but feel flattered yet nervous all at the same time. "You fit the description."

"What was the description?" It was like we played a game, where I had to guess why he was here, all while maintaining my disguise.

"Brown eyes, petite build, good with a knife, light colored lips—" At the mention of lips, his eyes dove down to my lips and I looked away. "And flawed skin."

"Flawed skin?" I raised an eyebrow. "Obviously it's not me because my skin is perfect." I meant it sarcastically, of course, because freckles covered me from head to toe. I suppose one could call it "flawed," though freckles were a natural part of my appearance.

Ali'i laughed. I hated that my insides weakened at the sound of it. "Exactly. The description doesn't fit you because your skin is absolutely perfect." He paused before adding, "It's beautiful."

Now embarrassment flooded me. I hadn't been fishing for a compliment on my skin. In fact, I often felt self conscious of the freckles covering my arms, face, neck, and chest. I used to wish I had less freckles and darker skin, like Melika and Kona. Why was I cursed with this many freckles and spots?

Aliʻi's compliment sounded genuine, and it made me even more uneasy. In fact, I felt all weird and mushy, like my legs were melting beneath me, and I was feeling hotter and hotter by the second.

"And what does the king want with the young woman who fits this description?" I asked, changing the subject.

"That, my lady, is only for me to know." He grinned at me, and I hated how laid back he looked. Because I was far from comfortable. In fact, the more I was around him, the more out of control I felt. His good looks, natural charm, and banter made me feel like I wasn't as shy as I'd always been, and that, maybe... I was kind of pretty. I'd never struggled with self worth or my appearance to the level that I couldn't do anything, but, deep down, I definitely enjoyed the validation.

"Has this young woman done something to charm the king?" I asked. "Or perhaps she has done something to displease him..."

Aliʻi remained quiet for a second, and I made my own guess.

The king is looking for me. But he didn't know it was *me.* Was he wanting revenge on Ua and I for tying him up and embarrassing him? After all, his men scoured the island looking for him, and they found him tied up deep in the forest, in his own vomit. It took them forever to cut through the amount of rope we tied Hua in. We even gagged him, a king!

Or perhaps the king knew about my operations. That'd be bad. Very bad.

But how would he know the details about my skin? It had to be that one night... Would the king recognize me if he came here himself? He'd been so drunk, Ua and I were sure he would remember nothing.

"The king's business is his own," Ali'i said, holding his hands behind his back, body language that signaled he was hiding the truth.

"Of course," I said, tipping my head. "But can you answer this one question?"

"Depends on the question."

"Did the king meet this young woman here, on Lanai?"

Ali'i nodded. "Of course he did. Why else would I be here, inspecting?"

Perfect. I was right. The king *was* looking for me... and Ua. I knew one day he'd want revenge on us for doing what we did.

"I suppose that was a silly question," I said, and bowed my head, as we now reached the fishermen. "Anyway, it was nice meeting you Ali'i. Good day." I whipped around, not giving him a chance to reply.

"Ka'ala!" He called out to me before I got far. I paused and glanced at him. "I hope to see you again," he said, and gave that winning smile. I nodded and pursed my lips to keep from saying, *I hope to* never *see you again.*

Because the more distance I kept from Ali'i, a servant of King Hua, the better off I, and my secret operations, would be. The lives and safety of people depended on me, and I wouldn't put any of it at risk by being around the king's flirty captain.

CHAPTER FIVE

*T*wo days passed and I didn't see Ali'i, but I knew he was around, because the gossip Ua and I collected always told us he was. He'd gone inspecting people's homes all over the island.

But he hadn't come to my home... yet.

Kona, as usual of his visits to Lanai, stayed at our father's home in the valley, spending time with our mother. Though Kalani, our mother, could hardly remember any of us, Oponui insisted Kona stick around.

"How's the baby?" I asked as I stepped into the hut and placed a bundle of food on the ground. It had been a busy morning on the shores. I saw Mailou once again, but then he disappeared, and I walked along the path with other women, so he probably didn't bother to stalk me today.

It was honestly exhausting watching my back at every step. It seemed a lot easier when the bounty hunters and creed left the island. Why did he have to come back?

Melika rocked the baby back and forth. "She seems a lot happier."

"Good." I took my turn, taking the baby in my hands. She cooed as I smiled and greeted her. "We should give her a name," I said, stepping into the bedroom. The secret back door was open so the children could play in the back of the hut, where nobody would see them.

The thick bushes, that grew back after the most recent storm, acted as a barrier so if anyone glanced around the back of the hut, they had to traverse through the bushes to see the back wall. It was clever.

"It's too much pressure to name a baby," Melika said with a laugh.

Ua appeared at the front of the hut, rushing in. "Did you hear the latest news?"

"What?"

"One of the visitors from Oʻahu said that two of the creed members were turned to stone by menehune. Akamu married a princess–"

"Boo!" Melika exclaimed, making pouty lips. She used to tease me about possibly courting Akamu. I'd never been attracted to him, and my father would be choosing my future husband anyway.

"Wait, who did he marry?" I asked.

Ua laughed at Melika's continued boos. "He married a princess in Waialua. And then Mailou was threatened to be turned to stone by menehune, so he's here... empty handed."

I closed my eyes, grateful, once more, that Mailou didn't succeed in his mission. Otherwise, he or I would be dead at this point if we were forced to marry.

"There's gossip about that inspector too," Ua said and, though I told my best friend and sister of my encounter with him the other day, I kept out the part where he asked me questions regarding my relationship status.

"Ooh, tell all," Melika said. We made our way to the front of the hut, where we sat in the grass and I played with the baby. Though this was a time for us to chat and relax, as nobody passed around here, Ua and I continued to glance at the gate and fence, watching for anyone who might sneak up on us.

"He's single, first of all," Ua said and Melika's eyes went wide.

"Ka'ala, was he cute?"

I frowned at her but before Ua could continue, Melika pestered her. "Is he good looking? Do you think we could set him and Ka'ala up?"

"I don't *want* to be set up," I said, adding, "And especially not with a king's man. You know that Melika."

She rolled her eyes. "So boring. Well, one day, when I'm old enough, I'll marry Prince Kekoa, and he's definitely a king's man." She grinned into the distance. "He's so dreamy."

Ua chuckled at Melika and I shook my head, returning to the topic. "What about the captain?"

"He's been to many battles," Ua said. "So he's a very well-known, well decorated war hero back in Hana. He's been trained in the art of lua."

Lua. The art of war. Perhaps there was more to the captain than I expected. He didn't defend himself when I pulled my knife on him though.

But he wasn't expecting to be attacked by you, a maiden, I thought.

The baby cooed and giggled as I rested her back on my legs and stretched her out.

"Wait, so is he courting anyone?" Melika asked. "If not, then Ka'ala is available..." She wiggled her eyebrows at me.

I sighed.

"Not that I heard of. Although, the young women are going crazy with *two* eligible bachelors on the island at one time."

Kona and Aliʻi. The mothers of the young women, too, probably were pestering the two young men. Because my father lived in the valley, however, I had no idea what was going on with Kona.

"Anything else?" Melika asked. Ua had always been better at gathering gossip than myself. She was more sociable, whereas I was reserved, feeling more comfortable being alone. I was also never good at egging people on, especially with gossip.

"Of course. The king is looking for eligible brides for his son."

"Prince Kekoa?" Melika nearly jumped up. "When? Where? I must go!"

At this, both Ua and I laughed. "Calm down," I said, and the baby giggled at Melika's outburst. The prince was a handsome young man, as was expected, but he and Melika wouldn't make a good match. He was reserved and serious, emotionally scarred from the war and growing up with such a wicked father, while Melika was bubbly and loud. Not to mention she was years younger than him, and I wouldn't let her get married so young. Maybe my father would, but not I.

"They say within the next year the prince should be married," Ua continued. "He's of age, and we haven't had a celebration or break from the war against Kohala in a long time, besides the Makahiki, which wasn't long enough."

"Maybe if the prince gets married, they'll send the troops home again for a season," I said. Melika lightened at this.

"And then *you* can find an eligible bachelor, Ka'ala."

"What about Ua? You never say anything about Ua finding someone."

The girls laughed at that. "I'm sure I'll find someone," Ua said, and avoided eye contact. I thought of Kona going to sit by her the other night, and the quiet that fell between them.

Should I ask? What if asking made it awkward? He was my brother, after all, and she was my best friend.

But it is *my business.* I'd never been the type to pry others. But, perhaps, should I start now? We told each other everything... or did we?

"Anything else?" Melika asked Ua, practically falling forward.

Ua grinned. "No. But don't worry Melika. I'm sure a messenger will come to every corner of Maui and Lanai, looking for an eligible young woman to marry Prince Kekoa."

"But don't get your hopes up," I warned, standing and taking the baby with me.

"Oh you're such a downer," Melika said, also standing. "Fifteen isn't *that* young."

"Yes it is," both Ua and I said. Melika rolled her eyes, but we knew she wasn't mad at us.

"I'll check on the kids." She wiggled her eyebrows at us once more before heading towards the back.

"I'll get the food ready," I said.

"I'll keep watch." Ua fixed the knife at her belt. As we stepped on the porch, she touched my arm. "Ka'ala?"

"'Ae?"

"Do you really think you won't fall in love? I mean... what if you do?"

I gave her a look. "I've never thought of it. Especially with all of this..." I motioned around us and Ua nodded.

"I agree. That's why I hesitate to get close to any man."

I bit my lip from asking if "any man" might be Kona. Ua held her arm. "We've kept this sanctuary a secret for so long, and we've saved so many people's lives. It would feel wrong to fall in love and... what if falling in love ruins all of these operations?"

"We've been taught to put others first," I said, thinking of how we both trained under Ua's late grandfather.

"And so if we put ourselves first, that's risky." Ua finished my thought. Bringing another man into the picture might be a good thing. He could help us save more people. But what if it complicated things? For example, what if he was called back to battle? Or what if he was deathly loyal to the king, and betrayed us?

Ua smiled. "Anyway, that captain is quite good-looking, don't you think?"

I shrugged. "Maybe a little. But... he's a king's man."

Ua nodded, the joke already over. "And those king's men aren't safe to deal with."

We finished our conversation there and I put the baby down in the living room of the hut to prepare the food.

She fussed when she wasn't held, so Melika came in to get her.

"This might be problematic," my younger sister said as she rocked the baby gently. "If one of us has to hold baby at all times, one of us always has to stay hidden."

I nodded. Melika was right, and we needed to get the baby out of here as soon as possible.

But we never knew when 'Eleu, also known as Nai'a, came around. Her stops on Lanai were unpredictable, which always gave us an advantage.

But please come sooner than later, I thought, as the image of the captain came to mind. Because sooner or later, he'd come to inspect my hut, and I could only hope that we kept the children hidden and safe.

CHAPTER SIX

A day later, storm clouds rolled in as I kept watch on the porch. The evening felt darker than usual, because of the heavy skies.

Ua and Melika were in the bedroom with the children, helping them prepare for bed. I listened to their songs and chants, and smiled to myself when the sound of the children's laughter filled the air.

It had been a lovely few days together, and the children seemed more at ease than the night they arrived.

In fact, even though they didn't know where they were going, they looked happier. We told them that a young woman named Nai'a would take them to another place, to safety, and they trusted us completely.

I hoped 'Eleu, also known as Nai'a, would find them safe homes. 'Eleu, our wayfinding friend, and her grandfather, stowed people on their large canoe, and took them to neighboring islands. Almost every neighboring island was sympathetic to the refugees, even if they were from Hana.

The only place that 'Eleu avoided, of course, was

Kohala itself, the place that Hana waged war on. She was from Puna on the Big Island, so often took refugees there.

I glanced in the hut, finding Ua on the ground with a gourd, beating it and chanting. The children danced hula under Melika's instructions. Ua caught my eye and nodded, a silent message that the children were happy.

That, alone, made my heart happy.

This is why I do what I do...

I stood and watched them, grateful that the children felt safe here. They knew that I, Ua, and Melika would do everything in our power to protect them. We hadn't been able to get much information from the children, but what we did get was that they had families in Hana. Whether their families gave them up for human sacrifice or the king ordered it, we didn't know.

Kona also wasn't able to tell me anymore about the children's history, as he only visited once, while I was absent.

I returned to my post and continued watching the forest for any signs of people.

Ua had been absent when Kona visited too, and I wondered if he was disappointed by that. Of course he'd be happy to see Melika, and happy to see that the children were alright, but... could there be something between him and Ua?

I wished I could have asked him.

A movement along the path caught my attention and I sat up, heart pumping. The figure looked familiar, and before he even stepped towards the gate, I knew that it was the captain.

He's here to inspect.

I stood and rattled the coral shells against one another, warning Melika and Ua inside. Hushes filled the air and the children went dead silent, the sound of Ua's chanting and the ipu beats on the ground stopped. Night crickets and the distant roll of thunder filled the space.

Melika's eyes went wide from within the bedroom and I nodded.

This is not a drill. This is real.

She closed the sliding door, and, just at that moment, the baby started crying.

Of all times!

The gate opened and the captain stepped in. I rushed to meet him, stepping on all the creaky parts of the porch to, hopefully, cover the noise of the baby's cries. Though, it became more and more distant. Did Ua take the baby and run out the back? I sure hoped so.

Please hide the children and their beds in the bushes. Hurry, Melika.

"Are you here for an inspection?" I asked, keeping my face even. I didn't want the captain to get any ideas of my heart fluttering from just the sight of him. It was a mixture of admiration and fear.

But I couldn't show fear. In fact, I needed to stay as calm as possible, giving my sister and Ua time to hide the children. We would protect the children and any refugees at any costs, including whatever it took now to cover their noises.

Aliʻi's hair was down, and it was wavy as ever. His clean cut beard had grown a little longer, but his facial hair made him look even more handsome.

I lifted my chin, trying to push away the betraying thought of him being labeled as "handsome" in my mind.

I am not attracted to a king's man. I am not attracted to a king's man.

Aliʻi ran his fingers through his hair, revealing toned biceps. My core, already tight from nervousness, weakened.

"It's a little late, don't you think?" I asked, looking at the sky. The sun had set, so everything around us had a blue-ish tone. A breeze blew by, and light raindrops began to fall.

Rain harder, I prayed, trying not to tense anytime I heard the distant cry of the baby.

"Do you hear that?" Ali'i asked.

I leaned forward, causing our faces to be close, as if listening, and he stiffened. I shook my head. "Just the lovely sound of rain." I folded my arms. "So... you realize the hour, right? Some people might spread rumors of you 'inspecting' my home at this time."

"I heard that you have a younger sister. Is she not here?" Ali'i asked and winked. "I didn't come here to inspect you... Did you think that's why I came?"

He was flirting. Again.

And I didn't want to flirt, but an idea crossed my mind. *What if I flirted back with Ali'i? Would it stall time?* Yes. Yes it would. I played with my hair and shrugged.

"Sort of." I then moved out of the way and motioned to the home. "But I'm assuming you're here to check my home." I looked at him through my lashes and he tensed. "My sister is home, yes. And I've got nothing to hide."

It was a straight up lie, but, at those words, he walked forward. I followed. The porch made the same creaking noises it always made. The bamboo chimes clashed against one another.

All of these things made the captain look about, studying my home. Could he tell it was specially designed this way?

"Who built this structure?" he asked, touching the poles that held the roof over the porch. Now it started raining, much to my relief.

"Akamu. He was one of the Nawao," I said, leaning

against the pole and studying the captain. Did I... *enjoy* flirting with the captain? Or was he nice to look at? Because I sure didn't mind staring at him. He folded his arms, studying me too. "He's gone now," I said. "The gossip is that he married a princess on Oʻahu."

Aliʻi raised an eyebrow. "Interesting."

"Have you enjoyed your time on Lanai?" I asked, eager to change the subject, to get him distracted. Aliʻi paced the porch, looking around. What did he expect to find? He paused at my question.

"It's nice here," he said, approaching and placing his arm on the post above me. If this wasn't flirting, I didn't know what was. My back was pressed against the post and I looked up at him, now able to get a whiff of him.

He smelled nice, like koa wood and ocean. "It's peaceful. The people are kind. Calm." He looked past me, to the garden. My mind flashed to the bundle of weapons hidden in kapa beneath the garden bed...

He'll never see it, I told myself over and over, knowing that it was an emergency stash, only to be dug up when we ran out of weapons, or when we needed the refugees to arm themselves. Sure enough, his gaze returned to me.

"Beautiful..." His eyes fell to my lips and my heart started pumping. The rain poured harder. Would I let him kiss me?

If it stalls time, yes... But what if I continued this conversation? It was obvious that he liked me. But I didn't like him. In fact, how could he ever want to kiss a girl that he hardly knew? My stomach twisted in knots.

Because he's like King Hua... he's probably kissed plenty of girls in his lifetime... and done more than just kissing too.

I shrank back, as if to warn him that I didn't want to be kissed. "And is beauty all that matters to you?" I asked. His eyebrows creased, receiving my message through body language.

"Of course not."

"It seems that way." I noticed a tiny dark red scar on his chin, the one I'd given him. I frowned and reached out to touch it, but he pulled away.

"Sorry about that," I said, and my breath hitched. He grinned, looking into my eyes.

"I know what you're doing," he said, almost a whisper.

"What are you talking about?" I pointed to the door of my hut. "I told you to check it out. I've got nothing to hide. *You* are wasting time, flirting."

"*I'm* wasting time?"

I raised an eyebrow. "You're hovering over me like you're going to kiss me. But you're not, so get on with the inspection."

"Do you want me to kiss you?" He leaned in closer.

"No, especially when we don't even know each other." At this, I slipped away from him, knowing I'd given Melika and Ua enough time to get the children out and scrub the bedroom clean. "Come on. Do you want a personal tour? Is that what you want?"

Ali'i sensed my immediate change of character, and I regretted being so cold. I should have played it smoothly. To cover my mistakes, I took his arm and led him inside. My legs were shaking though, replaying his question over and over. It was a question I'd never been asked before: *Do you want me to kiss you?* Did I? I never imagined what my romantic life would look like. Meanwhile, Ali'i seemed *too* comfortable with all of it.

Perhaps he's just overly confident. And he's kissed plenty of girls before. I told myself that my original intentions were right. Keep him far, far away. He was nothing more than a player who participated in King Hua's disgusting feasts and nights of unbridled desires.

"This is the living area."

"You've got a lot of food for two people," he said, glancing at the pile of taro, fish, and other ingredients in the corner.

"We like to make extras for our neighbors," I said.

"What neighbors?" Ali'i smiled innocently. We had no neighbors until town.

"In town, of course," I said as casually as possible. I paused before opening the bedroom door. "Maybe I should let my sister know you're here. She likes to go to bed early and I think it's rude to wake her with a young man in the house, don't you think?"

Ali'i nodded. "Of course."

I slid the door open and snuck in, finding the bedroom completely empty, except for two beds: mine and Melika's.

Well done Melika and Ua, I thought, knowing that the children were right outside the window, probably soaking wet by now, but well hidden.

"Is he still here?" Melika whispered and I gave her the look, warning her to silence.

"Act tired, like you just woke up," I said, keeping my voice low. Then I opened the door and motioned for Ali'i to come. He did so, with great hesitancy.

Melika put her kihei on and bowed to the captain. "Sorry, I like to sleep early," she said and yawned. It looked quite genuine. She glanced from me to the captain and a smile crossed her lips.

"What have you both been up to?"

"He's here to inspect the bedroom," I said, trying to make my voice sound awkward and embarrassed.

"Inspect the bedroom?" Melika giggled and muttered,

"Or maybe he was here for something else if I weren't around."

"Melika." I gave her a warning look, but all of this was staged.

A blush crawled up Aliʻi's face. "I'm not here for that, I assure you," he said to my sister. "I'm a man of honor."

She crossed her arms. "That's not what we hear about the king's men, especially his captains." Melika was good at this acting game, maybe even better than myself. If she made Aliʻi feel uncomfortable enough, maybe he'd be too embarrassed to come back or show his face to me.

"It is quite dark outside, don't you think, captain?" She added. "And Kaʻala is *very* pretty."

"Melika, that's enough." I grabbed Aliʻi's arm. "I'm sorry. She's only fifteen. Are you done inspecting the room?"

He looked very uncomfortable now. "'Ae." But he hesitated. "Why is the room so big?"

"We like our space," Melika answered. "And sometimes Kaʻala stores leis and floral arrangements back here for big events."

"I heard you make lei and decoration," he said, but spoke softer than usual, probably humiliated by Melika's comment and assumption. If I were in his place, I'd be uncomfortable.

"Is that all you'd like to see?" I asked.

He stepped out onto the porch, where the rain had lightened. It was now dark, and I hastened to light the torches in front of the home.

The cry of the baby rang over the sound of rain, freezing me in place.

I thought Ua went far... But perhaps not far enough. She probably ran as fast as she could, but the baby had to be wet and miserable. I didn't blame it for crying, but it made my heart pump.

I made eye contact with Ali'i, and I shouldn't have. Because he read me.

He knew that *I* heard the baby's cry too, and that I was hiding more than I pretended not to.

"It's getting late," I said. "Maybe you should get going... before people start saying things..."

"Only if your sister says something." Ali'i looked like he tried to laugh at the joke, but a darkness had overcome him, like a sense of heaviness.

My skin tingled all over.

He knows. He knew I was hiding something. And he probably knew that I was responsible for duping the king so long ago–my skill with the knife the other day had probably proved it. So would he tell my secret?

I stepped forward and his jaw tightened. My fingers shook, but I needed to do something... something to distract him from the baby's cry. What could I do though?

I stood on the tips of my toes and kissed his cheek, but I couldn't make eye contact with him after that. Shyness overcame me, and embarrassment.

That was a pathetic kiss. I should have made it more distracting, but when I looked up at him, his eyes were wide. And the heaviness that covered him now seemed to have disappeared. Perhaps my distraction worked... for a time.

Maybe that peck on the cheek would hold him off until he decided to reveal my secrets. Or... maybe I had to keep this game up, so he'd stay distracted forever...

If it's for the safety of these people, these children, and that poor baby...

He tipped his head. "Will I see you again?"

My heart pumped. "Only if you want to."

Aliʻi grinned. "I really want to... it'd be nice to get to know you better."

"Because you've kissed too many girls you *don't* know?" I tested.

He blushed. "I've actually only kissed one girl before."

I frowned. That had to be a lie. A big fat lie. There was no way the captain of King Hua kissed only *one* girl! Then, surely, he went beyond just kissing her.

"And she's in Hana?" I asked, not knowing why I cared so much.

I should be trying to get him to leave, not hang around...

He nodded. "I wanted to marry her but... she wanted something else."

I frowned and he looked as awkward as ever, the confidence he exuded earlier now seeming deflated.

"It's late, you're right. I need to be on my way. Good night, Kaʻala." At that, he whirled around and left along the path so quickly, I was sure I reopened some wound.

What did she want from him? I had a feeling it was intimacy, intimacy that was sacred and special in marriage. Yet many people lusted and wanted to have that pleasure outside of marriage... so was Aliʻi *not* as promiscuous and disgusting as I thought him to be? I'd find out.

No, I don't need to know. It's his personal life, and I have no reason to pry into it.

"Well that was cute." I turned to see Melika hidden in the shadows, watching.

"What are you doing?" Heat rushed up my cheeks. "Come on, let's get those children out of the rain."

"I think he really likes you," she said.

A lump formed in my throat as I passed her. "He does not."

"And I've never seen you kiss a man before—"

"I didn't kiss him."

"Yes you did."

"On the cheek, alright? I was trying to distract him."

"Well it was a valiant effort," Melika said and shrugged. "He heard the baby, there's no question about it." Heaviness fell on both of us, but we put on new faces. We smiled, opened the back door, and ushered the children in. We made it all seem like a game. In no time, the children, who had turned tense and nervous from being shoved out in the rain to hide, were giggling and chatting as they changed into dry clothes.

But as Ua stepped in with the baby, both of them soaked, the three of us young women exchanged worried glances.

We couldn't keep this charade up forever.

In fact, since Ali'i probably suspected me, I had to do something... but what?

CHAPTER SEVEN

*T*he baby had a high fever the next day. She didn't cry, but, instead, lied still as a rock.

And that worried me. While Ua, Melika, and I rotated the watch on the porch, we took turns caring for the baby. Her little brown face, overtime, grew hotter and redder.

Rash broke out on her cheeks, and that night, she began wailing. Ua kept watch while Melika and I did everything in our power to soothe the infant.

We tried poi, milk, singing, cuddling... but she wouldn't stop crying.

"What haven't we tried?" I asked, feeling her head. No doubt the baby caught a cold from Ua's desperate sprint into the rain.

"Medicine," Melika said. "But I don't know what medicine a baby can or can't have."

"What about the kahuna?" Ua asked, peeking in. We never went to the local kahuna's help, as he was loyal to King Hua. If he found out about our underground operations, he'd surely turn us in.

"I can go," Melika offered, but she was not as stealthy or

quick as myself. I could send Ua, but, looking at the skies, I could tell a storm was coming in. Ua had an affinity for getting into tricky spots during storms.

Once, she had to hunker down in the safety of some thick ti leaf bushes. Another time, she waited it out at someone's home in town. But either way, we didn't need Ua to get caught in yet another storm.

"I'll go," I said, grabbing things to offer the kahuna: Food, practical items like coconut bowls, lauhala weavings, and kapa.

"She just won't stop crying," Melika said, her eyes watering, overwhelmed. Ua stepped in.

"I'll take a turn."

Thunder rolled over the hut, silencing the baby for a moment. Her tear streaked eyes glanced up at us, afraid.

"It's alright," Ua said, holding the baby close to her chest and rocking her. "Kaʻala will get you medicine and it will be alright." Her soothing voice, also new and different from mine and Melika's, calmed the baby.

Ua wiped the baby's tears and glanced at Melika and I. Purple rimmed Ua's eyes. Strands of hair fell from the bun on top of her head. It looked like she hadn't slept in days... because she hadn't. Not really.

I was pretty sure Melika and I looked the same. We were all tired, not fit to raise such a young infant, but doing our best.

"I'll be back as soon as I can," I said, placing my bag over my shoulder. I knelt to rub the baby's back, hoping that the kahuna could give me something to help.

"Be safe," Ua said, and, as if on cue, lightning flashed the room with bright lights. A child from the bedroom moaned. Ua quickly left with the baby to tend to the frightened child.

"Thanks for keeping watch," I said to Melika as we stepped onto the porch.

"If you take too long, should we come looking for you?" Melika asked.

I shook my head. "I'll be fine. Promise." We kissed one another's cheeks and then I started on the path towards town. Thunder continued to move across the sky, followed by piercing streaks of lightning. Rain had not yet started, but I had a feeling it would soon. The air seemed unusually still, the calm before the storm.

And all I could think about was the sick baby. The poor, innocent infant had already endured so much: her mother dropping her off, leaving her in the hands of a murderous king; being rescued multiple times by myself, Ua, and Melika, and now... she was horribly sick. I wanted to give this baby the life and health she deserved, but I really didn't know the first thing. I was not in a position right now to do so, even if I did my best. My home was for refugees who could mostly take care of themselves (besides wounded soldiers and the like).

If things had been different, I might have gone to my father's house to ask my mother, Kalani, what to do. Growing up, she had been a natural herbalist. Kalani grew every type of plant and knew exactly how each could heal the body.

But my mother is gone. Though she was still around, the sickness took over her, wiping her memory. I wondered if Kona was doing alright during his visit to our parents. I wished he could come and help us more, but my father, Oponui, was so controlling. I had no qualms against Kona for not coming, but an extra set of hands would be nice.

If Kona did come to stay at my hut, Oponui might come

after him. And father meddling in our operations was the last thing we needed.

A few light drops of rain misted my skin. I kept looking around, making sure Mailou, or anyone else, did not follow me. So far I was alone, as anyone wise enough would hunker down and prepare to weather the storm. I wished I'd given Melika instructions on checking the thatch roofing. I hadn't checked it in days since Kona returned, and I liked to keep things in tip top shape.

Our refugees, who'd already been through so much, didn't need a roof leaking on them or walls flapping in the wind.

Maybe she'll check it, I told myself, knowing Melika to be resourceful and take initiative.

Rain started falling harder, until it became a downpour. Luckily the wind hadn't picked up, so I could still make my way to town quite fast without getting blown all over the place.

The kahuna lived on the outskirts of the town, closer to the ocean. His hut always smelled of incense and smoke when one passed it. Even as I got closer, I could smell it.

Sopping wet, I knocked on his door.

The kahuna was a peculiar sort, just like myself, because nobody had doors. The huts we built on the islands were usually very small, with no windows, but an open hole for the door.

The kahuna creaked open the door and an old, wrinkled face, with stringy gray hair frowned at me.

"It's me, Ka'ala," I said. "My sister is sick with a fever. Can I trade something for help?"

He looked me up and down, and I became aware of how wet I was. Everything clung to me, and my hair, which had been pulled up into a bun, had loose hair plastered to my skin and face. He rubbed his chin.

"A fever? Well... I might have something. Come in."

I stayed by the door, overwhelmed by the amount of scents: herbs, smoke, incense, body odor. The old man moved about the hut, looking through all sorts of his coconut bowls, gourds, and other box holders. He sniffed things, spoke to himself, and then, finally, found what he was looking for.

"I have only a little bit left," he said, holding out a coconut bowl to me, his fingers shaky. Inside the bowl was a gooey purple substance.

"What is it?"

"A mixture of sea ingredients. Rub the salve on her forehead, behind her ears, and neck. The fever should go down in a few hours."

I eagerly reached into my bag, ready to trade whatever was in there. "I have newly made kapa, recently waxed coconut bowls, lauhala weavings—"

The kahuna held up his hand. "My payment is only that you bring me a bundle of purple limu as soon as you can."

"Purple limu..." The limu, seaweed, was in the ocean, close to the reef. Though I couldn't get the limu now, I nodded. I could always get it later and repay the kahuna.

"There's enough in that bowl for two to three uses," he continued. "But I need more purple limu for medicine, in case another unfortunate soul stops by here."

"I will check after the storm and bring you as much as I can."

"The sooner after the storm, the better."

I tipped my head to let him know I had every intention

of finding his purple limu. After placing the coconut bowl in my bag, I bowed my head and stepped back."Good day."

"Don't forget to come back," the old man warned.

He was right. There were probably plenty of people who didn't pay him back. Even if he didn't *really* fix the problem, he still deserved payment for his time and resources.

"I won't forget," I assured him, then ran into the rain. The wind picked up, blowing the drops in every direction, making it difficult to see. I avoided palm trees, not wanting anything to fall and crack my head.

It had happened to other islanders in the past, and I'd seen huge leaves and coconuts fall from trees on any day. I would not be another one who was killed by acting so carelessly.

As I NEARED THE TOWN, I was going to pass by, not enter it. But a queasy feeling reached my stomach and I saw a shadow move in the path ahead. I didn't need more than a glimpse to catch the height and broad shoulders of someone waiting for me.

Mailou.

If I took the path, he'd grab me. The rain and wind would cover my cries for help, or, perhaps, I'd fight him, out in the open. I couldn't risk that.

I just need to get back. The helpless baby's sweet face came to mind. How were Ua and Melika doing with the baby? I hadn't been gone too long, but I still had a trek to get back to the sanctuary. Hopefully the baby was doing alright.

Calculating my chances, I decided to move through the village. I could take the long way home, which consisted of taking a different path on the other end of town.

Many of the huts had been sealed shut with lauhala woven or koa wood doors. I could imagine all the families huddled inside, with nothing but kukui oil lamps to light their homes.

Thunder boomed across the sky, and I kept my arm over my face to keep it shielded. Each passing minute it became harder and harder to see. Not to mention the skies grew darker now, as night fell.

As I reached the end of town, a figure ran out from one of the huts, a large cape over his head. I groaned to myself.

"Kaʻala, are you crazy?" Aliʻi looked nice today, his hair pulled back, his facial hair now cleanly trimmed. He covered me with his cape, providing some respite from the icy wind and rain. But, in no time, his cape was soaked through. I immediately noticed he wasn't wearing a kihei across his chest, and it made my heart skip a beat.

He was quite toned, and the battle scars across his body made it difficult to *not* stare.

"Come on!" He led us to his hut and stood in the doorway of it. I didn't dare go in, but stood across from him, catching my breath and wiping water from my face and arms.

"What are you doing?" he asked above the sound of the rain. It looked like he wanted to smile at seeing me, but, instead, concern crossed his face.

"Melika has a fever," I said, lying once more. "I went to the kahuna for medicine."

"It's that bad?" Now he looked even more concerned. It made my heart feel all mushy.

"She'll be fine. I just need her fever to go down so she can rest." I then glanced at the pathway. Did Mailou secure himself on this path? The brush between the two different

65

paths was quite thick with trees, ferns, and long grass, and he'd be a fool to traverse it in the rain.

But then again, Mailou did seem creepy and desperate enough to do such a thing.

"What did the kahuna give you?" Aliʻi asked, respectfully keeping his distance from me, though we were both crammed in the doorway. I was surprised he didn't place his arm above me, to hover over me like he did last time.

Perhaps he suspected me... again. My eyes moved from his face to his chest, once more.

So many scars... I remembered Ua's words, that Aliʻi was a war hero. Surely he was feared by many, both of his own men in Hana, and the men they fought in Kohala.

His face, both scarred and hardened from the war, also looked... compassionate. Or was that a look he only reserved for maidens like me?

I showed him the coconut bowl from my bag and he bit his lower lip. "Is that it?"

"'Ae. Do you have other suggestions?"

For a baby? Who knew if this gel stuff would work to help a baby? Was it even safe to use on a baby? I couldn't ask any of these questions though. Once again, I wished my mother was healthier. She would know.

He nodded and moved into the hut. Now I looked at his humble home, here in Lanai. The local chief had probably given Aliʻi this guest hut to stay in for the time. Aliʻi didn't seem to have much belongings, but the room seemed... cozy.

I thought about how inappropriate this would look, if anyone were to see me hanging out at the captain's doorway in the middle of a storm.

"I should get going," I said, not knowing why he went inside. He searched through a bundle and pulled out a small gourd.

"Here," he said, taking my hand and placing it within. "This is a remedy we used all the time on the wounded men in war. It works like a charm."

"What is it?" I opened the lid and peeked in, finding a thick purple liquid.

"It's like what you have, but even just a drop or two can help soothe a person from the inside out."

"Is it a drug?" I asked.

"One of King Hua's high priests, Luuana, made it. From using it on others, to using it myself, I assure you it's all natural, not addictive, and definitely not a drug." He eyed me again, as if trying to read *who* really needed this remedy.

I placed the gourd in my bag next to the coconut bowl. "Thanks," I told him, not trusting it, but glad to have a second option if we got desperate.

Now looking up at him, I realized he stood close to me. Not on purpose, as the door frame was small, but I couldn't help staring into his eyes. He had kind brown eyes, like the color of bright koa wood.

"Can I escort you to your home?" he asked, then broke eye contact by looking towards the path. It was dark out now, and I had no doubt it'd make it harder to see Mailou.

But what if Melika is out keeping watch and he sees her? No. That wouldn't be possible, because Melika would see us coming up the path long before he glanced at the hut. She would go in and hide, no questions asked.

And I didn't want to risk getting pounced on by Mailou. My stomach fluttered a little at the thought of the captain being my protector that night. Was I really trusting a king's man?

I nodded. "If you don't mind."

The captain tipped his head. "It's my pleasure." At that, he grabbed a rain cape that hung on the wall. The rain cape, made of dried ti leaves, was thick and warm as he held it over our heads. I was aware of his bicep behind my head, and his body close to me.

We stepped into the pouring rain, the wind immediately pushing us to the side. Ali'i let one hand off the cape to wrap his arm around my waist, steadying me.

Heat overcame my body, and I was glad he couldn't see me blush.

No words passed between us, but, instead, we focused on the darkened path, planting our feet firmly so the wind wouldn't blow us away.

Ali'i kept looking up at the trees, watching for palms or any other things that might potentially fall on us.

In a strange way, it felt good to have someone looking out for me. I always looked out for others, keeping watch, but now... someone did that for me.

Though I was chilled to the bone, it warmed me a little.

By the time the hut came into view, I concealed a smile that the porch was empty. Melika or Ua must have spotted us and hid inside. We stepped onto the porch, the creaks and groans still loud enough against the rainy weather.

"Thank you," I said, wiping wet hair from my face. Ali'i put his thick ti leaf cape around his shoulders and nodded.

"Of course. Will you and your sister be alright?"

I patted the bag at my side. "We will now. Thanks for escorting me and for the remedy. I'll return it when she's better..."

We stood in an awkward silence, while both of us searched for words.

"Well, I should get going then..." Ali'i seemed to have lost his flirty, player self. Why? Was that act not working, so he had to try something else?

"Sure..." I didn't know what to do with my hands. Or

my legs. Or where I should look. I was just glad the baby wasn't crying, or that Melika and Ua had cleared the area.

"Good night then," Ali'i said, tipping his head. But before he left, he swallowed and smoothed his hair back. "Will I see you again?"

"Only if you want to." I repeated the same words I said to him the other night.

"I'd really like to." A smile crawled up the sides of his lips and my girly heart swooned at it.

Stop it... my thoughts said. I would have *nothing* to do with Ali'i, a servant to King Hua.

I held my hands behind my back. "Well, then maybe I'll see you around."

The captain now grinned. "'Ae. See you around." Without warning, he kissed my cheek, his hand lightly brushing my shoulder, then he turned and left.

He left me speechless. Kissing someone's cheek was an island custom, no big deal... but it felt like a big deal.

My heart was beating so hard and fast, I took a deep breath and hurried into the hut.

"It's me," I said, knocking on the sliding door.

Melika opened it and peeked out. "Is he gone?" she asked.

I nodded, and she opened the door more.

Ua sat in the corner, rocking the baby. It was awake, but whimpering quietly. Some of the children sat up, unable to sleep, while others seemed completely content with the sound of the storm.

I brought out the kahuna's remedy, still not knowing if I could trust Ali'i's remedy from the high priest. I heard King Hua's high priest was very powerful, so it made me distrust him even more.

Ua and I applied the dark purple gel to the places that

the healer recommended, then I changed into dry clothes before taking the baby into my arms and hoping her fever broke overnight.

THE STORM RAGED on into the next day, flooding the pathways and keeping us stuck in the hut. Ua and Melika played games with the children while I held the baby.

But nothing worked. Her fever did not break overnight, and she didn't look one bit better.

By midday, she was silent as ever. She would spit up the water we tried to give her and not eat anything. Ua, Melika, and I finally broke into tears as we realized how helpless we were.

The children all napped as Melika put a meal together. Ua and I took turns holding the baby, trying to chant words of comfort and healing.

But nothing worked.

Then I remembered Ali'i's gourd. Should I use it? What if it was a trick?

Why would the captain give you something to poison your sister? He wouldn't, right? I just never trusted any of the king's men, and I didn't want to start now.

I told my sister and best friend about Ali'i escorting me, but I didn't mention the remedy.

We have no other choice, I thought.

I brought the gourd from my bag, and, after explaining what it was to Ua and Melika, dipped my finger lightly into the gourd.

"He said even one drip helps soothe the body." I gently opened the baby's mouth and let a few drops fall onto her tongue. She swallowed and tried to spit, but the liquid went down.

I blinked multiple times, hopeful.

"It probably doesn't work right away," Ua said, letting out a sad sigh.

"Wait." I kept a few fingers on the baby's forehead. Within minutes, the fever broke. While Ua and Melika celebrated, I was baffled.

The high priest is powerful. Was the high priest the reason King Hua was so invincible? Did the high priest give the king all sorts of remedies like this to heal his body after bloody battles? And what about spells on the king? Could the high priest do that?

And does Ali'i know about all of that? The thought crossed my mind that he did. With a scar like the one that went across his face, shouldn't he be dead? Perhaps the high priest did something to help Ali'i, one of King Hua's prized captains, to heal and survive.

Though I should have been celebrating with Ua and Melika, an overwhelming feeling of anger fell over me.

This baby would never be in this situation if it wasn't for people like Captain Ali'i and King Hua. This was all the captain's fault. People like him, who were loyal to the king, prolonged this bloody, endless war. People like him caused others to be used as sacrifices, or to flee Hana in hopes of escaping the war.

This was all his fault, and he'd pay for it.

The second realization washed over me with clarity.

Ali'i is attracted to me. I didn't like him (or so I told myself), but what if... what if I *used* him? What if I played him to get to the king? Surely the captain knew the king's secrets, like how he was so invincible.

The king kept his captains close to him, treated his captains the best out of all his subjects. Surely Ali'i knew

71

how to make the king vulnerable. Perhaps he even knew how the high priest and magic and all of that worked...

As Melika and Ua clapped and hugged and cheered, I seethed.

I'm so sick of this war. And tired of innocent people, like this baby suffering. Especially when the king has resources like this remedy that should be used for his people, not for war.

I made a decision right then and there. *Ali'i knows about the king. I'm going to get close to him... and I'm going to discover how to kill King Hua. If nobody else can end this war, then I will.*

CHAPTER EIGHT

*D*ebris littered the entire island. Fallen trees blocked paths. Mud and landslides covered large areas. Brown, murky waves broke onto the shore. Branches, torn pieces from huts, and leaves covered the once white, sandy beaches. The waterfalls overflowed with brown, rushing currents.

But the people of Lanai were resilient and smiling, as always. We emerged from our homes, many of us checking up on one another. A few people from town ran up to my hut, asking if Melika and I were alright.

Ua went to her own hut, gifted by her grandfather, to see if there might be any damage. The air hung in heavy humidity, and a messenger from the chief came up the porch to speak with Melika, who kept watch.

The baby slept peacefully in the corner, while I combed through and braided one of the little girl's hair. Ua, Melika, and I made an effort to treat the children well, doing small acts of service like making their hair, listening, and playing games.

Melika slid the bedroom door open a little and smiled at the children who waved to her, silently, as we told them to.

"The chief says there will be a beach cleanup tomorrow morning," Melika said. "And then whoever needs the most help patching up their homes... we'll divide and conquer." She sighed. "Ka'ala, can I please go?"

I knew Melika had been feeling cooped up lately. Usually 'Eleu came a little more frequently, so we didn't have to host the refugees *this* long. I understood 'Eleu's delay, as the storm was probably raging across the sea. Perhaps she encountered it and had to land somewhere else, like on Maui or Molokai. Or perhaps it drifted her and her grandfather farther from here.

I did feel bad for Melika. Because when we didn't have refugees, I usually went around doing my errands with Melika, except on days that Kona arrived with new people.

I suppressed my own sigh. As much as I would have enjoyed staying at home, watching and tending to the children, I knew I had to go.

Ali'i will be there, helping. It'd give me a chance to be around him. *To flirt...* though I didn't want to, no matter how handsome he really was.

"Melika, I promise after we get these children to Nai'a, you and I will go surfing, swimming and do *whatever* you want every day until the next batch of people arrive," I said, offering a smile.

My younger sister's shoulders sank, but she nodded. "Alright."

Guilt panged my chest. I wanted to let her go, but I also needed to take my chance with the captain. Who knew what he would do now? Because... if he figured me out, would he arrest me? Take me to the king? Kill me?

I remembered kissing him on the cheek, and how he

froze, wide eyed, like he was under some spell. Although I didn't want to play bad games, I wanted to learn how to kill the king, how to finish his invincibility, and end this war. Ali'i was the way to do that.

These children deserved a better life. If King Hua were gone, Prince Kekoa would become King of Hana, and I had no doubt he'd make a better ruler by a thousand times. After all, he was the one keeping these children and people safe from his father's murderous hand.

"My turn," said the next girl, who waited patiently in line. She sat in front of me as I combed through her hair and began braiding. The other girls, as usual, circled, watching my hands work. The young boys, meanwhile, built little huts with sticks in the other corner.

"Are you married?" asked the girl, barely whispering. We taught the children to speak quietly, unless we told them otherwise.

"No."

Silence. Her thick, midnight hair wove through my fingers into a beautiful braid at the back of her head, curving against her small back like a waterfall. "Why do you ask?"

The other girls giggled, but covered their mouths to keep quiet.

"Because we saw 'Apapane kiss someone."

I frowned. Ua... kissed someone? "Who?"

"He came to the door here..." One of the girls pointed to the sliding door. "And they talked for a little while."

"Then they kissed!" Another little girl, who had to be about six years old, covered her mouth again to keep from giggling.

"When?"

"When you were gone, and 'Elepaio went for a walk."

75

Melika went for a walk? When did this happen? I hated to feel out of control. Melika knew better than to *not* keep watch. Unless...

Unless Kona came here. Kona could have told Melika to take a break while he kept watch.

I must have been gone, in town.

"She thought we were all taking a nap," said another little one.

"It was so romantic," an older girl, about ten years old, said, smiling wide.

"Ew, gross," said a boy in the corner.

"Was it 'Ake?" Was it Kona then?

The girls nodded, big smiles on their faces.

"Was this just a few days ago?" I asked, recalling a time Ua and Melika had been here during the day, while I'd been gone. They mentioned Kona had stopped by, but I missed him.

"'Ae." The children spoke in unison.

"Have you told anyone else?"

They shook their heads.

"Oh... it'll be our secret, alright?" I smiled and covered my lips with my finger. The children giggled and covered their own lips. My heart pumped though. Someone was to keep watch, *always*. And while it was alright if Kona spoke to Ua for a few minutes, how could I be sure?

A few minutes was enough time for *anyone* to come up the path and discover this secret, this sanctuary I worked so hard to build. Any of these people could be in danger at any moment, if we let our guard down.

Ua and Kona kissed? It was weird to think, and made my head a little dizzy. Ua, my best friend since childhood, and Kona, my older brother... *kissed?* Was this going to ruin our operations? What if their relationship *didn't* work out?

What if they "broke up?" It'd make things incredibly awkward for all of us. Did Melika know about this secret romantic relationship between the two? And what did she think of it? I had no doubt she'd be alright with it, because she was a hopeless romantic and wanted to see Ua and I married off to handsome men, living happily ever after.

But I figured I should speak with Ua first, as Melika was only a second-hand observation. And, of course, I was not one to gossip, especially not about my best friend.

BUT NOTHING HAPPENED. Ua didn't stop by that night, and I figured I would see her the following day at the clean up. She had probably been busy helping her own family patch things up and get everything re-situated after the storm.

It made me feel antsy inside though. Why did I feel so anxious to ask Ua about her relationship with Kona? Was it because their relationship might ruin everything? Was I afraid she'd be mad at my disapproval? *Did* I disapprove? Because, at the moment, it certainly felt like it.

But why should I withhold Ua from happiness? Especially if she finds that happiness with Kona. It was still all weird to me, but I kept my feelings and thoughts close to my heart.

For now, I braced myself for the clean up and spending time with Ali'i... because I'd be sure we spent ample time together. And who knew? Maybe I'd get all the answers out of him faster than I expected.

Or, at least, *I hoped* to get the answers out of him.

. . .

THE HOT MORNING sun made the air feel even more sticky and wet with the storm's aftermath. I joined the throng of people on the beach as they listened to instructions from the local chief's advisor. I didn't see the yellow cape of Ali'i and wondered if he went to a different volunteer group, as there were a few spread across the island.

A tall figure stood next to me, and when I looked, thinking it might be Ali'i, I saw it was my brother, Kona.

"Long time no see," I muttered.

He rolled his eyes. "Father is getting worse, you know."

I did know what he meant: father was getting more controlling. We spoke softly to one another, keeping our eyes open for any potential dangers around us.

"Has he been setting you up with different young women?" I asked.

"He doesn't even have to try. They come on their own."

"Has anyone caught your eye?" I glanced at him. The corner of his lip turned up.

"I've had my eye on someone for a while now."

Did he mean Ua? And how long? Kona had returned from battle years ago, so had he and Ua been courting in secret? Or did they recently discover their interest for each other? Before I could ask, a familiar voice spoke softly next to me.

"Nice to see you here." Another tall figure slipped on the right side of me, his arm brushing against mine. My cheeks warmed of their own accord, though I had no reason to blush or feel embarrassed.

Kona's jaw tensed as he looked from me to the captain. "This is my older brother, Kona," I said, motioning with my hands. "Kona, this is Ali'i, a captain to King Hua."

Kona looked ahead, saying nothing. His coldness was apparent, and Ali'i read it immediately. "Nice to meet you," he said, but Kona ignored him. I met Ali'i's eyes and quickly looked away, not knowing what to say or do. The awkwardness settled around us.

"What did I miss?" Ua now squeezed between me and Kona, causing more of a rift between us. I'd never been terribly close to my older brother, but now it felt like Ua literally and figuratively wedged herself into the picture.

Ali'i glanced from me to Ua, frowning. He could see the resemblance between us, the same build, height, even the same kind of hair.

"Are you related?" he asked.

Ua's eyes went wide, as she hadn't noticed him standing there. And then she secretly squeezed my wrist, apologetic. She knew, as well as I, that the captain seeing us together was only evidence to support his investigation. He was looking for two girls who looked alike, yet one had "flawed skin." He was looking for two girls who duped the king.

"We're not related," I said, adding. "But we're best friends."

Much to my relief, the chief's assistant began dividing up the crowd. He sent me, Ali'i, Ua, and Kona, to start cleaning at the north beach, moving all the debris into a large pile to be burned later.

Like a protective older brother, Kona stayed beside me. Ali'i got the hint loud and clear, so he offered his arm to Ua and they walked in front of us. Kona scowled as Ali'i and Ua started an easy conversation.

Much to my own annoyance, seeing Ua and Ali'i together made my own heart flare.

Why in the world am I jealous? I thought. I decided I didn't like Ali'i, but I'd use him. The two walked ahead, picking things up along the path.

Kona and I followed.

"You should stay away from him," Kona said, once the other two were out of ear shot. We picked up branches and moved them to a pile off the sandy beach.

"Why?"

My brother picked up a particularly large log and dragged it, as I walked beside him, my hands full of debris.

"He's one of the king's highest captains."

"I know. And... so?"

"I can tell you're up to something–the way you're observing him," Kona said as he dropped the log. He let out a breath. "I've known you long enough not to doubt you though... whatever plans you have with this captain... just be careful."

We walked to gather more black, brown, and green logs and branches. The gooey, mushy wood kept crumbling everytime I tried to pick them up, as the rain had soaked everything through.

"You're right not to doubt me," I said. Kona pursed his lips, knowing that though we had a good childhood together, he always teased me for being too shy.

I was always a quiet person, but that didn't make me any less brave. Ever since he joined my cause, he promised to never doubt me. It was an honor I greatly appreciated.

Kona paused to watch Ali'i and Ua, and he frowned.

"What do you know of the captain?" I asked.

"He broke a young woman's heart. She's from the upper class. Every young man in the battle pined after her. There's rumors that Prince Kekoa might marry her."

"What's her name?"

"Noni."

"And the captain was... courting her?" I remembered the captain saying he wanted to marry a young lady. He said she was the only girl he kissed. Though I hated to gossip, I couldn't help but indulge in my brother's words. What, about this captain, did I need to know?

"She said she waited all those battles for him, and, finally, he dumped her in front of a huge crowd. Noni was so embarrassed, and so she opened up, sharing all sorts of horrible things he did to her."

My eyes went wide. "Like what?"

"Most of it was words, but she said he attempted to physically hurt her a few times."

I didn't really believe it, but then again... anyone could be right. And some men, like Ali'i, were charmers on the outside, monsters on the inside.

"And you trust this... Noni girl?" I asked.

Kona shrugged and looked back at the two, his fists clenched. "Come on."

"Excuse me?"

"I said, come on." He started marching towards Ua and Ali'i, leaning on his crutch and moving fast. I ran to catch up.

"What are you doing?"

Ua saw us approach, and, upon seeing Kona's face, the smile that spread across her face, faded.

"Ua, will you come with me to start the area up there?" Kona asked, pointing to the northern spot of the beach, where there seemed to be large deposits of seaweed. As far as I could tell, none of it was purple seaweed, which I needed.

"Of course," she said, taking his arm and glancing back at me, shrugging. But why would she shrug? Wasn't she courting Kona? Or was Ua putting on a front too?

"Is your sister doing better?" Ali'i asked, picking up some logs and heaving them over his shoulder.

"Oh, um. Yes." I picked up my own pile and followed

him. He and Ua had worked quickly earlier, their pile very large and tall already. I looked back at my brother and Ua, catching my brother rubbing Ua's back.

That's definitely romantic. All my suspicions were right then, and now... what could I do? I should be happy for them. Yet... I felt sort of annoyed. What were they thinking? This could ruin *everything,* everything I worked so hard to build.

"Ka'ala?"

I whirled around, seeing the captain smile at me. "You seem distracted. Is something wrong?"

"Oh no..."

Ali'i followed my gaze. "Ua is really nice. I can see why she's your best friend." My stomach tightened. What was he trying to say? That she was nicer than me?

Why am I being jealous? I asked myself once more. There was no need for that. I cleared my throat and smiled back at him, which froze him in place.

"'Ae, she's wonderful. We've been friends since childhood." I had to change the subject, fast. Before he asked any questions about Ua, or her family. Because if he knew that Ua's grandfather was a master at the art of lua, the captain might guess that Ua and I trained under her grandfather. That's why I knew how to use a knife, how to defend myself, and more.

"Anyway, I wanted to thank you for the remedy you gave me. Here are the extras," I said, pulling the gourd from my bag.

Ali'i shook his head. "Keep it. I have plenty."

"I would feel guilty. Really." I took his hand and placed the gourd in it. He stared at our hands touching, and I cleared my throat, which broke whatever spell came on him.

"You mentioned it's from the king's high priest?" I asked.

"'Ae. It's powerful stuff. It saved many warrior's lives in battle." He placed the gourd in his own bag and continued cleaning.

"If you don't mind me asking... is that what was used to help you?"

Ali'i paused, studying me. "What do you mean?"

A blush spread up my face. Was it rude to inquire about the scar across his face? I dropped the contents from my hand into the pile, wiped my hands, and touched his cheek. "This scar," I said, knowing that I was completely flirting with him, and he was stunned in place.

He stepped back, breaking the contact. "I don't know if I want to talk about it."

We stared at each other, and I couldn't keep my heart from weeping for him. So many men had not only physical scars, but emotional and mental scars from battle. None of them were the same, including my own brother. He left with a sense of humor and came home somber as ever.

I nodded. "Of course. Best not to reopen wounds." I turned to pick up more trash, but the captain gently grabbed my arm.

"Wait."

I stepped closer, my heart pumping as his thumb caressed my skin. "I almost died... several times." He pointed to the scar on his face. "This one was the worst. It was given to me by the crown prince of Kohala. He was going to kill King Hua, but..." He paused. "I stepped in and defended him. My men pulled me out before the prince could finish me."

"I'm so sorry," I said. His hand dropped from my arm and he placed it on his hip, looking past me to the sea.

"It taught me a valuable lesson."

"And what is that?"

"Life is short."

I nodded, as I couldn't agree more. It was one of the biggest reasons I started my sanctuary, helping fleeing warriors and refugees. They all deserved a second chance, and, because I'd been born a woman, and was safeguarded here on Lanai, I had to create an opportunity to help.

"After I healed from this, with the high priest's help," Ali'i said, "I intended to marry."

"Why didn't you?"

He shook his head. "It's a story for another time. But... I just don't want to miss an opportunity." At that, he stared into my eyes. "Do you ever feel that way?"

He doesn't want to miss an opportunity... with what? With me? My knees felt weak, and I wondered if I did feel that way. When I started my sanctuary, I certainly didn't want to miss my chance to make a difference. And now. Well... it was all going relatively fine.

Except that I had a more important task, and Ali'i was a part of this game to help me kill the king. I nodded.

"I feel that way all the time."

We studied each other, a deep, intense moment of connection, my insides feeling like they suddenly lost all strength. He looked into my eyes, then down my face, to my lips, before he gently touched my cheek.

A light smile touched his lips. "We're not going to get anything done if you keep asking questions," he said.

I gently pushed him, and he caught my hand, pulling me close. I didn't expect it, and I blushed, glancing at Ua and Kona to make sure they didn't see us flirting. The two were busy talking and gathering things in the distance. I looked into Ali'i's eyes and the realization came over me that he was buying my act. I didn't even have to try.

"Well then get back to work captain," I said, and whirled around, my head feeling dizzy. Ali'i looked at me in a way that no other man looked at me, and it was terrifying. Unlike all the people in my life, who couldn't read me, who didn't understand my true emotions, Ali'i seemed like he really, deeply saw me. And that made this game even more dangerous than I imagined. I would have to put up several fronts, several disguises and distractions to keep him from getting to me. Because if he got to me, this whole act to get close to him, to get to know him and his secrets... it wouldn't be an act. It'd be real.

CHAPTER NINE

We didn't speak much the rest of the time, as we all worked hard to clean the beaches. A few other volunteers joined us, so I eventually separated from Ali'i, working with other women. Ali'i, Kona, and other men were employed to take care of the heavier debris covering the pathways across the island, so they disappeared.

Ua and I walked home after a long day of work, our backs aching, hands and arms raw from picking up and carrying loads of itchy island debris.

Awkwardness settled between us, and I knew it shouldn't be that way. Ua was my best friend, after all, and we grew up doing everything together.

Before I could say something, though, she talked about her family and the condition of their hut that morning. Everything looked good, her siblings and parents were fine. Her grandfather's hut, the one he gave to her, and where she stayed when not helping out at the sanctuary, was in great shape.

I listened and responded, but my stomach kept getting tighter and tighter.

Ask about Kona.

When silence fell between us again, I swallowed hard and said, "Did you notice Kona acting kind of weird today? If I didn't know him any better, I'd say he was jealous..."

Ua faltered in her step but shrugged. "He's always like that, isn't he?"

Silence. *No.* Kona was usually really chill about everything.

"Not around you..." I meant for the words to come out playful, but they came out edgy. Ua tensed, and I hated that I was causing this rift between us. We trusted each other in every way, and now...

"I'm sure he's just being protective. He's protective of you, isn't he?"

"In a brotherly way, ʻae."

More quiet. Was Ua ever going to tell me?

"Maybe he was trying to help you with your plot," she said, and I wanted to pull out my hair. Why couldn't she just tell the truth?

"What plot?"

"The one where you're paying special attention to Aliʻi?" Ua grinned, but it didn't have the heart behind it. Ua, Melika, and Kona knew something was up with me, but I usually kept plans close to my chest. It was easier. When I started the whole sanctuary thing, if I said something, they would have probably discouraged me. But now they all trusted me, even if I didn't say much.

"I've got it sorted, even without Kona's help," I said.

"I know you do." Ua's confidence touched my heart, but I knew we were avoiding the topic of her and Kona. Should I bring up what the children said?

She's making this difficult.

"It just seems like..." I began to say, hating that I wasn't supportive of this relationship. "It seems like Kona's been paying extra attention to you."

"Kona has plenty of women to look at—"

"Ua." I stopped in our tracks and faced her. She was a mirror image of myself, except for the few different features, like her flawless skin and slightly wider nose. We could have been twins in the womb for all I knew.

She chuckled, but it sounded nervous.

I wanted to say, *It's alright if you and Kona like each other...* but then I'd be lying. I didn't *like* that they were interested in each other. It would ruin everything.

Ua hesitated, as if reading my thoughts. "Kona has been showing some... interest," she finally said, fidgeting with her hands. "But I'm just not sure."

"What are you not sure about?" I sounded more annoyed than I meant to. Or, perhaps, my true emotions were showing. I put my emotions in check, putting on a blank face.

"I can't help but..." Ua took a short breath. "I can't really help it, Ka'ala."

"Help what?" Why wouldn't she just say the words?

"I really like him." At this, she blushed. "I've liked him since we were little girls. But he's never paid me any attention. Probably because we look so alike, you know?"

The part of me that was Ua's best friend wanted to melt with and comfort her. That was sad to know—I had never realized she had a crush on Kona. But then again, Kona wasn't around much, as he trained under a grandmaster wayfinder, disappearing for years during my adolescence, and reappearing as a young man.

I'd never paid any attention to the way he and Ua inter-acted... maybe because he didn't notice her. Until now.

The other part of me was plain annoyed. Why would Ua go after Kona when he ignored her all those years? And though I loved my brother, I knew nothing about his love life or self control. All I knew was that he trusted and helped me get refugees out of Hana safely.

And if he was distracted by a girl, then that could ruin our operations.

"We do look alike." I should have said something else, something kind, but I worked *so* hard to start this sanctuary. It even took me a while to let my siblings in on the deal. Ua was the first and only person to know about it–besides Prince Kekoa in Hana–until Kona and Melika came into the pact.

"I'm sorry Kaʻala," Ua said in haste, trying to read me. But I was difficult to read, and her confused look told me I kept my annoyance in check.

"Well... who am I to stop you?" I said, walking again. "If you both like each other... and if it works out, I suppose it should be fine."

"But it's not fine." Ua sighed. "He kissed me the other day..." So the children were right. Ua blushed and avoided eye contact. "And, well... I told him we shouldn't be together."

"What?" I turned on her.

"I told him it wasn't right, and that if we got too attached to each other, it would ruin everything." Ua walked ahead of me and I followed, my heart torn between relief and sadness.

"But you just said you really like him," I said.

"I know, but there are some things in life more impor-tant, like running this sanctuary." Ua motioned to the large hut as it came into view. Melika waved to us from the porch. Ua slowed down so we could finish our conversation before Melika got involved.

"If Kona and I were to..." She hesitated, her cheeks a rosy color. "If we were to, say, marry, then I'd want to go everywhere with him, including to Hana."

And she'd leave me and Melika behind to take care of everything. It wasn't impossible, but it also wasn't easy. Having three of us there ensured that someone was always on watch, while the others got supplies, made food, and tended to the refugees. Just thinking of two people to do all the work made my head spin.

But you've done it with just you and Ua before... That's right. Back in the day, it had been just both of us. No Kona. No Melika.

Prince Kekoa would bring the refugees himself, and then we'd do all the work. Perhaps I'd gotten used to the way we ran things with more of us on board the secret.

"I thought, maybe we have to sacrifice... at least until the war is over." Ua avoided eye contact.

"So you told him you wouldn't court him... until after the war?" I asked.

Ua nodded. "If the war ever ends," she muttered under her breath.

And she was right. The war had been going on for years. I remembered the war starting when I was a young girl, and I couldn't recall a time of peace.

But a new idea crept into my head, even more reason and push to get close to Ali'i.

If he tells me the king's secret to being invincible, I will kill the king. And then everyone will be free. No more refugees. Ua and Kona could feel secure in their courtship and marriage.

Yes. My idea was right all along.

"I admire your patience," I said and squeezed her arm. "Maybe the war will end sooner than we think."

Ua shrugged. "Everyday we hoped the war would end. It's probably only a matter of time before Hua orders his wounded men back to serve." That meant he'd call back my brother, even my father.

"Or he commands women to go to war," I suggested.

Ua rolled her eyes.

"I'm sorry you have to wait." I returned to the topic of her and Kona.

"The question is, will he wait?" She stared at her feet. "There are already so many beautiful girls on the island going after him—"

"Ua, he'd be a fool not to wait for you."

She didn't look one bit comforted.

"What are you all doing? Come on! Tell me everything!" Melika's voice broke our conversation as she stood by the gate, beckoning to us.

"Coming!" I said, then squeezed Ua's arm once more. But she didn't smile or meet my eyes, the concern about winning Kona plain on her face.

I wanted to say something more, like, *He kissed you. Doesn't that tell you enough?* Or *Kona is patient.* But I didn't know if those were true or encouraging. After all, she didn't tell me how Kona responded to her request to wait.

"Come on, I'm dying!" Melika said. "What are you two being all hush hush about? Tell me, please!"

I hurried to the gate, and Ua trailed behind.

"She's just tired. There was a lot of debris to clean up," I said, knowing that Ua probably didn't want Melika meddling in her business. A fifteen year old *and* a hopeless romantic, Melika would talk about it nonstop.

"Well come eat then," Melika said, taking Ua's arm and leading us inside. I shared the happenings and news of that morning with Melika as I held the baby. All the while, Ua kept quiet, deep in thought.

I felt sorry for her, but I also felt a new fire inside of me.

I will play Ali'i's heart... and then I will kill the king. This war had gone on long enough. People, like Ua, the baby, the children, all the refugees who came here, didn't need to suffer anymore because of it.

Ali'i's kind eyes flashed through my mind, and, for a moment, my heart skipped a beat at the way he seemed to see me, beyond my shyness, beyond my masks. *But I will keep a front. He'll never know what he's in for...*

CHAPTER TEN

"I'll be back before dark," I said, kissing Melika's cheek and heading on the path once more. I felt sorry for how long she'd been cooped up at the hut, but we had no other choice.

I needed to pay my debt to the local kahuna for the medicine he let me try, and keep an eye out for 'Eleu. A few days had passed since the storm and, much to my surprise, Ali'i did not stop by, though he was still on the island.

He could be on the other side of Lanai, which explained his absence.

Or he was avoiding me.

A part of me worried that he was no longer interested in me. What if he found some other girl to flirt with?

I intended to cross paths with him that day.

And avoid Mailou. Because having a stalker weighed on my mind at all times. In the past, I considered going to the local chief to voice my concerns. But since the local chief used Mailou for his dirty, secret business, he'd probably side with Mailou.

I told my father multiple times that I was afraid of

Mailou stalking me, but he said I was a woman and being dramatic.

So I took matters into my own hands. Seeing Ua learn self defense, I asked if I could join her. Her grandfather happily took me in to train in the art of lua.

As I walked onto the shores, my feet sunk into the soft sand. The water still looked a little murky from the storm, but it had cleared up significantly. It had cleared up enough to go swimming for some purple limu, at least.

I felt a presence behind me and looked, knowing right away that Mailou must have followed me. My heart pumped.

Get into the water. Now.

Mailou wouldn't chase me into the water. Where was the fun in that? With my knife on my belt and a small pouch over my shoulder, I hurried into the water. It was a little colder than usual, both from the dirty leftovers of the storm and the overcast clouds. But I wasn't afraid.

I wish Melika could come with me. She loved the ocean as much as I did, and when we weren't tending to our duties at the sanctuary, we went surfing, swimming, and, on occasion, borrowed a canoe from another local. Ua would come with us too. As the oldest in her family, she'd been raised by her grandparents and was not close to her parents or siblings.

Melika and I were more like her sisters than her own family.

I dove under the water, opening my eyes, but feeling disappointed that I couldn't see anything. I'd have to swim out farther, no big deal.

When I'm done collecting this stuff, I'll stop by Ali'i's hut, I thought. I walked through the town earlier but found no sign of him. Yet he was on the island, because when I passed his hut, I noticed his things were still there.

But he was not around. So where could he be?

I swam deeper, keeping an eye on my distance from the shore. I was also aware of the rock jettisons reaching out from either side of the bay. If the waves or current were to pull me out, I could make my way to the rocky areas and stand, then walk safely back to shore.

When I scanned the woods for Mailou's shadowy figure, I saw nothing. He must have left.

Does he really have nothing better to do? He was the last of the creed and the last of the Nawao around here. Didn't he want to do something with his life besides follow me around? I shuddered and looked around at the blue ocean surrounding me.

I miss this so much. It felt like forever since I went swimming. I remembered meeting Moana, the same day I first saw Ali'i. She was so lucky to swim in this everyday. It was healing, and calmed my troubled spirit.

A honu, turtle, swam by, taking a breath of air and looking at me.

"Hello there," I said, smiling. It stared at me long enough for me to feel that it returned the greeting, then it dove underwater.

I dove underwater with it, grateful, as it led me straight to a thick cluster of purple limu growing along the reef. I swam away to give the honu space as it ate, finding another cluster nearby. After using my knife to cut a good amount, I broke the surface for air and stuffed the limu into the pouch at my side.

I was so busy fitting the limu into my bag that I didn't notice the waves push me out... further and further away from shore. The currents swelled around me and I frowned as I finished putting away my knife and looked about.

This isn't good. The current pulled me out to sea... fast. I needed to reach the rocky reef, so I swam parallel with the waves, telling myself not to panic.

Panicking would only make things worse and could even cause me to drown. I'd been caught in the current a few times before, and all I had to do was swim with the waves. They'd bring me to the rocks or shore. Eventually.

Yet even as I followed the waves, they continued to pull me out, further and further. Usually the currents had some consistency, but it was a strange day in the water. I didn't blame it. A storm had just come through the area, so it seemed that the ocean was trying to readjust itself. I'd get pulled out, then in, back and forth. I finally had to rest, as I'd passed my rocky reefs long ago, and now aimed to swim with the waves towards a cliff area.

I floated on my back and took some deep breaths. This would be a story to share with Melika, for sure. She'd probably be jealous that I got to swim for so long too. She'd been so sad that morning, wanting to come with me. I wanted her to, but Ua had errands to run and I needed to repay my debt. I didn't want too much time to pass before giving the old kahuna his payment.

Knowing that I needed to get back to swimming, I slowly let my legs down and calculated how far the cliffs were. They'd be hard to scale, but I could do it. Just getting out of this strong current was more important than being stuck on the side of a cliff.

I glanced towards the shore, now so small in the distance. I was along the side of a different beach, and a figure in the water caught my eye.

I squinted to try to get a better look, hoping it wasn't Mailou.

It's someone on a surfboard... paddling out.

My heart skipped a beat as I realized the form and shape of the man paddling. *Ali'i.*

How did he know I was out here? I waited patiently for him, treading water, until he arrived. He was completely bare chested, and, again, the scars across his body were prominent reminders of his time in battle. Water glistened across his muscles and I tried hard not to stare.

I *tried.*

"I noticed you were out here," he said, looking around and shaking his head, as if surprised. "What are you doing?"

"Collecting purple limu for the kahuna."

"The currents are strong today."

"I know. But I had a debt to pay."

Ali'i challenged me. "And the water is murky. You know what that means." Sharks. But I'd never been afraid of sharks.

I frowned. "Are you just going to stare at me swimming, or did you come to help?" Obviously I could have said something more clever or flirtatious but I was too tired to think of something.

At this, he grinned and scooted back, patting the front of his board for me to sit. There was a paddle on the board that he moved to the side. "I was hoping you'd like a ride," he said.

I hoisted myself up and let out a breath, not realizing how tired the swimming and treading had made me. My fingers were pruny and wilted looking, and I wondered how long I'd been out there.

"Your lips are purple. Are you alright?" Ali'i asked, his hand on my back as he placed the paddle behind him.

With his question, my teeth chattered and my body trembled. I tried to stop the shivers, but it was uncontrollable. "I guess I'm a little cold," I said, wiping my wet hair from my face and pulling my knees onto the board.

Before I could protest, Aliʻi pulled me into his arms, my back against his chest. I stiffened, resisting the urge to flinch or yank myself away. This was *not* normal. Or appropriate?

But... his arms, wrapped around me, felt so warm.

"Is that *all* you were doing out here?" he asked. "I noticed Mailou leaving the area."

I was quiet for a moment. After telling my father, repeatedly, that Mailou was stalking me, and after getting rejected, told I was delusional and crazy, I didn't tell anyone except Ua and Melika. I knew they believed me, at least. Yet I vowed never to tell any *man*. Because they frowned down on me, like I was an idiot or wanting attention.

"And you follow Mailou around?" I teased.

"Only because I noticed he follows *you* around," Aliʻi said, leaning his head over my shoulder to look me in the eyes. His face was so close, my heart couldn't handle it.

I'm not attracted to him, I'm NOT attracted to him, I told myself over and over. But he was so warm, his arms so comforting. His chest was hard, and each time the waves bounced us up and down, I fell against him. But I continued to hold myself stiffly, because I didn't want to succumb to falling into him. This was just an act, after all and I didn't need to go *all in*. Right?

Wait... *he* noticed Mailou following me around? So Aliʻi was watching me.

Exhausted from holding myself, as not to fall against his chest, I gave up. My back rested against him, and he shifted, noticing I'd given up the fight within myself.

"I promised myself I'd never tell another man about Mailou. Nobody believes me."

"What do you mean?"

"I told my father many times, and he said I'm making it up."

"Well if he spent even one day following Mailou, he'd know it's not made up." Ali'i shook his head. "That man does nothing *all* day, but keeps an eye out for you. I've been watching him."

"You've been watching him..." I smiled at the shoreline ahead of us, testing the captain once more. "Not because you're curious as to him following me around, but because of the inspections, right?"

I could feel Ali'i's grin as he leaned forward once more, his cheek against the side of my head. "Of course."

"I think I'm warm enough now," I said, sitting forward and grabbing the paddle, breaking his grip from my body. "We're drifting farther from shore."

"I'll paddle, you rest," Ali'i said, taking the paddle from my hand. His fingers brushed against mine and my whole body tingled. In fact, I felt warm from the inside out. Having his arms wrapped around me caused feelings within me I'd never had before.

Excitement. Hope. Lightness. Was it bad to want more?

Yes, very bad. Remember the end goal. Get close to Ali'i so I could discover how to kill King Hua. *Right.*

Ali'i knelt behind me and started paddling. I kept my arms wrapped around my knees, wondering if my back looked alright.

What am I thinking? My hair was a mess, strands plastered to my face from the messy bun. My clothes also stuck to me, and I felt incredibly vulnerable. I thought of all the freckles along my back, and covering every inch of my body. Did Ali'i find that attractive?

It doesn't matter. Focus.

"Well if you ever told me Mailou is following you around, I'd believe you in a heartbeat," Ali'i said.

"Why?"

"Because I've watched him myself." The waves started getting choppier, so I held onto the side of the board for balance. Ali'i was right. The currents were strong, so we might be paddling to shore for a while.

At least we had a board.

And each other. I glared ahead, trying to silence my thoughts.

"Why does he follow you?" Ali'i asked again.

"I don't know."

The waves bobbed us up and down.

"When did you notice him following you?"

I hesitated before answering. "When I started becoming a young woman..." At this, I blushed, realizing how tacky that sounded. But I continued anyway. "I mean, when I was *growing,* I think he started noticing me."

"Did he hurt you?"

"No."

"Touch you?"

"No. Well..." I paused, not wanting to share the moment I realized Mailou had started to become obsessed with me. Ali'i waited, patiently at first, but when I didn't continue, he rubbed my arm.

I froze up, not used to someone touching me this much. I would hug Ua and Melika, squeeze their arms for comfort, and we'd kiss one another's cheeks, but the way Ali'i touched me was completely different. And the sensations it gave me were a whole other level.

"What happened?" Ali'i asked, then resumed paddling.

I swallowed, finding a lump in my throat. Nobody had ever asked when it all started, not even Ua or Melika. It wasn't because they didn't care, but rather that they were afraid to even bring up anything to do with the creed or the Nawao. Did I dare tell Ali'i?

Maybe if I share this, he'll open up to me. I had to take the chance.

"One time I was walking along the beach." I paused before adding, "Alone."

Ali'i didn't say anything, and I wished I could see his facial expressions, but I kept my eyes on the shore ahead. I also didn't need to add that the reason I was alone was that I had been going on my usual stroll to the fishermen, wanting to trade kapa or other materials for fish. At the time it was just me and Ua running our operations, and Prince Kekoa would be by that day with refugees.

"He, and some other creed members—you heard about the creed right?" I asked, interjecting my own story.

"'Ae."

Fortunately the creed was gone now, making me breathe easier. But years ago, when they were on Lanai, everyone walked on eggshells. "They came walking onto the beach. One of them started asking me questions. I was kind of scared, but I knew if I needed to, I could run away."

I dipped my fingers in the water, not wanting the salt to dry and make them sticky.

"Well, they asked me if I was interested in their kind. I told them I wasn't. I asked them to leave me alone. They teased me and said inappropriate things. Some of them asked if they could... do things with me and I told them I would never do such a thing. They laughed about it. And then Mailou grabbed my wrist and said one day I would be very interested in their kind."

At this, I shuddered. "I broke free of his grasp and ran away as fast as I could. But ever since then, Mailou has followed me around. I didn't notice it at first, but it became apparent he was set on having me... but for what purpose, I don't know." At this I glanced back at Ali'i, finding him frowning.

"Did he do anything else to you?" he asked, not looking at me. Was he angry at me? Panic rose within me. Maybe Ali'i thought I was being dramatic, just like my father. I shouldn't have told him. This story would ruin the game between us.

"Well, when he was assigned by the Lanai chief to capture a local chief and return the goods, he requested me as his reward."

"And your father agreed to it?"

"'Ae." I let out a breath, worried now that I'd said too much. The shoreline never looked so far away. Were we even moving?

"Anyway, it's not a big deal. I don't know why I shared it with you."

"It *is* a big deal," Ali'i said, kneeling behind me so he was at eye level with me. "Ka'ala, that is *not* normal. Mailou stalking you is *not* normal. No woman should have to deal with that."

I swallowed once more. "But my father says I'm crazy–"

"You're not crazy." Ali'i's voice was so reassuring, it almost made me want to cry. "Ka'ala, I'm going to make sure that monster stops following you. And I'm going to make sure he *never* touches you again, understand?"

How could he care so much about this? And how would

he ensure that? Sure, he was a high captain to King Hua, but why would Mailou listen to an order from the captain?

Although I wasn't sure how Ali'i would protect me, the fact that he *believed* me and wanted to protect me made my eyes watery.

Don't cry. I nodded and looked away. Ali'i stood, once more, and began paddling. "I'm sorry you've had to deal with that... especially for so long."

How could he be so nice? Not even Ua or Melika had said something like that before. Everyone assumed I was fine, because I put on a front that I was fine. I focused on the sanctuary and making sure everything ran smoothly.

But they didn't really understand what it felt like to have to watch my back at every second. They didn't know how exhausted I felt from being on high alert all the time.

We continued in silence for a while, then Ali'i sighed.

"We're not moving very far. Are you alright swimming?"

I nodded, and slipped off the board. He got in next to me. We held onto the board and swam towards shore. With both of us, we were able to get there in a significantly shorter amount of time than if he'd been paddling the entire way.

When we stepped onto the sand, I collapsed on the shore and stared up at the sky.

"Feels good to touch the ground," I said, the waves brushing up beside me. Ali'i lied next to me, and I realized this might be a good opportunity to flirt.

But I didn't *feel* like flirting. He was so kind to me earlier, it almost felt wrong to play his heart. He'd been so protective of me, something I'd never experienced before. That compassion pulled at my insides.

It's for the people though, I thought. *For the baby, the refugees, the people of Hana, and Ua.*

"Thanks for rescuing me," I said, rolling onto my side and facing him. He grinned at me.

"My pleasure."

"What do I owe you?" I asked.

At that, his eyes fell to my lips.

Oh no. Maybe I should have thought the question through before asking it. "I think you know," he said and winked. Before I could say something, he added, as he sat up, sand covering his back, "But I'll wait until you want it too."

"How do you know I don't want it?" I didn't know why I felt embarrassed, but it was hard not to feel that way.

"I think you'll know when you want it." At that, he stood. "Can I escort you to the kahuna's hut, or..."

"I'm good, thank you," I said, standing and brushing myself off. I then looked up at him. "Really, thank you. That was kind of you to listen to me."

He smiled, his eyes the nicest thing I'd ever seen. "I wasn't being kind, Ka'ala. I really like listening to you."

I had to look away, shyness overcoming my entire body. "Well... I'll see you around?" I asked, unsure of what to do next.

"I sure hope so," Ali'i said as he picked up his board. I nodded and hurried away before I fell into the beauty of his eyes, his kindness, his heart.

Though it had been a meaningful time together, I still had a lot of work to do. None of my questions about the king were answered, but I'd get them out of Ali'i. Somehow.

Unless he gets answers out of me first. Because based on this sweet interaction, I realized it was easy to fall for him.

And I will not *fall for him.*

CHAPTER ELEVEN

*M*elika and I walked in silence through the thick woods, the evening sun falling over the treetops. Kona had been here a few weeks, and he needed to return to Hana to serve the king. He wasn't gone long when he went to the king, and he really didn't do much. In fact, because of his injury, Kona took goods from the people of Lanai to aid in the war. He sometimes took longer coming back because he waited for refugees: injured warriors or prisoners of war from Kohala, innocent citizens being taken for sacrifices, and people fleeing Hana in general.

It worked out well, as Kona was an expert in wayfinding. And because he traveled alone, it was an easy opportunity for him to stowaway the refugees. But he couldn't stay here forever. The people of Lanai each offered their taxes and goods, and, with his canoe fully stocked, he was ready to depart the following morning.

With his departure, our father, Oponui, fully expected a family dinner. Though, I didn't always understand why. The sentiment didn't make much sense to me, because father didn't care to have me or Melika around. Mother didn't bother with us, but she had an excuse, as the sickness took over her mind.

The torches lit up the hut in the distance and Melika sighed. "I hope this goes quickly," she muttered. Earlier, as I told her about Aliʻi, she squirmed and squealed in delight. I left out parts, like how he asked about Mailou, because I didn't want to make her feel bad. And I definitely did *not* want to explore how his care and concern affected me.

But one thing was sure: I would never hear the end of Melika reminding me that I was in Aliʻi's arms.

"How romantic!" she said, over and over. But as we drew closer to our old home, dread weighed on both of our shoulders.

It's not that we didn't like our mother. Kalani couldn't help her sickness—it had just overcome her and her memory of us. But Oponui... he was all about "show." He wanted to look good, no matter the cost. I was not pretty enough for him, and he always made that known, because of my freckled skin.

Meanwhile, he treated Melika as an annoying teenager... which she was sometimes. But she could be as responsible and independent as myself, something I found to be the case as she blossomed and grew.

Father sees what he wants to see, I reminded myself, in case he said something tonight that would sting. I had trusted him growing up, tried to please him, but I was simply never "pretty" enough. And I wasn't a boy, like Kona, so father saw me and Melika as useless and worthless.

The sound of laughter came from within.

"Ugh, are there guests here too?" Melika asked. "Why doesn't he ever have just a 'family' dinner? Why call it a family dinner, if it's not just family?"

Father *always* had people over. It was as if he couldn't stand to be with his own children. Whether he invited a neighbor, friend, distant relative, or even strangers off the side of the road, father never really had a "family dinner." He called it that, probably to sound good to others, but I came to realize he didn't know how to talk to his own children. Hence, he invited other people over so he could talk to them.

We have no real relationship with Oponui.

I reached my arm out to Melika and she linked hers with mine, understanding my meaning: we'd get through this together.

"The whole time I'm just going to be daydreaming about you and that handsome captain," she said, winking at me. I rolled my eyes, but couldn't help myself from thinking about him. His arms, pulling me close to him, how warm he felt, the way he looked at me, the kindness he showed in listening *and* believing me...

It's all just a game, I reminded myself. *Get close to Ali'i, learn the king's secret to invincibility, and kill the king...* I still didn't know much personal information about Ali'i, except that he kissed some other girl, some girl he hoped to marry. And, based on what Kona said, Ali'i could be dangerous, especially when it came to women.

Melika and I wiped our feet before stepping into the hut. Neither of us bothered to announce our arrival, but Kona stood as we walked in.

"Finally," he said, relief clear on his face. "What took you so long?"

I wanted to tell him: the baby and children needed tending. Ua couldn't get them all ready for bed alone, before she had to keep watch. In fact, the baby had been crying and I didn't want to leave Ua with the task of soothing the baby, not when Ua had to keep watch on the porch *and* tend to the children.

"Sorry," I said and shrugged. Melika and I hugged Kona, but the entire time I checked who my father invited over.

It was a family from the upper class. The daughter, around my age, was beautiful, her brown skin completely flawless. She wore richly dyed kapa, and her hair was made into a fancy updo, with flowers hanging out the back.

I brushed back loose hair from my own messy bun.

Melika went to Oponui, our father, and kissed his cheek. I did the same, exchanging no words. Melika and I then greeted the guests, and made our way to the back room, paying respects to our mother.

She looked like a wilted flower, her skin sagging, body skinny. Not only had she lost her memory of us, but she even lost her memory of how to care for herself. She forgot that she needed to eat or drink.

I wanted to care for my mother, but Oponui said it was better that the local healer do so. My frustration against my father only grew at his insistence on someone else caring for her than her own children. So it was better that I lived away.

Strips of lauhala covered the floor, and beautiful weavings sat around the room. Mother's hands worked on a lauhala basket, her skill and speed unmatched by anyone on Lanai. Weaving lauhala was the only thing she remembered.

"And who do we have here?" she asked, smiling at us. A pang struck my heart, just like it did everytime she asked us to introduce ourselves. We were complete strangers to her.

"I'm Melika."

"I'm Ka'ala."

"Are you cousins? Friends?"

I had to suck in a breath as Melika answered. It only got harder and harder to see Kalani like this. She was too young to have such problems. Nobody else on Lanai lost their memory, forgetting even their own children. People said she must have drank or ate something poisonous that affected her mind, while others whispered that she must have done something to displease the gods. My mother had been a good woman though, and I couldn't imagine her doing anything against the gods.

"Sisters," Melika answered. She sat next to Kalani, observing her fingers as she worked. "Are you enjoying that?" she asked.

"I believe so." Mother smiled, her face looking so old since the sickness took over her. Gray and white wisps of hair fell from the loose bun at the back of her head.

"What have you been up to?" Melika asked. I sat on the other side of my mother. No doubt Oponui would call us soon to help entertain *his* guests. But, for now, I'd try to enjoy this time with my mother, no matter how painful it was.

"Oh nothing much. Just brushing leaves, cleaning water, and changing flowers."

Melika and I exchanged glances. Kalani's condition was probably getting worse. She had started saying gibberish the last time we came, but not like this.

"Do you get to spend time with friends?" I asked.

"Of course. There's Kekoa who lives around here."

"Like Kekoa, the prince?" Melika asked.

Mother nodded. "'Ae, the prince. And also the sky." She grinned. "My old friend Nalani comes by often."

"Who's that?" Melika asked. Mother hadn't had many friends as we grew up in this home, because she was too busy tending to all the household duties for Oponui. He was a greedy man, always wanting to look good but not wanting to put in the work. Perhaps mother just... burnt out after a time. I couldn't remember a time when our family didn't host a dinner.

Father seemed to be the one who invited neighbors, extended family, and even grandparents, as though he were connecting everyone to each other. But what really happened was he disconnected his own family.

"Nalani is my old friend. She's an expert at making shells."

"Making shells?"

"You girls ask a lot of questions, don't you?" Kalani smiled, but it looked weak and tired.

"We do," I said, placing my hand on her back. "We're just glad to see you're doing well."

"And glad that Kekoa and Nalani visit you often," Melika added. No doubt mother had probably heard the names Kekoa and Nalani once, and her mind must have imagined stories about who they might be in her life.

"Girls."

Melika and I looked up to see Oponui standing at the door frame, hands folded. "Our guests are waiting."

As much as I wanted to open my mouth and say, *They're* your *guests,* I kissed Kalani's cheek, and followed father to the dining area. Melika did the same, trailing behind me. As we sat on our mats, putting food on our leaf plates, Kona looked absolutely miffed and impatient.

The lovely-looking girl watched us, and when I noticed her staring at me—probably at all my freckles—she looked away in haste.

"These are my daughters. Ka'ala. She has that impressive hut in the woods," Oponui said. I wanted to roll my eyes. In private he used to question my hut and ask why it needed to be so big. Now he simply boasted about it.

"And this is my youngest, Melika." He didn't add anything about her and Melika glared as she ate.

"Girls, this is Chief Haka of the valley. He has a son who is away right now at war."

"May the gods watch over him," said the chief's wife, a portly woman with small eyes. The chief was a lesser chief, meaning he answered to the high chief of Lanai. And the high chief of Lanai answered to the king of Hana. I didn't know all the politics, but it did drive me a little crazy that we were not more sovereign on Lanai.

"This is his daughter, Liha."

Melika and I tipped our heads to the guests, acknowledging them.

"Are your daughters betrothed to anyone?" the chief asked, studying us both.

"No." Father cleared his throat, quickly adding, "Not yet," as if to challenge the chief. The man simply rubbed his chin and I had no doubt he was watching us, trying to decide if either of us was a suitable match for his son fighting in the war.

I wouldn't be able to avoid marriage my entire life, so if his son was a good match, I was sure I could make it work. The question, though, was that of the sanctuary. Marriage would change everything, or would it? Perhaps the chief had a kind son, one who would probably be as tired of the endless wars as everyone else. If he was tired of the wars, he'd support me, I was sure of it.

I'd never thought too deeply about marriage, not the way Melika did, at least. I couldn't even hope for a romantic marriage... Mostly because father would pick out our suit-ors, and that was that.

Perhaps, deep down, knowing that my father would have given me to Mailou–had he succeeded in finding the thief and stolen goods–had probably ruined whatever hope for a romantic, happy marriage that I once had.

The image of Ali'i's arms around me flashed through my mind, making me feel warm inside.

No, no, no, I told myself. Ali'i was *certainly* not an option for marriage.

"Well we have wonderful news," Oponui said, addressing Melika and I. He never did that, and I wondered if this was another part of his "show" for the guests, trying to make it seem like he had a relationship with us.

When we didn't reply, he continued. "The chief and I have made a betrothal agreement." My stomach sank. Had they already agreed on a betrothal for me... or worse, for Melika? She was too young to be betrothed. I didn't doubt father would betroth her before me, as she was much pret-tier. Melika turned pale, probably thinking the same thoughts as myself. I restrained myself from placing a hand on hers for comfort. Everyone would see that.

Oponui grinned. "When Kona returns from his next trip, we will have a grand ceremony for his and Liha's wedding!"

My jaw dropped as I looked from my father to Kona. He grimaced, then nodded. I looked at Liha, who stared at her plate. Was she shy, or did she not want to get married to Kona? She was a commodity, like me and Melika, and I felt sorry for her.

I realized that Melika and I remained silent for a few seconds, aggravating my father. His genuine grin turned into a fake smile, plastered on his face, as if forcing us to react.

"Oh, that is..." I started to say, then sat straighter, finding the only words I could say. "Congratulations Kona and Liha." I didn't want to say I was happy for them, because I wasn't. Ua said she would wait until after the war for Kona, and now... my father just went ahead and signed up Kona to marry this random girl, a girl my father didn't know. But, because of her status, my father heartily consented to betroth his son. Kona was also one of the only eligible bachelors on the island, so I wasn't surprised that the chief would stoop to our status.

"Congratulations," I said once more, when Melika stared at both of them. She was a better actress than myself, but her stunned look spoke volumes. Did she know about Ua and Kona? Perhaps I underestimated my sister's observations.

"Well, we are happy to have spent the evening with your family," said the chief. "But it is getting late so we better head on our way before it gets too dark."

Lanai had once been known to have ghosts, but long ago a chief from Maui cast them all out. However, people still moved about with caution in the night, in case a ghost returned. We all stood to kiss one another's cheeks and see them out. Of course father was the last to walk them out, leaving me, Melika, and Kona behind.

"But I thought..." I started to say and Kona frowned at me.

"I guess I don't even get to decide for myself," he said. "And this marriage is about status."

"You'd rather marry for status?" Melika asked, appalled. Kona avoided looking at us, annoyance clear on his face.

"We better get going," I said, noticing Oponui say his

farewells to the family. I didn't want to hang around long with father and deal with his negativity and criticism. We used to stay and help clean up, but Oponui since hired a maid, paying her with mother's beautiful creations.

I had so much to say about it all, but none of it was worth it. I had tried before, and it only ended up being a big drama between father and I. So we didn't need to make things worse than they were.

"You could have at least smiled in your reaction," he said to both Melika and I as he walked in, his eyebrows deeply creased.

Melika looked like she might mutter something, but, much to my surprise and admiration, she kept her mouth shut.

"We need to get back as well," I said, though we really hadn't stayed long.

"I will call on you to get things ready for the wedding," Oponui said, ignoring me. "Leis, floral arrangements, kapa..." He looked from me to Melika. "You both don't do anything up there all day, so might as well make yourselves useful."

If only he knew.

But he'll never know.

"Let us know whatever you need," I said, then motioned for Melika to follow me. "Good night father. Thank you for inviting us to dinner."

"I'll walk you out," Kona offered, and we three walked into the darkness together. The night geckos chirped while the island breeze made the palm trees above sway back and forth. Moon lit the path ahead.

"Safe travels back," I said to Kona, once we were out of earshot from the family hut. I didn't know what else to say, my thoughts a confused mess: the memory of Ali'i, the topic of marriage, and my concern for Ua's feelings.

"You don't *have* to marry that girl," Melika said, bringing up the subject we *all* thought of but struggled to bring up.

"It's probably better," Kona said.

"Why?"

"Because she's of a higher status. If I marry her, you two will have better options for marriage in the future."

"I don't care about status," Melika said, folding her arms. She didn't add that she had a big crush on Prince Kekoa, who was obviously a young man of status. But the chances of Melika marrying the prince were slim—she was too young, and he was already old enough to choose a bride.

"I'm sure you can convince father to cut off the betrothal," I said, wondering if any of us would mention Ua's name.

"It's too late now." Kona shook his head, and from the way his shoulders sank, I could tell he gave up the fight. "Father's been conjuring this deal up for way too long, and they finally agreed on it last night. The high chief of Lanai will be performing the ceremony—father asked him today and he said he would be honored to do it."

Melika and I stood in silence. Involving high chiefs, and then going back on one's word with them, was very serious.

Instead of continuing the conversation, I hugged Kona. "Be safe, alright? Thanks for all your help."

"You be safe too," he said, sounding relieved to be done with the marriage conversation. "And I hope it all goes smoothly getting those little ones to 'Eleu."

"Me too," Melika and I agreed. We then parted ways, the darkness enveloping us. Melika and I said nothing the entire way home, both of us wrapped in our thoughts. The helplessness that weighed on my shoulders was more than I could bear.

I had controlled many things throughout my life, namely creating a sanctuary. But, in the end, I couldn't control everything, not even who I got to marry.

But can I control whether or not I kill the king? It all depended on if I could get answers from Ali'i. He seemed to know more than anyone else about the king, and if I could get answers from him, I could possibly end these wars.

Yet it won't make a difference... Because ending the wars didn't prevent Kona from marrying Liha. Father got to decide that. I rubbed my forehead in frustration as we neared the gate and Melika squeezed my arm.

We made eye contact and she bit her lower lip. It was time to tell Ua the news.

Ua broke into tears, sobbing while I wrapped my arm around her shoulders. I didn't try to offer words of comfort or consolation, because I didn't want to be a liar. Maybe things *wouldn't* be ok between Ua and Kona. There didn't seem to be a way out of this unless Kona disrespected our father, which would make him a dishonorable subject in the eyes of everyone else (even if they didn't know the situation).

"It's all my fault," Ua said. "I pushed him away..." But I didn't blame her. Ua, Melika, Kona, and I ran this operation, and each of us had a duty to perform. Ua had "pushed" him away by sticking to her duty, putting others first. I wish I knew what to say.

I was sure Melika would have said the right thing, because she believed in romantic love and the sort. But even Melika remained quiet, facing the reality of the situation.

One day I'd be married off to someone. So would Ua. And so would Melika.

But what if there was a way for love to prevail? After all, my sanctuary had started out of my own desire to care for people. Could romantic love be just as powerful (or more) than compassion for one's fellow men? Could two people, who were in love, defy the odds, social norms, and the rigidness of our society in order to be together? Was it worth it? I didn't know.

CHAPTER TWELVE

A hot, muggy day encompassed all of Lanai as I scanned the horizon for the blue sails of Nai'a and her grandfather's canoe. Kona had left a few days ago, and the storm had long passed, so where was she? I felt sorry for the children, who had gotten used to staying in the hut. They had a routine, and we taught them valuable life skills, including etiquette, courtesy, cleanliness, respect, and, of course other cultural things like dancing hula, weaving lauhala, and making kapa. I had no doubt that wherever they went, they'd be fine. They developed their skills, so when 'Eleu took them to a family—wherever that might be—to stay until the end of the war (or, possibly, forever), then the children would already have some independence and confidence.

The baby was a whole other ordeal. She had become quite attached to all three of us caretakers, and as long as one of us held her, she didn't cry. In fact, it was probably the first time the baby had started feeling safe.

It broke my heart that we'd have to send her away with 'Eleu. But we had no choice, because we couldn't raise a baby, and, in less than a month's time, Kona would be back with more refugees.

Unless I end this war before that happens. I hadn't seen Ali'i around, and, as usual, I worried that he was disinterested in me.

The ocean blinded me for a moment, the sunlight reflecting on the water. I usually came to this cliffside, because it gave me a better view of the horizon, instead of going to the shoreline by the canoes. I had checked it earlier that morning anyway.

As I stood at the cliffside, staring at the ocean, my skin tingled.

Someone is here.

I quickly turned, seeing the tall figure of Mailou approaching from the distance. He wore his usual outfit of a long brown skirt, brown vest, and sandals made from koa wood. The straps of his sandals wove around his ankles. In his hand he held a long leiomano, the white shark teeth shining in the sunlight.

Oh no. What was I thinking? Had I let my guard down for too long? I glanced down the cliff, knowing that if I jumped, I would die. Could I sprint past Mailou?

What was he going to do to me? I had long imagined that he would kill me, maybe do something inappropriate and evil to me before that but...

I have my knife. I always did. I felt the handle of it beneath my skirt.

I'll defend myself.

I decided to get away from the cliff edge, because what if he decided to simply push me over? I had a feeling he wanted more than that, but one could never be sure.

There was a little forest trail, with dry trees that led to

this cliff edge, so Mailou must have followed me. Why was I such a fool to come here?

I marched towards him and stopped, keeping a safe distance. But at least I wasn't close enough to be pushed off the cliff.

Mailou stopped and folded his arms, then a smug grin appeared across his face.

"Well, well," he said, his voice deep, dark, and cold, the voice of a murderer.

"What do you want from me?" I asked, holding the strap of my bag to keep my fingers from shaking.

"I told you that you'd be interested in me one day," he said. "You think you're better than the Nawao. You think you can just walk away unharmed after encountering a group of our kind."

So he was mad that I walked away, unscathed, from him and his friends? Disgusting. Did they usually hurt other people they encountered? I wasn't sure, but they were strong and big enough to do so. Everyone avoided members of the creed at all costs. I had relaxed since all of the creed left the island, but putting my guard down, even for a moment, placed me in this situation.

"I'll teach you," he said, smiling, advancing towards me. I took a step back, readying myself to fight. I didn't pull my knife out just yet though. I needed the element of surprise.

"Don't touch me," I said. "Let me pass."

"You think you got away from the creed that day, but I'll show you who's in charge," Mailou said. At that he lunged forward to grab me. I evaded him, easily, moving to the side. He reached for my wrist but I stepped away.

His eyes darkened, as I continued to step away from his advances. He was slow, sloppy, and his large size made him step hard, shaking the ground. I checked the path, wondering *how* I would escape this situation. I couldn't duck away from him all day, but if I ran, that would give him an advantage. I'd seen the creed men running in the morning, training, as always. Because of their height, they were fast, definitely faster than me, even though I was petite.

Mailou let out a growl. "You slippery, snarky little girl–"

"Kaʻala!" The voice, coming from the distant path, caught me off guard, and Mailou grabbed my wrist.

Out of self defense, I moved my arm up, folded my wrist over, then pulled straight down. The action freed my wrist of Mailou's grip and now gave me the advantage. With my hand over his large, oversized wrist, I yanked as hard as I could, pulling Mailou to the ground.

At that, I grabbed my knife. Mailou, who had fallen, used his leg to trip me, and I fell, but caught myself with my hands. My knife scattered away as Mailou jumped up, his own knife in hand.

"I should have finished you off a long time ago, you disrespectful–"

"Stay away from her!"

A tall form with a yellow cape shoved Mailou away from me. Two men, with red capes followed, weapons pointed at Mailou.

"Are you alright?" The captain hovered over me, wiping hair from my face. He helped me up and then stormed off to Mailou, saying words I'd never heard before. Perhaps the people of Hana were a rude lot, as the words were definitely inappropriate.

I grabbed my knife and placed it in my bag, wondering if Aliʻi had noticed it on the ground.

"I'll kill you right now!" Mailou exclaimed, grounding

his feet and facing the captain. Aliʻi, too, looked like he wanted to fight.

"If you kill a captain of the king, he has every right to have you executed," said one of the men in a red cape.

"Then let that king come to me. I'll tear his head off," Mailou said. I didn't realize how muffled everything sounded until Mailou said those words. Perhaps it wasn't a bad idea to get Mailou in King Hua's business. Perhaps the bounty hunter would kill the king, so I didn't have to.

But he'd have to kill Aliʻi. No. Aliʻi had come here, sparing me.

"Enough," I said, stepping forward.

"I want to duel him," Aliʻi said, ignoring me. At that moment, I saw a different side of the captain... the dangerous side. It was the fighter part of him, the one that led armies to battle, the one that probably shed innocent blood of Kohala warriors.

I couldn't help from shuddering as I reached for his arm and gently pulled back. "Let's go," I said.

Mailou looked at Aliʻi, the men in red capes, and then growled at me. "Just wait," he said, and spit on the ground. Then he put his knife away and walked off.

Aliʻi didn't move for a moment, focused on Mailou's form. For a few intense seconds, we stood there, my hand on his arm. Then he turned his attention to me.

"I can take him," he said, his eyebrows creased in anger. "Easily."

"It's not worth it—"

"Not worth it?" Aliʻi looked like I said the most horrible thing in the world. "Kaʻala, *you* are worth it. You shouldn't have him following your shadow anywhere you go."

"Captain, should we head back?" One of the men in the red capes interrupted. I studied them now, recognizing them as servants to King Hua. All servants of the highest class also wore red. Their capes were made of kapa, not feathers, though, to distinguish them as royal servants.

"ʻAe," Aliʻi said, and motioned for them to lead the way. He paused before following, and looked down at me.

"Are you alright? Did he hurt you?"

"No."

The captain moved a loose piece of hair from my face, and I became aware of all my freckles. I probably should have been evaluating my fight with Mailou, or thinking of the next way to get close to Aliʻi and learn King Hua's secrets, but insecurity covered my mind. Was he looking at how many freckles I had? I'd never been heavily insecure about my freckles but... for whatever reason, being around him made me wonder.

"I'm sorry I didn't come sooner. I had an eye on you, but there's someone coming who I've been expecting so I was distracted."

My stomach tightened. He'd been expecting someone? Who was it? Was it a woman he was interested in?

I shouldn't care if it's a woman... He even said he was keeping an eye on me, so why would he wait for some other woman? Yet I couldn't help myself.

"Who were you expecting?"

"They'll be here soon. But..." He paused. "My business is my own."

I wanted to fight him on it, to get the answer out of him who was coming, but the adrenaline from my fight already started to wear off. A sluggish feeling overcame me.

Aliʻi offered his arm. "Can I escort you back?"

I nodded and took his arm, loving how warm and muscular it felt. And not long ago, his arms had been wrapped around me. My heart skipped a beat at the memory.

Stop Ka'ala. But I was tired, and I allowed myself to lean against him more than I should.

"Who are these men?" I asked, nodding to the two servants in red capes.

"They arrived just earlier."

"King's servants," I said, remembering years ago, when the king and his army stayed here. Two servants in red capes, just like these, were in charge of getting everything set up: the king's camp, food, bathing area, everything.

Wait... does that mean...

"Is the king coming?" I asked, wide eyed.

"No. Well..." Ali'i paused. "No." Then he changed the subject. "I'm worried about you Ka'ala. What if I didn't show up? Mailou looked like he was about to..."

"Stab me?" I was still wondering if King Hua of Hana would set foot here. Perhaps he wanted to personally get his revenge for what Ua and I did to him that night.

"'Ae." At this, Ali'i slowed down, giving us space from the red-caped servants ahead. "Ka'ala, you have to tell the local chief what Mailou did to you."

I groaned. "He won't believe me."

"Mailou *just* attempted to hurt you. I'll stand as a witness."

"Did you forget that the high chief of Lanai asked my father if Mailou could have me for a prize?" I met Ali'i's eyes and the sadness in them made my heart melt. How could he care about me so much? We still didn't know each other very well.

And I don't intend to get to know him for romantic purposes... but only so I can learn the king's secrets.

I itched my leg, then frowned when blood covered my hand.

"You're bleeding." Ali'i knelt immediately and checked my ankle. When Mailou tripped me, the straps from his sandals must have cut me.

"I'm fine," I said, but Ali'i stopped me.

"I'll bandage it really fast."

Before I could protest, he pulled a clean piece of kapa from his small lauhala bag and gently wrapped it. Each time his fingers brushed against my skin, I had to keep from gushing internally. He was so handsome, so kind.

And so not what I'm looking for. I remembered the other side of him earlier, the fighter side. He was capable of causing great harm, and I needed to be careful. Kona told me he was dangerous.

"My brother is betrothed," I said, not knowing why I said it. Ali'i didn't need to know.

I'm trying to find out about Ali'i! I told myself, wishing I had kept my mouth shut. Perhaps Kona's betrothal bothered me more than I believed. Ua, Melika, and I had said nothing on the topic since Kona left. In fact, Ua seemed more quiet than ever before, and I did what I could to help her cope with the loss.

"Really? How do you feel about it?" Ali'i rubbed the back of my calf before standing, and my heart beat so hard from it, I thought I might faint. What was he doing? Was that even appropriate? He offered his arm again, and I took it, forgetting everything.

What did he just ask? Oh, how I feel about Kona's betrothal....

"I guess I feel indifferent. One day I'll be in his place. My father intends to sell Melika and I to men of high status."

"Oponui?"

"'Ae." I frowned. "Have you met my father?"

"'Ae. I met him again, recently, during my inspections. Years ago he was also under my command in a specific battle." Ali'i went quiet.

"And?"

"He didn't obey orders so..."

"So what?"

"So he was punished."

I frowned. My father? Disobeying orders? "Were they *your* orders?" I asked.

Ali'i nodded. "I shouldn't have told you that. You probably despise me—"

"No," I said, squeezing his arm. For all the times I squeezed Melika or Ua's arm for comfort, there was nothing quite like feeling Ali'i's arm.

What is wrong with me? Was I obsessed with arms—no, *his* arms—all of a sudden?

"My father is a stubborn man. He must have been really fed up to *not* want to please his commander."

"A lot of the men purposely try to displease their captains," Ali'i said. He sighed. "It's so they can get sent home."

"My father was sent home."

"Honorably, though. He was injured in a battle, almost died, so..." The men in the red capes walked fast, so they were far ahead now. I liked the solace of just Ali'i and I, being alone.

No I don't.

"Aren't the wars still going?" I asked.

"There's been a small break now, because of the Makahiki." Tree branches and leaves rustled against one another, and I moved hair from my face, wishing I'd made my hair a little nicer that morning.

Stop Kaʻala... Flirt with him. Get the answers, and then get out of there. Right. I was wasting time.

"Will you have to return to battle?"

"Unfortunately, yes. After I finish my investigations, I'll report back to the king. If all gets resolved, I should be leaving within the next couple of weeks."

"And what are you hoping to get resolved?" At this I leaned my chin against his shoulder and looked up at him through my lashes, hoping to get him to like me. But he did like me, right? Why else would he keep an eye on me, be overprotective?

He grinned, as if enjoying my game. "I've told you before but... There's a young lady I'm looking for. You seem to fit the description."

"So are you saying I'm the one you're looking for?"

"Well, I hope you *aren't* the one I'm looking for..." His jaw tensed as he said this, and I squeezed his arm again. I waited for him to say more, but he didn't.

"I hope you don't have to go back," I said, and Aliʻi relaxed a little.

"Why is that?"

"Because... who will watch Mailou's shadow?" I should have thought of something more clever, but that was all I had.

Aliʻi laughed and I loved the sound of it. "Maybe you can marry me, then you'll be far away from him."

Aliʻi's bold words made me falter, and I had nothing to say. *Maybe you can marry me?* Did he just... ask to marry me in an offhand way? I had never thought I'd be attracted to someone who wanted to marry me.

Hold up. I'm not attracted to Aliʻi. And we are not

getting married. But then... another idea crept into my mind. Was marriage the thing it would take to get the secrets from Ali'i about Hua? I opened my mouth twice to say something, but couldn't think of a comeback.

Instead of playing the game, the one that I should have flirted with him, I became somber. "I thought you were going to get married... to someone else. You told me yourself."

Ali'i sighed. "It was a long time ago. She was not what I wanted, and I wasn't what she wanted."

"But I was told you... did things to her."

"I never hurt her," Ali'i said, frowning. "She lied, and her lies almost cost me everything. It was because I didn't compromise my standards for her."

"What are your standards?"

At this, he blushed. "Not to sleep with someone outside of marriage."

"Oh."

"And that's all she wanted. Not only that, but I found out she had been cheating on me... Every time I went to battle, she worked her way to the upper class of the ali'i." He shook his head. "I wouldn't be a part of that. She was mad that I discovered her secret. She was also scared that I'd tell everyone she only became part of the elite society because of, well, her promiscuity."

Silence.

"And you didn't know this about her when you met her?"

"I thought I knew her when I met her, but I was young. And dumb. Naive. I was an easy target for someone like her, wanting to make her way to the top. I was already well advanced in rank for my age, and only rising higher and higher."

"I heard she's going to marry Prince Kekoa. Does he know about her?" I knew the prince personally, and if he was going to marry a promiscuous girl, he should know that. He had been through a lot, with his father, and being at the front of war his entire life. The prince certainly didn't need a horrible wife to make his life even more miserable. Or, worse, she'd ruin all the undercover operations.

Instead of answering my question, Ali'i glanced at me. "You know who she is?"

"My brother sort of... told me stuff about you."

"And you believe him?"

"I'm not sure." I stopped and faced Ali'i. "Which is why I'm asking *you*. Aren't you glad I don't take people's gossip for truth?"

Ali'i nodded, as if apologizing for his impatience. "I am glad, Ka'ala. You're wise. You're kind. You're a good person." With those words, he stepped close to me and stroked my cheek. My legs started shaking as he looked into my eyes. He was doing that thing again where he saw me. *Me,* the girl with feelings beneath everything, the girl who had to cover everything up to be brave enough for the refugees and hosting the sanctuary.

"That's why I'll probably never be good enough for you," he said, the words causing every part of me to lose balance.

Not good enough for me? What was he talking about? He seemed so confident, so sure that he'd win me over. And now he was here, confessing that I was too good for him?

"What are you saying—"

"You've never killed anyone, Ka'ala. You've never done the horrible things I've done. I've led so many battles, trained and disciplined many men... You're pure. You're good. You're the complete opposite of me." At that, his hand fell to his side, leaving my cheek feeling cold. Empty. "I shouldn't ever hope to be loved by you, but I can't help it.."

Stunned in place, I didn't know what to say. Because of his past, his career, and, quite possibly, his failed relationship with Noni, he probably saw himself as the vilest of creatures, most unworthy.

But I was not perfect. No. Here he was, being honest and open, while I was playing his heart. I wanted to be honest, to say I was pretty sure I'd never have a loving relationship with a man, mostly because my father would betroth me to someone.

I wanted to be honest and say I also didn't dare hope for a romantic relationship, especially after my father easily agreed to give me to Mailou if he succeeded on his quest.

But, instead, I chose to continue the game, to keep luring Ali'i in... and all to kill the king.

"Don't say that," I said, taking his hand. It felt warm and rough and my hand fit perfectly in it. "The past is over. We're here now." He slipped his hand out of mine.

"I'm sorry. I shouldn't have done any of this. I don't want to hurt you—"

"Shh." At that I stepped on the tips of my toes and kissed his cheek. This time I did it slower, not a quick peck like last time. I placed one hand on his other cheek, and one hand at the back of his neck, pressing my lips gently against his cheek, my forehead lingering against the side of his face after I kissed him. Then I stepped back and quickly put my hands away, afraid that he'd feel them shaking. It was just an innocent kiss on the cheek. But... was it?

He froze. "Really, Ka'ala, it's probably better that we don't—"

"Give us a chance," I said, and hugged him. At first he

was tense as I rested my head on his chest. But then he relaxed and held me for a long moment. I never felt so safe.

He kissed the top of my head and rested his chin there. "You're right. I need to give us a chance." He rubbed my back, and it made me feel dizzy all over.

This is just for the answers, just for the answers, I said over and over to myself. But as we stepped away from each other and headed back towards town, I couldn't help but wonder what it would feel like if it were all real.

CHAPTER THIRTEEN

"*Y*ou won't believe what I found out today!" Ua came rushing to the porch. Melika and I taught the children how to weed the garden while the baby lay on her stomach, cooing and watching. The children knew what to do if we told them to run and hide in the back, in case someone came up the path.

It was a normal, hot day on Lanai and there was no reason for anyone to come. Two days had passed since I last saw Ali'i and I continued to question my plot: would I have to pretend to *want* to marry him, in order to find out the secrets of the king?

"Ooh tell all," Melika said, interrupting my thoughts and wiping sweat from her forehead. Dirt streaked our cheeks, and the children had gotten considerably messy, but I was glad they enjoyed this work.

Ua placed her bundle of food and goods on the ground and knelt by us, digging her hands into the dirt to help.

"There's another inspector on the island."

"Who?" Melika and I asked at the same time.

"Captain Kaaiali'i isn't the only one. Apparently this other inspector is here to verify the captain's findings."

"But nobody knows *what* the inspectors are trying to find," Melika said, though she frowned. "Except, if Ka'ala is right, they're looking for both of you."

"And if the captain has his eye on Ka'ala, he can't turn her in or else..." Ua replied, raising an eyebrow. If the captain turned me and Ua into King Hua, he would kill us. Nobody was allowed to mock the king, even though he completely deserved it in his drunken, disgusting state.

And even if he wasn't in his drunken state, he deserves death. I glanced at the sweet little baby who smiled at me, her brown eyes glistening in the sunlight. I leaned over her and tickled her stomach.

"You're so cute," I said softly.

"So is the investigator handsome?" Melika asked, grinning at both of us. At first I worried about Melika's comment—it was too soon for her to play games like this. Ua had just experienced a deep heartbreak, and now Melika teased her about courting again?

"Melika—" I started to say but Ua waved my warning away.

"No, he's as old as ever. He's old enough to be one of our fathers." We giggled as Melika looked bummed. Ua winked at me, and I knew she was slowly—very slowly—overcoming her grief. I admired her for it, though it pained me that she had to go through such a sad struggle.

But this was our world, our lot, after all. One day each of us would be betrothed to whoever our fathers chose for us. Kona had no choice. Ua, Melika, and I, likewise, had no choice in the matter. It was best to move on, though deep down I wondered if one *could* choose who they married.

Ali'i had suggested we get married the other day. I swallowed hard to keep from blushing. What would a life with him look like?

That's not something to think about. Certainly not. I would never marry Ali'i... but if I did, it would be for the purpose of finding answers and killing the king.

"So is the inspector coming here sometime?" I asked, changing the subject to move my thoughts away from marriage and romance.

Ua shrugged. "I can assume he is. We should be on the lookout. I don't think he'll be as distracted by Ka'ala as the other captain." She placed her hand on mine. "I still don't know what you're up to Ka'ala, but are things going the way you hoped with the captain?"

Melika smiled, that annoying, sneaky smile.

I shrugged. "Sort of. It's taking some time."

"Well let us know if we can help." Ua and Melika would not let me down, I knew it. But I was too ashamed to tell them my plan. It wasn't like me to play with someone else's heart.

Yet I have no choice. King Hua must die, or these wars would never end. And if nobody else had the bravery or skill to do it, I would do the deed. I tried once and failed, but not this next time. Ali'i would have all the answers I needed. Just thinking this reminder gave me the boost I needed.

"I'm actually going to see him tonight," I said, nodding as I made my decision. I hadn't seen him since the encounter with Mailou, and maybe tonight I'd get the answers I needed. "And 'Eleu has to be here sometime soon, so I'll check the shores once more."

Ua and Melika studied me, and, for a moment, I could tell they tried to read me—to read my plans. But I'd never been so easy for them to read.

"I'll keep watch tonight then," Ua said.

"And I'll get these children all cleaned up." Melika giggled as she pointed to the kids. Mud and dirt covered their hands, arms, and legs... but they looked happy. I smiled and picked up the baby.

"Have you thought of any names for the baby?" I asked.

Ua and Melika shook their heads.

"If there's anyone who's wise enough to name a baby, it'd be you," Ua pointed out.

"I'm not wise."

"Psh, says the one who built this thing from nothing." Melika shook her head. "You underestimate yourself way too much Ka'ala." I rolled my eyes at my younger sister and then smiled at the baby. She was so cute. So innocent.

I remembered Ali'i calling me innocent, pure.

But I'm not. I had secrets in my heart, and he was the key to all the answers I needed.

As the evening sun hung over the island, I made my way to town. The entire time I kept an eye out for Mailou. I originally thought of having Melika come with me, but there were too many children for Ua to tend alone. And maybe the captain could escort me back home after we spent some time together.

I rehearsed the questions in my mind, and the scenarios of how I could bring things up naturally and in a flirty way. Ali'i shouldn't have any reason to suspect my plans against the king... unless he had somehow figured out that it was me, after all, who duped the king years ago.

But he probably does know that it's me. He saw me wield a knife and attack him, and he possibly saw me defend myself against Mailou... But if Ali'i really cared about me, he would try to keep that other inspector far from me and Ua, right?

As I approached his hut, a chill ran up my spine. Two of the king's servants stood outside of it, their red capes reminding everyone of the status of those within. One of them glanced at me when I stopped before them.

"Is Captain Ali'i here?" I asked. I wanted to look past him, to see if Ali'i was inside, but they were bulky servants. The sound of voices came from inside, and I immediately recognized one of them as Ali'i. The other voice was older, gruff, and had an accent of those from Hana.

"He's busy," said the guard.

"I just need to ask him something. It won't take long." I hadn't thought of some excuse at this point. I really had no reason to be here, but Ali'i would make time for me, right?

"You can ask him when he's not busy."

"But it's important."

"Then we can relay your message."

The guards and I stood there, and I let out a sigh. "Alright, fine. Is there a time when he's *not* busy?"

"He's busy until he leaves," said the other guard.

"What's going on here?" An older man stepped between the guards and looked down at me. He had a hooked nose and white hair pulled back into a bun. Like others who had gone to battle, scars lined his brown face and body. Wrinkles showed the sort of sun exposure he'd received over the years.

"Who are you?" he asked, immediately studying my features. I hoped he didn't link my freckles with the king's description of "flawed skin."

"I'm Ka'ala. Is Captain Ali'i here?"

"Ka'ala." Now Ali'i stepped through the guards and gently touched my arm. "What are you doing here?"

Though he tried to sound calm, there was a hint of alarm in his voice.

"I..." With all the eyes of the intimidating men on me, I faltered. It had seemed so easy to waltz down here, grab Ali'i, and take a stroll along the beach. But now... what was the best excuse?

"I was hoping you'd have a few minutes to talk..."

The older man's eyebrows creased and he folded his arms. "Ali'i is busy. He doesn't have time for peasant women like you."

It was a personal stab to my status, and I swallowed hard because it was true. This older man, who I assumed was the other investigator, was not wrong. My rank didn't compare with Ali'i's rank.

"Naha–" Ali'i started to say, and the man, who I now knew as Captain Naha, glared.

"We don't have time for her. Come on."

"Give me a few minutes," Ali'i said, gently pulling me away. Naha frowned, folded his arms, and watched until we were out of earshot and out of view.

"Ka'ala, is everything alright?" Ali'i asked as we stepped into the forest, the light getting darker and darker. If he couldn't escort me home, I'd better leave now... in case Mailou tried to follow me.

"I just..." All the things I rehearsed in my head earlier started to disappear. What were my lines again? "I just missed you," I stuttered, looking away, knowing that if I didn't look convincing, which I certainly didn't right now, then Ali'i might catch onto me. "Is everything alright with you?" I asked, stroking his arm. It felt so strong and muscular, smooth, yet textured from the war scars.

Feels so nice. No. No, it really didn't, and I hated that I'd become so obsessed with his arms.

137

"'Ae. There's just another investigator here and..." He hesitated.

"What is it?"

"He's looking for the same young woman I was looking for." At this, he stroked my cheek. My heart started pumping again. "Ka'ala, I really want to spend time with you. But, for now, it's probably best if you and I kept a distance. At least until I can get this investigation resolved."

"You mean... when you find the young woman you were looking for?"

Ali'i nodded. "Or... hopefully we *won't* find her." At this, my heart sank. The way he stared into my eyes, his eyebrows creased in concern, studying me... he knew it was me. He knew Ua and I duped the king. So why didn't he say it? Why didn't he confront that truth? Would this be a gaping, unspoken truth between us?

But why does it matter? I shouldn't care about anything hindering our relationship. All I needed to worry about was getting information from Ali'i about the king.

"Will the king come here to... meet this young woman?" I asked, though we both very well knew the young woman was I.

Ali'i nodded. "Ka'ala, as much as I want to be with you... we need to stay apart for some time. At least until Naha and I return and report to King Hua. Maybe he won't come here if we can prove our case that the young woman was a ghost."

Ah, so that was the story Ali'i came up with. It made complete sense though. Lanai had been full of ghosts long ago, so why wouldn't a ghost make fun of King Hua? There was nothing he could do about it if it was a ghost. I should have said thank you to Ali'i for covering for me and Ua, but

I didn't have the heart. The truth sat like a huge lie between us.

Instead, my mind went back to my mission: get close to Ali'i and find out the answers about King Hua.

"But when you return to Hana... then you won't ever come back." Panic rose in me. What if he left? Since the time of Makahiki was over, when Ali'i returned to Hana, he would have to return to war.

And I won't get any answers. I had to end this war before it started once more.

Ali'i sensed my anxiety and stroked my arms. "It won't be long."

"But what if you get sent to war again?"

"I won't. I'll come back for you. I just need to... sort things out." At those words, his hands dropped, and I wondered if he meant he needed to sort his feelings too. He was loyal to the king–he always had been. So would he fall in love with a girl who tied up the king and left him in his own vomit?

Or was there a possibility that Ali'i didn't *want* to serve the king? Perhaps he was like so many others, serving out of duty and responsibility. Was it possible that Ali'i was like Prince Kekoa, keeping his true feelings about the king under disguise?

"Ali'i..." I searched his face, trying to find answers. How could I ask such question? "Is your loyalty more important than me?" I regretted the words as soon as they came out of my mouth. They were selfish, and we both knew it.

Ali'i tensed. "My loyalty is to King Hua, and you know this. When I became a captain, I swore to protect him, including finding those who might want to kill him. Even if it happened years ago, there's an unsolved mystery and killers might be on the loose, like a young woman who wants to kill the king." At this he stared into my eyes, and I wished I could look away. But I could feel him reading me. Intensely.

Oh no... he's going to find out why I've been trying to lead him on. If I didn't do or say something, he'd read right through me, see my true intentions. Because Ali'i read me like nobody else could. Was he trained to be like this, or did he disarm me? And why?

"Ka'ala, I've met a lot of people in my life," he said, stepping away from me. The distance between us felt like miles. "I know an intent when I see it."

A chill ran down my spine. *I know an intent when I see it.* Did he see my intent? From his body language, and the way he tensed up, I knew he could see my desire. How did he know, so quickly, that I intended on killing the king?

Because he's been to many battles. He's not lying. And I'd lied to him for so long. Guilt welled up in me. This man, who served the king, who had shown me such kindness, and who now would do what it took to keep the king from killing me and Ua... I lied to him.

And what could I do? He probably realized, at this moment, I had been playing games with him. The overwhelming feeling of guilt made my shoulders sink. Try as I might to find words, nothing came.

"It's probably best that we part ways," he said, his voice now distant, cold.

"Ali'i..."

"I knew it was you the instant I met you," he said, then let out a little sigh.

The truth.

He finally said it.

But it wasn't the truth about Ua and I trying to kill the king years ago, it was the fact that he must have felt something for me. The feelings he had for me caused him to decide to protect me, instead of turning me in.

And I felt something for him. No no no... I couldn't. I wouldn't.

As I looked into his eyes, the despair, disappointment, and sadness that filled them, my heart crumbled inside. I knew playing with people's hearts was a dangerous game, and I shouldn't have done it, but I couldn't help it.

Aliʻi had the answers I needed. And now the game slipped right through my fingers. He'd known all along about me, and no doubt Naha now suspected me. Aliʻi would have to come up with even more lies to cover for and protect me... because I felt his deep care for me. But why?

"We should stay away from each other."

"But I don't want to," I said, stepping towards him, realizing that I wasn't lying now. That terrified me.

"I don't want to either." The defeat in his voice made me want to hug him, but, instead, I started shivering.

"But it's better this way, Kaʻala. We shouldn't have ever gotten involved with each other. You have your business, and I have mine." Did he know about my sanctuary then?

But he's telling me he's still loyal to King Hua... My insides rolled.

So there we stood, two people on opposite teams, yet longing to be together.

Maybe he's right. Maybe it is best to part ways. Pretend like nothing ever existed between us. Sure, we'd been attracted to each other. But we were loyal to different causes, and that would make it impossible to be together.

Not to mention I came from a lowly rank, while he was part of the elite, and one of the closest to King Hua. He wouldn't tell the king about me, nor would I ever rat him out to others. So it was better to part ways. Ali'i was right all along. We'd never work out.

Yet... why did I hurt so much inside?

"So... this is goodbye?" I asked, my heart pumping so hard it felt like it would crack. Unless it already did crack.

Ali'i looked down, his fists clenched, like he had to think long and hard about it. "I think so."

"I'm sorry we didn't work out," I said, choking back tears. Why did I want to cry? There really was nothing to cry about. He and I hadn't connected much... or did we?

I remembered how much he cared about me, how he listened to me, kept an eye out for me... nobody had ever done that for me before. His actions had spoken volumes about how he felt about me, while I'd been busy playing my game.

I thought of his arms wrapped around me, keeping me warm when he rescued me from the ocean currents. I thought of how he cared and stepped in when Mailou tried to attack. I swallowed hard, as if hoping that it would swallow away all the feelings and emotions.

But I was now in the same boat as Ua. She started falling for someone, and duty had called him another way.

And, in a way, I started falling for Ali'i, but duty called us both in separate directions. He served the king. I repelled the king, and took people into my safe haven.

"I'm sorry we didn't work out too," Ali'i said, breaking the silence. He looked like he wanted to hug me, or gather me in his arms, but he kept his body tense, his fists clenched together, as if restraining himself.

I nodded then turned and brushed past him, afraid that if I stood there any longer, I'd break down into tears.

There's no need to break down, I told myself over and

over, but my heart ached. It had never hurt like this before, and the sensation was overwhelming.

Ali'i stood there, still as stone, and I hurried on the path back home.

I should have known better.

There were other ways to find out about the king's secrets, not just through Ali'i.

As I ran home, I swiped away tears to keep open eyes and ears for Mailou... because Ali'i would no longer watch after me. We were done, and my plan had failed.

But it wasn't the failed plan that felt the worst of the situation. It was that my heart ached so much. I'd never experienced this before, and I didn't understand it. Did it mean... I *really, truly* liked Ali'i? If it did, that meant I fell for him. And my game was not actually a game. It was real.

My real feelings didn't matter though. They never had, because duty had always come first—for me, for Ali'i, for Ua, for nearly everyone who lived on Lanai or Maui.

Ali'i swore an oath of loyalty to the king when he became a captain. Meanwhile, I had a duty to provide refugees with safety. Ali'i and I would have never worked out, and the realization of it cut to my core.

But it doesn't matter now, I told myself. The plan to get secrets from Ali'i failed. *I have to move on.*

Perhaps there was another way to gain access to the king, and I'd find it. As I stepped towards the gate, I made sure to recompose myself and show no evidence of tears.

Two figures stood on the porch talking to Ua, and, though night had fallen, I wondered if the people were some folks from town, visiting. As I got closer, the aching in my heart lightened for a moment.

"'Eleu!" I exclaimed and ran to hug the girl with sun-darkened skin, big blue eyes, and short, wavy hair. "You made it," I said, relief flooding through me. We'd get these children to safety, far away from here, far away from King Hua.

But when I met 'Eleu's eyes and looked to her grandfather, a grandmaster wayfinder, I knew that it wouldn't be easy.

"There are two king's men on the island," said 'Eleu's grandfather, Naula, his white hair glowing in the moonlight. "We've crossed paths with them before. They're dangerous, and powerful."

Ali'i and Naha were captains, inspectors, and men of war. Naula was right.

"We'll have to be careful," 'Eleu said, looking from me to Ua, who stood on the porch. "Very, *very* careful."

CHAPTER FOURTEEN

"*A*re you alright? You've been really quiet today," Ua said as we packed the children's belongings, the midday sun turning to evening. The children and baby played in the back with Melika, while Ua and I took turns walking to the front porch, making sure nobody snuck up on us.

Though the thought of getting the children safely to 'Eleu and her grandfather's boat filled me with anxiety, my heart still hurt from the conversation with Ali'i.

I'm sorry we didn't work out, I'd told him. His response stuck with me.

I'm sorry too. The longing I had inside my gut wouldn't go away, no matter how much I tried to think of something else. Nobody had cared for or protected me like Ali'i had. Nobody had understood or read right through me the way he did.

I have Melika and Ua. That was true. They would look out for me, and I would look out for them, just as we always had. I didn't need Ali'i.

I have to move on. I'd been telling myself the motto all

day, but every thought directed itself back to his kind eyes, gentle touch, and protective nature. He was sorry we didn't work out too, which meant... he had hoped, somewhere deep down, that we would. Ali'i had even proposed—in a joking way—but he proposed nonetheless.

"I'm fine. Just a little nervous about tonight," I said. It wasn't a lie, at least.

But I lied to Ali'i. I kept trying to play him, and he read right through me. So why did he care so much about me? Was it because I *tried* to play him but fell for him instead?

"Are you sure?" Ua asked, rolling a kapa blanket. We'd make new beds for the next refugees, as it'd fill up our time until Kona arrived.

I nodded.

'Eleu and her grandfather kept their visits on the island brief, as in three days or less, because their voyages took longer than others. They had to take refugees to safety and return as soon as possible for the next set of people fleeing Hana.

We had the operations down to nearly the perfect timing.

"I was thinking about those inspectors, the captains," Ua said. I didn't share much with Ua or Melika about my conversation with Ali'i. And because 'Eleu was on Lanai, we had to hurry and make preparations for the children to leave. It was a welcome distraction from my thoughts of Ali'i, and Ua and Melika hadn't had much of an opportunity to inquire more into the conversation.

However, when I told them that Ali'i knew Ua and I duped the king years ago, my best friend's eyes went wide, and she immediately said, "We have to silence him."

But I wouldn't hurt Ali'i. He had done nothing to hurt me, but rather did what he could to protect me. Could him, covering for us, possibly mean that he felt something for me? He had no duty or obligation to protect me.

I also realized how precarious the situation could be. At any time, Aliʻi could change his mind and turn us in.

When I said nothing, and continued rolling up the beds, Ua sighed. "I was thinking that all three of us should go tonight."

"All three of us?" I frowned. Usually only Ua and I took the refugees to safety. While Melika trained under our mentorship, because Ua's grandfather passed away, she wasn't nearly as stealthy yet. She had a ways to go before guiding people to safety in the night.

"You should take the baby. She likes you the best," Ua continued. "Melika and I can take the children in waves. I'll take the four. She takes three. You come at the very end. Stay here until we've cleared out and stowed the children."

I stared at the rolled kapa bed. Ua and I had been rolling and tying them as tight as we could with food and clothes for the children. ʻEleu had to somehow fit all of them on her grandfather's canoe, and stow the children in the hulls. ʻEleu and her grandfather had a large, majestic waʻa, and the fact that they manned it alone continued to amaze me. Usually a boat of that size took at least four or five people to man.

"I know we discussed just you and I going but..." Ua shrugged. "I have a bad feeling about those inspectors." She leaned in. "I feel like we're being watched." She didn't mean now, in the moment, but I had the same impression as her.

When I passed through town, Captain Naha followed me for a short time. Ua said he did the same for her. No doubt he sized us up, comparing us, using the details that King Hua had given him.

"I think if the captain happened to see us together, alone in the night, he'd know," Ua said.

"But Melika—"

"Have more faith in her," Ua cut in. "I know she's not as... quiet. But it's better. If we were caught at some point, it's better that the captain find Melika and I. Not you and I."

Ua was right. Captain Naha would see the resemblance between Ua and I. He'd observe my freckles, and realize we were out at night, just like the night we duped the king.

"Alright, let's tell Melika."

"And Ka'ala..." Ua gently placed her hand on my wrist. "You know what we have to do if we're caught, right?"

I nodded. We had vowed, long ago, that we would do anything to protect these refugees. They'd been through great abuse, violence, and aggression through no fault of their own. The least we could do was fight for them.

That meant we *would* fight. If either of the captains caught and wanted to turn us (or them) in, we would defend ourselves and the refugees at all costs.

"If Captain Kaaiali'i sees..." Ua raised an eyebrow. "Are you sure you can fight him?"

I hesitated. I didn't want to fight Ali'i.

"He won't see—"

"But if he does?" Ua frowned. "Ka'ala..."

"I know." I looked away.

"Ka'ala, I don't know what happened but you must put your feelings aside and remember our loyalty to these innocent people, this operation, this sanctuary and system that you've worked so hard to build." Ua softened and placed her hand on my shoulder.

"I know," I said once more, staring at the rolled bundle below me.

"So if he does happen to see or confront you—especially if you have refugees, will you fight?"

I nodded. "You're right."

She nodded too, squeezed my shoulder, and returned to the kapa she left half rolled.

My insides tightened.

Please don't follow us tonight, Ali'i. Stay far, far away... you and Captain Naha.

NIGHT FELL ON THE ISLAND, but there was no breeze, making the air hang in humidity. Crickets and geckos chirped in the woods, and I prayed the winds would pick up. The trade winds made the leaves rustle against each other, and that would help mask our sounds... well, Melika's sounds.

I worried the most about her as I handed her the lauhala bag, stuffed with the children's things.

Everyone was barefoot, as it made the walk to shore quieter.

"Will we see you again 'Iwa?" asked one of the little girls as I fixed the kihei tied at her shoulder. The baby slept in the back room and we brought all the children to the front room, preparing them to leave.

My heart ached, but I smiled. "I hope so." I hugged the little girl, trying not to cry. "But wherever you go, don't forget what you learned here, alright? And remember that we care for each one of you. Deeply."

One of the younger girls started crying, which made another little boy join her. Ua hurried to comfort them. We didn't need the tears to start falling now. They could cry all they wanted on the boat, with 'Eleu to comfort them, but not now.

"It's gonna be alright," I heard Ua say to the children, her voice calm and quiet. "I need you both to be brave. Be brave for us, and for each other. Understand?"

She gave them hugs and left kisses on their cheeks. "Tell 'Iwa goodbye, all of you."

I didn't know saying goodbye to the children would be so hard. It was one thing to tell adult refugees goodbye, but innocent children? I trusted 'Eleu to take them to good, safe homes, but I couldn't help the aching within my heart.

They're just children. They should never have to deal with something as horrible as what they went through. Now they had to flee again, but hopefully, for the last time.

Melika came from the room, her hair pulled up in a tight bun. We all wore our hair up in tight buns, so we could hear everything, and our hair wouldn't fall into our faces, blocking our view.

She had to excuse herself for a moment, unable to hold her emotions while saying goodbye. But now she looked fierce and determined as ever. Though Melika was only fifteen, she looked older now, more mature, ready to fight.

As I hugged and kissed the last child goodbye, I stood and embraced Ua and Melika. We hugged for a good moment, holding back tears.

"No matter what happens tonight," I said, trying to keep my hands from shaking with nervousness, "I'm so grateful to have worked side by side with you."

"Same." Melika's frame trembled but her eyes were on fire.

Ua nodded. "Good luck to both of you."

We separated, not wanting to make the children more anxious than they were. Ua went first, while Melika waited a moment. Chills ran up my spine as they disappeared down the path.

Melika took my hand and we stood on the porch, waiting in silence, giving Ua time and space before Melika departed. The three children under Melika's care waited inside.

"You know the call for help," I said, all thoughts of Ali'i gone, my mind completely focused on the present task of getting my sister, best friend, and children all safely where they needed to go.

"'Ae," Melika whispered.

"I need you to use it if you're in danger, understand?" I looked at her and she nodded, her eyes on the path ahead. "Let's get the children." I brought the last three out. Melika held the youngest in her arm while the other two, the older ones of the group, carried extra baskets of food. I didn't expect 'Eleu to have all the supplies and food for their journey and always tried to pull our load to help make her journey easier. Seven children was a lot to feed for a voyage to another island.

"See you at the shore," Melika said, kissed my cheek, then headed with the children on the path. My heart pumped, watching her leave.

My sister... If anything happened to Melika, I wouldn't forgive myself. She was so young, innocent...

And a fighter. Though doubts and anxiety pressed against my mind, I told myself that she could take care of herself. Ua and I had trained her, and we trained her enough.

When she finally disappeared from view, I went into the back room and scooped the baby into my arms. My heart pounded even louder.

Please stay asleep, I coaxed the baby in my mind, rocking her back and forth. As I stepped on the porch, I glanced at the palm trees.

151

Come on wind... Even 'Eleu and her grandfather must have been praying at that moment, because they needed good winds for sailing, departing this very evening. Why was tonight such a dead night?

A chill ran down my spine as I thought of the inspectors, the two captains closest to King Hua. Were Ali'i and Naha out there, waiting for us?

And what about Mailou? The man who always followed my shadow, no doubt, had to be out there now. It seemed like the island was awake, because we were awake. I hated that the nights we took refugees to 'Eleu always felt like this, even though we'd never been caught, not even once.

I felt the stone knife hanging from a belt around my waist. I never took caution to hide it on the fleeing nights, because I'd need it handy.

Sweat made my hands feel clammy, but I took a deep breath and started on the path. My skin prickled at every noise in the bushes, every rustle. Even when a gecko chirped a little loudly, I jumped, and the baby moved.

"Oh it's alright," I whispered, rocking her, trying to stay calm as I walked on. The path always seemed long on these nights, because anxiety panged my chest. I had to be extra alert, keen on any sounds, any slight deviation from normal.

The moon shone through pockets of the tree canopy above, and, soon, I stepped onto the hot paths of Lanai.

I'm getting closer to the ocean, I thought, seeing it on the horizon. As the shoreline came into view, I let out a quiet breath of relief. 'Eleu and her grandfather already gathered the lines, preparing to leave.

This meant that Melika and Ua made it safely, and that the children were now hiding in the hulls of that grand wa'a. Light shone through the golden sails, and the canoe looked majestic on the water.

I scanned the trees, knowing that Melika and Ua had long disappeared, going to our secret meeting place not far from here. We would watch the boat leave together, and safely make our way back to the hut.

The baby shifted once more and her eyes opened. I gasped.

"Not now," I whispered and tried to rock her asleep, but she smiled up at me. "Are you hungry?" The last thing I needed was for the baby to cry right now. 'Eleu didn't need a wailing baby to wake the island as they departed.

I hurried into the water, hiding at the back of the boat, where 'Eleu met me.

"Can you grab the poi from my bag?" I asked, turning to the side. 'Eleu dug her hand in and pulled out a small coconut bowl, with the other half as the lid. As she pulled the lid off, the baby squealed.

"Oh hello," I said, trying to smile, but internally freaking out. "Nai'a is going to feed you, don't worry."

'Eleu dipped her finger into the poi and offered it to the baby. "What's her name?" she asked.

The baby stared at 'Eleu, an unfamiliar face.

"Hey cutie," she said and smiled. The baby didn't eat the poi, but continued staring. 'Eleu had pulled her hair back into a tight bun today too, accentuating the sharp features of her face. She had dark skin from being in the sun all day, angled cheekbones, and coral lips. We had met long ago, on the shores of Lanai, when I learned her grandfather served as a messenger for the queen of Puna.

We became fast friends and I took the chance, asking if she'd help with my operations. She and her grandfather, both of them master wayfinders, were imperative in the smooth running of the sanctuary.

"Oh no, I'm so sorry." I tried not to panic. The fact that the baby was now awake remained out of my control.

"It's alright. Here, let me try holding her." 'Eleu was calm as ever, but I knew she was as worried as myself. They needed to get out of here.

Now.

Before someone showed up, like the inspectors, and asked to look through their canoe. Even though it was the dead of night, I had no doubt the inspectors would do such a thing.

"Ua said she might have been followed," 'Eleu said, then smiled and held out her hands. "Hi sweetheart... do you want to come to me?" The baby pulled back into me, alarmed.

"It's just Nai'a," I said, but I kept glancing around. 'Eleu's grandfather came around to the back of the boat.

He grimaced. "She's awake?"

"She doesn't want me." Eleu's voice thinned, like she couldn't breathe. "Grandpa, can you try?"

"I'm scarier than either of you," he said, trying to make us laugh, but I was on full alarm now.

Ua said she might have been followed. I kept scanning the trees along the shoreline, hoping that nobody watched us now.

"Hey there." He tickled the baby's tummy and flashed his big Hawaiian smile, but the baby turned and looked at me, as if wondering what I was doing.

"What's her name?" Naula asked.

"She doesn't have one."

"You should give her one then," Naula said, his voice

deep and rich. "Perhaps she won't leave until you have gifted her with that."

I swallowed hard. "I can't name a child, and she's not mine—"

"It's only fitting that you, of all people, do it," said ʻEleu. "If it wasn't for you, she wouldn't be here."

My hands felt even more clammy. Giving someone a name was no light thing. I looked into the baby's big brown eyes. She had been through so much in such a short time of her life.

Her mother, who was unjustly forced on, left the baby at the king's hut. He didn't want the baby either. Prince Kekoa had saved the baby's life. Then Kona. Then me.

She was a symbol that every life was precious, and everyone deserved a chance at life.

"Ola," I said, then nodded. "Her name is Keola."

"Life." ʻEleu smiled. "Beautiful."

The baby cooed, as if pleased, and my heart ached again.

"Come here, Keola..." ʻEleu reached her hands out again. The baby stared for a moment then glanced at me.

"Go ahead, go on, Keola. She'll take care of you."

With that permission, Keola leaned into ʻEleu, who smiled and rocked her. "Good girl, you're coming with us now. We'll take care of you." She kissed the baby's head and nodded to her grandfather. He placed his hand on my shoulder.

"Thank you, again, Kaʻala."

I placed my hand over his and nodded. "Safe travels."

We then placed our foreheads against one another and breathed in. I didn't usually do this custom with peers my age, but with older kupuna, like Naula, I breathed in the *hā*, the breath of life.

He then moved past me to push the boat to sea. 'Eleu kissed my cheek and half hugged me, the baby in her other arm.

"Good luck Ka'ala."

"You too. Thank you again."

'Eleu stepped back and looked at the horizon. "Good. Tide's coming up, and the breeze has finally arrived." She looked so relieved, it made my own anxiety a little lighter. "We are in the favor of the gods, I suppose. Now be careful heading back," she warned me. "And I'll take care of these little ones, I promise."

"I know." I nodded and stepped towards shore. I needed to get out of the water as soon as possible, and hide in the bushes. But I watched as 'Eleu climbed onto the wa'a and, with one hand, pulled ropes to tighten the sails. The baby, Keola, remained in one arm.

Naula pushed the boat as far as he could before jumping on.

Sadness panged my chest, though I should have been happy. The boat pulled away and skimmed towards the sea, the wind, indeed picking up.

We did it... I sloshed out of the water and hurried towards the trees, where I could hide. I didn't want to keep Melika and Ua waiting, though I knew they'd be patient. Not far from here, they should be on a cliff, watching until the boat made it to the horizon.

Once it disappeared from view, *then* we knew we'd really been successful.

Keola is gone. The children are gone. I don't know why it seemed extra emotional this time. Usually I felt light and excited after getting refugees to 'Eleu and safety. But this time it felt... sad.

Maybe because I kept thinking that the children didn't

deserve this. They should have been raised in loving homes in Hana. They should have *never* been taken to the altar as a sacrifice.

They will be taken to loving homes though. I wiped a tear that had escaped and swallowed hard, knowing my task wasn't over yet.

Ua, Melika, and I still needed to return safely to the sanctuary. And after that, I needed to figure out how to get to King Hua. Innocent people–innocent children–should never have to suffer like these ones did.

I trudged up the hill, eager to find my sister and best friend hiding behind the bushes, watching the canoe. This area was full of orange bird-of-paradise flowers, a perfect symbol for the freedom that our innocent refugees would now taste.

As I approached the hiding place, I froze. The skin at the back of my neck tingled.

Something wasn't right. Ua and Melika weren't there, hunched over, necks craned to see the canoe flee over the horizon.

But someone else was there. A man.

I stepped back, hoping I wasn't too close for him to see me. Surely Melika and Ua must have seen him and went to our second hiding spot, our second meeting place.

The man turned and stood, his eyes on me. From the confused look on his face, I could tell he didn't recognize me. He probably hadn't expected anyone to find him here. But what was he doing here? Did he see 'Eleu's canoe sailing over the moonlit horizon? I reached for the knife at my side, my insides churning as he held a knife in his hand. He didn't hesitate, but ran towards me.

It was Captain Naha, and if he recognized me, I'd have to fight.

CHAPTER FIFTEEN

*M*y instincts told me to fight, but a second thought passed through me, possibly a better option.

Run.

If I could escape him, he'd never know it was me, never suspect anything. I'd been careless, expecting Melika and Ua in the hiding place, instead of keeping my eyes open.

Adrenaline pumped through my veins as I turned and bolted in the opposite direction. Though shorter than others, I could still sprint pretty well, and I felt myself gaining distance from the captain.

The breeze picked up, blowing the palm leaves against each other. The air felt less humid, but sweat still formed along my forehead and arms. Heavy clouds began to cover the moon and sky, meaning that possible rain showers could pass through.

For a moment, it made me think of 'Eleu getting through another storm, but I had to focus on getting myself out of here. 'Eleu and her grandfather were master wayfinders. They'd weathered many storms and would be fine.

As for me... well, *I* was in a completely different boat now. At least the heavy clouds made it harder for the captain to see me.

"Get back here!" Captain Naha called after me. Ferns, leaves, and branches scratched my arms, cheeks, and legs, but it didn't matter. The shuffling from behind me meant he wasn't going to give up this chase.

He wasn't as fast as me, and was probably slower because of his age and build. But he kept a good pace. I looked back to check on him.

Captain Naha cursed, holding his knife out to me, telling me to slow down, that I was under arrest. He still didn't recognize me, and I hoped having a tight bun on top of my head made it less obvious as to who I was. Many men and women wore their hair in tight buns.

My foot got stuck on a branch and I tripped, tumbling onto the ground.

"I've got you now!" He advanced so quickly, I hardly had time to turn around and scramble up. Before I could stand, he jumped and grabbed my ankle.

I didn't dare turn around, afraid that if I did, he'd see my face and there was no turning back. I'd have to fight.

Captain Naha suddenly let out a surprised "oof!" and his hold on my ankle loosened. I turned around and gasped.

Ali'i caught Naha's arm to keep him from falling to the ground. In the darkness, I could make out Ali'i's eyebrows, creased in anger, his fighter side in full life now.

I scrambled back, not knowing what to do. Ali'i, one of the king's loyal captains, now saw me.

But I can't fight him.

Ali'i checked Naha's pulse then gently placed his head on the ground before making eye contact with me.

"What are you doing?" he asked, his tone cold and annoyed.

"What are *you* doing?"

"Saving your life." He paused, before adding, "Again."

"I didn't need saving."

"Did he see that it was you?"

"I don't know."

Aliʻi held the bridge of his nose. "Did you make eye contact with him?"

"No." My whole body trembled as I stood and held my knife so tightly, my knuckles were white. I wiped sweat from my forehead. "What did you see Aliʻi?"

"Everything."

"Everything?" My heart pumped hard. I didn't want to fight Aliʻi, but what if he knew? And what if he told the king? It would ruin everything.

He won't tell the king about the sanctuary. He wouldn't, right? After all, he knew it was Ua and I who duped the king but he came up with a valid excuse as to why it wasn't us.

But, at the same time, I couldn't handle the thought that my secret could be exposed. Aliʻi had too much power with this knowledge. If Naha had seen me, I would have had to fight. So why was there such a gaping difference in my attitude towards Naha versus Aliʻi? They were *both* loyal to King Hua. They *both* intended on investigating me and, possibly, turning me in.

"I saw you take the baby to those wayfinding messengers from Puna," Aliʻi said. "I saw Ua and Melika with the children. I saw all of it."

I now noticed that Aliʻi held a knife in his hand too, his body tense. Was he prepared to fight?

"So you're going to turn me in?" I asked, stepping back, getting ready to fight.

"I should." He didn't move. "Not only did you tie and mock the king, but you are running illegal operations. I found out that you've even housed fleeing Kohala warriors in your sanctuary."

How did he know all this? Did some people on the island rat me out after all?

I tried to swallow but there was a big lump in my throat.

I've done nothing wrong, I told myself. Because I didn't. I rescued many people's lives.

"I can't let you take me," I said, my voice shaky and airy.

"Ka'ala–" He stepped forward and I hated what I had to do... but it was for the people. Ua had reminded me that very day, and I committed to taking the necessary steps to protect these people. I had sacrificed so much in my life to save other people's lives, and if Ali'i was one more thing to sacrifice, then so be it. It didn't make my heart feel any better though.

I dropped to the ground and swung my leg, tripping Ali'i. He caught himself with one hand, but the split second gave me an opportunity to swing my arms around his neck and flip him to the ground.

Before I could put my knife to his throat, though, he grabbed my wrist and twisted me to the ground next to him. Then he rolled over me, pinning my arms in place.

"What are you–" he started to ask, but I wrapped my legs around his waist and bumped my forehead against his. It disarmed him, once more, giving me space to yank my arms free of his grasp and flip us over so I was on top.

"I can't let you stop all of this," I said, panting as I held the knife against his neck.

A tiny trickle of blood started down his nose, and he let his head relax. "You're an excellent fighter, Ka'ala."

"Don't patronize me."

"I'm not–I mean it." His voice sounded sad. "So you're going to kill me?"

My white knuckles clutched the handle of my knife and, again, I tried to swallow. But the lump was still there.

"You've left me no choice."

"And you're going to kill Naha?" Ali'i glanced towards the unconscious captain not far from us.

"I have to."

Ali'i studied my face, then his eyes glazed over my body. I became aware of how inappropriate this looked, my legs straddled, sitting on top of him, my clothes plastered to my body in sweat and humidity, the knife pressed against his neck. The strangest feeling overcame my body, making me feel hot all over.

"You don't have to. I never planned to tell the king," Ali'i said. "From the first time I met you, I knew you were good, Ka'ala. You deserve protection."

His words were soothing, even sweet. But I kept my knife in place, hating that things had to end this way.

Ali'i moved so suddenly, I didn't even realize he'd used his words to distract me. He grabbed my hand with the knife and leaped up, which made my own two feet find solid ground. Before I could get my bearings, he twisted me around, taking the knife from my hand and pressing my back against a nearby tree.

With my knife in one of his hands, and his other hand holding my fingers above me, I was stuck.

I grimaced in pain at the way he pulled my fingers, causing him to loosen his grip, but only for a moment.

It was then that I knew Ali'i let me win earlier. He

probably wanted to see my fighting style, and now that he knew, he could use my strategies against me. Now the knife was pressed against my neck and he drew close to me, using his body to pin me against the tree.

The intense heat between us was almost suffocating. His chest was hard and muscled.

"Fine. Take me to the king," I said. "I've wanted to meet him."

"No, you've wanted to *kill* him," Aliʻi corrected, his face so close, I could kiss him if I wanted.

"Then kill me. But don't touch Ua or Melika."

"I already told you, Kaʻala. I don't plan on turning you in." He drew closer, and I gasped, wondering if I should use my legs to keep fighting.

But for some reason, I didn't want to keep fighting. There was something strangely attractive about Aliʻi pinning me against the tree. It was almost as if I *wanted* him there, our bodies touching. He seemed to realize this too, and his eyes fell to my lips. But only for a moment before they returned to my eyes.

"You're too good, Kaʻala. I can't turn you in."

"Why?"

"I don't know." We were both breathless, quietly gasping for air. "Maybe it's because I want to do something good," Aliʻi said, "for once in my life." He kept looking at my lips, and it made my stomach flutter. "After all the bad I've done, maybe sparing you is a way I can redeem myself."

"You don't have to just *spare me*," I said. "Help me. Help the sanctuary, Aliʻi."

At those words, his eyebrows creased.

"You don't have to go back and serve the king. You've done plenty—"

"I swore a lifetime of service."

"Then break it—"

"I'll die before I break a promise—"

"You're stubborn."

"Not stubborn. Loyal. I pledged an oath of loyalty. One doesn't simply break that."

"Even if the oath of loyalty is to a murderer? Ali'i, King Hua was going to murder children. *Children*." At that, my eyes watered. Those sweet, innocent little ones were safe with 'Eleu now. Keola, the baby, would be raised in a loving, good home. "How can you be loyal to someone like that?"

Ali'i looked down, and I felt self conscious of my chest. Was I dressed modestly enough right now? A light rain began falling through the trees. The droplets mixed with my sweat and streaked my face and body.

The captain had gone quiet, staring into my eyes. My heart beat so hard, I wasn't sure what to do.

Kiss him. My whole body wanted it. It seemed so easy, to lean in, to give into the feelings I'd been burying. Ali'i's face drew closer, his eyes moving down my face to my lips once more.

I ached to kiss him, to feel that this thing between us was real, and maybe, just maybe we'd work out.

Because Ali'i didn't have to serve King Hua. He didn't need to serve a murderer for the rest of his life. Wasn't it more honorable to leave his position and do something that was worth it, instead of miserably serving an evil warlord for the rest of his days?

We'd make it work out. We'd find a way.

And, with Ali'i, I can get access to the king. King Hua deserved to die, especially for all the lives he ended or ruined.

Just as I thought Ali'i might close the gap and kiss me,

he said, "I'm sorry Ka'ala. I'm not the man you want me to be. I'll never be good enough for you."

He then released me, dropping my knife to the ground and stepping back. Without his body against mine, everything felt icy cold.

"You don't believe that," I said, picking up my knife and shivering.

"We part ways here." He picked up his own knife and took another step away from me, as if he had to coax himself to do so. "I truly am sorry we didn't work out."

"Ali'i..."

"You don't have to worry. Your secret's safe with me." He tipped his head. "I promise, and I don't break my promises."

"I wish you would though," I said, my heart hurting more than the aches in my body. "You don't have to keep serving the king."

"Ka'ala, an oath is an oath."

"It's a cowardly oath," I came back, about to march up to him again. But he held up his hands.

"Don't come close. There's nothing—there can't be anything—between us."

I froze, wanting so badly to be around him again, to feel like we could work out. But maybe he was right. Maybe oceans separated us because our loyalties were to different causes.

"If you try to kill the king, I would have to stop you," the captain said. A warning. Naha moaned and Ali'i tensed.

"Hurry, get out of here."

I wanted to say something, to further prove my point as to why Ali'i should never, *ever* serve the king. But Ali'i sheathed his knife, wiped his nose, and knelt by the other captain.

"Serving the king is cowardly," I said, unable to find any other words.

"Ka'ala..." The way Ali'i said my name made my heart ache in ways I'd never felt before. "Please. You're making this harder. Go."

"Why won't you just do the right thing?"

At this, Ali'i stood and approached me. "That's enough."

"Stop fighting, Ali'i. You know it's not right. You know the king is wicked. These wars are nothing but evil–"

"Ka'ala." Now he looked stern, maybe even angry. I certainly felt angry.

"You're a coward–"

"Ka'ala, that's enough." He turned around, his jaw tense as he went to Captain Naha and shook him awake. I wanted to scream, to argue more with Ali'i, but I did need to get out of there.

"Fine." At that, I turned and ran as fast as I could, not even looking back at Ali'i. Rain began to pour, mixing in with my sweat and tears. Why did it hurt so bad? Ali'i had never been mine, and I had never been his.

Even though there was something between us, obvious feelings of attraction, maybe even care and compassion, I had to let it go.

Ali'i saved my life tonight... again. He'd protected me... again.

But just because those things happened more than once, didn't mean we'd fall in love again. This was the end of us, because we were on opposite teams.

I'd have to forget about him and move on. He would do nothing to end these wars, to save and preserve the lives of men, women, and children. Well, perhaps my secret was safe with him, but he'd always serve the king because of his oath of loyalty.

Ali'i would do nothing to end these wars. But I would do something. A mixture of sadness and anger swirled within my heart. *It's over. We're over.* But my plight to kill the king was far from over.

CHAPTER SIXTEEN

$\mathcal{U}$a, Melika, and I cleaned the hut in silence, returning to our usual duties of making new kapa bedding and sheets, clothes, and building up our food storage. We were back to normal: preparing for the next set of refugees.

Without the merry presence of the children and baby, it felt unusually quiet. Though none of us said it, we missed the children and their sweet spirits. I hoped, with each passing day, that they were doing alright on 'Eleu's boat and that they were safe. But, unlike with other refugees, the aftermath of this experience left us feeling down and sluggish.

How could we keep the morale up? All of us seemed to move about in a strange mixture of emotions. Perhaps we were sad because the children should have never experienced this. They should have had safe homes. Yet we were happy that we had a chance to cross paths with the children, to care for and love them, and then to send them to a new home.

But the heaviness of it all weighed on us, especially me.

I couldn't stop thinking how unfair this whole thing was for the children, and that one person remained responsible: King Hua.

Ua and I returned to our daily walks through town and the shores, watching the happenings of the people, listening to gossip, and keeping an eye out for Kona. I saw Ali'i, but avoided him as much as possible. Mailou seemed to have gone missing, and it made me suspicious. Did he decide to stop following me, after all? Did Ali'i say something to a local chief that made Mailou keep his distance? Ali'i said he'd make sure Mailou didn't touch me, but after our last conversation, he obviously didn't like me, right?

I didn't want to admit it, but every time I caught a glance of Ali'i, my insides tightened. Our argument replayed over and over in my mind. I tried to think of all the possible ways we could work out, but, in the end, we were on opposite teams.

He served Hua.

And I did not.

If given the chance, I would put my knife through the king's heart for all the injustices and bloody wars he caused.

I told Melika and Ua what happened with Captain Naha and Ali'i the night we took our refugees to 'Eleu. They both worried that Ali'i would say something, and Ua even volunteered to "silence" Ali'i, but I told her I trusted him. At first she gave me a questioning look, but several days later looked annoyed as ever.

"Why?" she asked as we sat on the porch, the evening sky dark and heavy with clouds. "You can't possibly still have feelings for him... not after he made it clear he is deathly loyal to King Hua. He even said that he would stop *you* if you attempted to kill the king."

"But he let me go free."

"That's not good enough for me," Ua said, shaking her head. Melika remained quiet, not used to hearing Ua and I argue. "Ka'ala, you've worked *so* hard to build this sanctuary. If a king's man—a captain, someone so close to the king—knows about all of this, why wouldn't he tell Hua? Maybe he's tricking you."

"What do you mean?"

"Maybe he wants you to think you're safe, but he's just going to tell the king anyway."

"But he hasn't gone back to Hana yet," Melika muttered.

She was right. Captain Naha, with a wicked head wound, had been escorted to Hana, and Ali'i was still in town.

With the two servants of the king. Rumors began floating around Lanai that the Captain and king's men stuck around because the king, indeed, was coming to Lanai. When asked why they were still here, Ali'i gave the islanders the vague answer that his investigations weren't complete.

"Why hasn't he gone back yet?" Ua rubbed her forehead, annoyed. "What else does he have to investigate if he knows it was us who mocked the king?"

A chilly evening breeze made the hairs on my skin stand on end. Ua continued. "Maybe the captain is just holding out so when the king comes he can get his revenge on us."

"Good. Let him come," I said. Ua and I looked at each other, and a silent understanding passed: we both wanted to kill the king. I could see it in her eyes, the fierce desire to end these wars. She probably felt as strongly about the king as I did, especially after rescuing the children.

"No, don't let him come," Melika cut in. "If you couldn't kill him last time—and that was years ago—why would things have changed?"

We both looked at Melika, surprised that she had picked up on the plans too. Did Melika know I wanted to kill the king all along, and I was using Ali'i?

She's more observant than I thought... Why did I doubt my sister so often?

"He's probably more invincible and powerful now than before," Ua said. She sat straighter. "Send me to Hana, Ka'ala. I'll talk to Kekoa. He probably knows the answer to kill the king."

"What? I want to go with!" Melika, sitting on Ua's right, squeezed her arm. "Take me!"

"Nobody is going to Hana," I said.

"If the king is coming here, we need answers." Ua let her hair out of its bun, and it fell down her back, long and wavy, similar to my hair.

For the first time since my failed conversation with Ali'i, I felt the fire inside of me again. Talking to Melika and Ua about finding a way to kill the king made it all so real.

But if there was anyone who should go to Hana, it was I. Kona would be there, and he could take me to Kekoa. The prince *had* to know something about killing the king, right? And what if I could do the deed right there, in Hana? Nobody would ever know it was me, and the wars could end. We were wasting time, waiting around here on Lanai. Meanwhile, since Makahiki, the time of peace, was over, King Hua could be gathering his troops right this moment for another attack on Kohala.

And if he was gathering troops, no doubt he was gathering sacrifices.

"Let's just think about it, alright?" I said, standing and stretching. As I did so, I noticed Ua frowning into the distance. A thought came over me.

Did she want to go to Hana to, possibly, see Kona? He

wouldn't be back here for another week or two, with new refugees. When he returned, he'd have to marry Liha. But maybe... just maybe, Ua still longed for him? Maybe there was a chance love could prevail?

I opened my mouth to ask, but Melika groaned and sat back. "You guys never let me do anything..." Her complaints filled the air and distracted me.

"We couldn't do this without you though," I said, kneeling and stroking her hair. We ended the night, as though we were just normal friends and sisters. Ua returned to her home in the woods, while Melika and I went to sleep. Neither of us bothered to keep watch.

But sleep didn't come over me.

I was too distraught about Ali'i, too distraught about Kona and Ua, too distraught because the king was still alive, and the wars were going to continue.

"Ali'i is leaving!" Ua came rushing up the hill. The beating sounds of kapa stopped immediately as Melika and I looked up from our work.

"What?" My heart raced as I processed. If he was leaving, would I never see him again?

Good. It's better that way.

Yet my heart hurt. Should I try talking to him one last time? Maybe he would change his mind and break his promise to the king. Was love powerful enough to conquer all?

"Why?" Melika asked.

"From the gossip, it's because he's completed his investigations. The king was supposed to come here in a few days, and he's leaving to stop the king in his path and return to Hana."

So Ali'i was still protecting me. He was leaving *now* so that the king wouldn't even land on Lanai.

"And..." Ua blushed.

"Your cheeks are getting awfully rosy," Melika said, leaping up. "What happened? Did you meet someone handsome?"

"No..."

"What?" I stood too, as Melika and I rushed to Ua. I wasn't used to seeing her flustered like this, and it made me anxious for her. Did something happen? Did someone else catch her eye?

"Last night I stopped by my parent's hut."

My heart ached for Ua. She was not close to her parents, as she'd been raised by her grandparents.

"And?" Melika looked like she might explode.

"I asked him if he'd speak to Oponui about... well..." She looked so embarrassed yet hopeful, I couldn't help but grab her hand. Melika grabbed her other hand.

"Did you ask him to speak to Oponui about reconsidering the marriage agreement so you can marry Kona?" Melika asked, speaking so quickly that her words slurred together and she ran out of breath.

"'Ae." Ua's whole face turned red and the color spread to the tips of her ears. "I don't know if anything will come of it. Kona's betrothed is a chief's daughter, a woman of status—"

"And you're incredible!" Melika piped in. "Not to forget your grandfather was a master of the lua. He taught and trained many men of Lanai how to fight."

"'Ae, Oponui would be a fool to overlook that point of status," I said, hope rising within myself. Maybe it *could* work out between Ua and Kona.

As Melika squealed and giggled and Ua finally allowed herself to join in, something moved within me.

If Ua was so brave to fight for her love... could I fight for Ali'i?

Wait. I'm not in love with him. Then why had he been on my mind for... who knew how long? Why did his kindness and care make me want him more and more?

"If Oponui doesn't reconsider, you should run away with Kona!" Melika exclaimed.

"Well I don't know if I'd be that drastic—"

"Why not?" Melika jumped up and down. "I'm so happy you spoke to your father! Something has to come of this!"

"I have to go," I suddenly said, wiping my skirt.

"Where?" Melika's eyes went wide. "You're going to talk to Ali'i?" She screamed in excitement and my cheeks turned as rosy as Ua's.

"Hurry," Ua said, pulling me into a quick hug, then stepped back and fixed my hair.

"And wipe your face," Melika said, motioning to her forehead. "You're sort of sweaty—"

"Alright alright," I said, nervousness and panic building within me.

"Run!" Melika and Ua both said, laughing and jumping in delight. I sprinted down the path, towards the shore, not knowing what to say, not knowing what to do... but hoping, maybe, that Ali'i would talk it out with me.

Ua's bravery had inspired me. Maybe Ali'i and I were a possibility. We hadn't given ourselves a fair chance, seeing ourselves on opposite teams. But was love more powerful than that? I had to know, because if Ali'i left now, I'd probably never see him again. The question of, *Could we have worked out?* Would stay with me forever, unanswered.

No. I'd get my answer now.

ONE OF THE king's servants noticed me first and approached before I even reached the canoe. It was a larger canoe, definitely not the one Ali'i came on. Captain Naha must have taken the other one back.

"What do you want?" the servant asked, looking annoyed, like I'd interrupted something.

"I need to speak with Captain Ali'i."

"We're about to depart. What do you wish to say?"

"It's personal."

"Then you'll keep it to yourself." He turned to leave and I followed, trying to find Ali'i's yellow cape. The wa'a was taller than most, so I craned my neck. The servant turned around.

"Stop following me. Get out of here, peasant."

The entitlement made me want to punch the servant's face but I kept calm. "I just need a few minutes with the captain."

"You're too late. Now get out of here or I'll force you." The servant's eyebrows creased and I knew he was serious.

I covered my eyes, hoping to see Ali'i's form on the boat.

"Go," said the servant, his fingers tightening on his spear. Anxiety panged my chest.

No. I couldn't just go, not when I was so close to the captain. Why was the servant being so resistant? They had all seemed so friendly and kind with the Lanai locals before. When they came to rescue me with Ali'i, from Mailou, they also seemed unbothered... but maybe it was all a facade.

Was Ali'i wearing a facade too?

"Ali'i!" I caught sight of his yellow cape as he moved on top of the canoe, getting things ready.

"Annoying girl, get out of here." At this the servant seized my arm and dragged me up the shore to the forest path.

"Hang on!" Aliʻi splashed into the water and came jogging up to us. The servant released me and I rushed to Aliʻi. At first I wanted to hug him, but felt awkward with the servant watching. Aliʻi made no motion to embrace me. If anything, his whole body tensed and he stepped back. My stomach dropped at the distance he created between us.

"What's going on here?" he asked.

"She's delaying our trip." The servant folded his arms.

"How?" Aliʻi kept his eyes on me, and he felt so, *so* far from me.

"Says she needs to have a few words with you."

Aliʻi looked around, as if making sure nobody watched, then nodded. "It will be quick then." The servant looked annoyed as ever, but Aliʻi ignored him, gently took my arm, and started walking along the shore.

We climbed over some rocky reefs, stopping on the other side, out of sight and out of hearing from the king's servants.

"What is it?" he asked, avoiding eye contact, folding his arms and looking to the ocean. Seeing him made my heart pound. The other night we had been so close to each other. I wanted to even kiss him the other night. Not only was I emotionally attracted to him, for all the kindness and protection he offered, but I was definitely physically attracted. I looked at my feet.

"I just wanted to talk."

"About?"

"Us."

He shook his head and started walking back.

"Aliʻi wait!" I grabbed his arm and stepped close to him.

"I just..." My cheeks turned hot as I didn't even know what to say.

"We've already established that we won't work out, alright?" He kept shaking his head, getting ready to leave but I held firm.

"Wait. I just... I want to know how you feel. Because, maybe, if we both feel the same... maybe we could work out."

"Our loyalties are to our duties," Ali'i said, glancing at my hand on his arm, and then looking back out to sea. He had the nicest brown eyes.

"But what if we chose loyalty to one another? To... love?" My voice went dry and I couldn't get myself to meet his eyes. Shyness overcame me. It was too easy to feel insecure. If I admitted my feelings, would he mock me? How could Ua make such a bold move?

I had to be brave, even if Ali'i's response crushed my heart, even if he rejected me. At least I was trying to be honest.

"You've been so good to me..." I rubbed his arm, remembering my weird thing for his arms. "You've shown me what it's like to be cared for, protected, seen... and loved."

He remained quiet.

"I want to show you how I feel," I said, blushing, "But I don't know how. I've never been expressive or... able to show my real feelings. Even my sister and best friend can't read me. But you can." I looked up at him, hoping he could see the emotions beneath the surface.

His jaw tensed, and he looked away once more. He was hardening his heart against me, I could tell. His loyalty ran deep.

"Ali'i..." I felt like a beggar, wanting some sort of reaction.

"Please stop, Ka'ala," he said, still not meeting my eyes. "You shouldn't have to ask to be loved."

"I'm not asking—"

"What I mean is that you *are* loved." He looked down at me now, and my heart beat so hard, I had to focus to hear his words. "But I don't deserve you. Your secret is safe with me, and that is the greatest service I can do for you. But I'm not fit to be someone you love—"

"Don't say that." I wanted to cry. Why did he think so low of himself?

"I've thought about *us* over and over. From the moment I first saw you, talked to you, and got to be around you, I've wanted to be and do better." He looked away. "But I can't. My loyalty is to King Hua."

"Why can't it change? Am I not *enough* for you?" I tried not to feel like something was stabbing me, but it was obvious he cared more about his status with King Hua than he cared about me.

"Ka'ala..." My words cracked him, as he immediately took my shoulders and stroked my cheek. "That's not what I mean at all. I just don't feel like I can ever change—I've done so much evil, led battles, killed men... You're so good, and so pure. I'm not worthy of redemption. It's too late for me now."

"But you could change now. You could help me, help the refugees. We could save people together..."

At this, Ali'i stared into my eyes, believing my words.

"I think I..." I wanted to say the words, to make sure he knew how I felt about him. But I was so embarrassed by my shyness, I looked down. I wanted to show him that I didn't despise him. He had been doing what everyone else throughout Hana and Maui did: serve King Hua, fight in the war.

But he could change, right now.

I stood on the tips of my toes and kissed his lips. It was a peck, like the first time I kissed his cheek, and I looked down, embarrassed at my own romantic inadequacies.

"You just... kissed me?" A smile crept up Ali'i's lips and he wrapped his arms around me.

"Not very good at it," I mumbled, unable to meet his eyes. Why was I so awkward, so embarrassing?

"Maybe you should try again," he said, stroking my cheek as he tucked back a loose piece of hair.

I looked into his eyes, wondering what my life would look like without him: I'd probably get along fine. I'd get over the disappointment of not working out. Oponui would marry me to someone else. I'd still run my secret operations. Somehow I'd find King Hua and kill him. Meanwhile, Ali'i would return to Hana, find someone else, get married, and return to battle.

But that's not the life I wanted... or at least, I was sure it could be better than that.

I wondered what my life would look like with him: someone to love, to talk to, who understood and cared for me, someone who wanted to protect me...

I stood on the tips of my toes, wrapped my arms around his neck and kissed him again. This time, he pulled me close to him and kissed me back, as if he had anticipated this. I'd never felt so alive, my stomach fluttering in excitement as our lips moved over each other.

"You didn't say... what you were thinking..." Ali'i said between kisses.

"Shh... I'm showing you," I replied, and kissed him harder, feeling his smile. For a moment, my insecurities left: it was just me and Ali'i standing on the beach, our arms wrapped around each other, our bodies melting into each other, our lips moving over one another.

And then my insecurities returned as self consciousness sunk in. What if someone saw us? I'd never kissed anyone before, and what if I looked silly? I broke away and hugged him.

"I don't want you to go," I said.

"And now I really don't want to go." Ali'i chuckled and my stomach fluttered at the sound of it. I rested my chin on his chest and looked up at him.

"If we really do love each other... we can make it work, right?" I asked.

Ali'i nodded. "You're so brave, Ka'ala. I need to be more like you." He kissed my forehead and held me tight. "I'm going to stay, and ask your father for your hand."

My heart skipped a beat. "Really?"

"'Ae. Maybe things won't be perfect at first—maybe you'll have to come to Hana with me while I figure things out and step down from my position."

"Or maybe your position as captain is a good thing. Maybe it'll be more beneficial to the sanctuary—"

"Unless I have to lead men in battle." He kissed my forehead again and I nodded.

"Right. It's best if you find a way out of the position."

"Would you be..." He hesitated. "Would you be happy being married to me?"

I nodded, smiling wide, thinking of a life with Ali'i: protection, care, kindness, love. "Yes, I'd be very happy."

He grinned. "You have made me happy since I arrived here in Lanai. I hope to be a good husband and take care of you for the rest of our lives."

"You will." I felt so happy *now*, like a huge weight had been lifted off my shoulders. Ali'i and I were going to work out, and he'd even ask my father to marry me. There was no way Oponui could resist that offer of marriage, because of Ali'i's status.

"You're so good." Ali'i kissed my lips again, then stepped back, rubbing my arms. "I'm going to speak with him now."

I couldn't stop smiling. "Alright."

"See you in a bit." He kissed my forehead then turned and hurried towards his boat, probably to tell his men they weren't leaving after all. I stood there, in a daze, too excited to even think.

Ali'i loves me. We're going to get married. Life was good. Too good.

CHAPTER SEVENTEEN

*M*elika, Ua, and I danced around as we worked and made preparations, a lightness in our steps that hadn't been there before. After I watched Ali'i leave, I ran home, bursting with excitement. Melika and Ua, supportive as ever, celebrated with me.

And then we waited.

Though we were excited over the revealed romances between myself and Ali'i, and between Ua and Kona, we still moved with caution. Oponui had the final say, though I hated to think it. Hopefully Oponui said yes to both offers: the offer from Ua's father, and the offer from Ali'i.

"We're going to have *two* weddings!" Melika kept saying, over and over, telling us what flowers we should use, what we could wear, how to make our hair, and so forth.

Meanwhile, I couldn't stop thinking about how nice it was to be in Ali'i's arms, to hear his confession. And it felt good that I told him the truth too. My question was answered: we could work out. We both loved each other and wanted to commit, and maybe our future together would start off a little rocky—he had to somehow step down from his position, and I'd probably go to Hana with him. That left Melika and Ua in charge.

But if Ua and Kona got married, Ua would probably travel with Kona. This part worried me. I trusted Melika and felt she was competent but... there were so many things to do. Could she hold the fort on her own?

This thought seemed to pass through Melika's mind as we ate our evening meal together around the campfire in the front lawn. Ua and I kept looking towards the path, hoping, waiting. It killed me inside, because a day had passed since I saw Ali'i and I wondered if he got an answer from my father.

Perhaps my father was playing tricks and didn't want to answer right away. That seemed typical of my father. He liked to be in control.

"So... if you both get married, you'll probably be off in Hana, huh?" Melika asked, then took a bite of her purple poi.

I nodded, staring at my bowl, too anxious to answer. Where was Ali'i? What did my father say? And what did my father say about Ua and Kona? How long would we have to wait around for answers? Should I seek out Ali'i myself?

Patience. Deep breaths. I took a steadying breath while Ua answered.

"I think so." She placed her hand on Melika's shoulder. "You are completely capable, I know it." She glanced at me for another affirmation.

I swallowed hard. "Ua is right. You're responsible, hard working, smart, and well trained. I have no doubt it will work out."

"Well..." Melika sighed then nodded, slowly. "You're right. It will just be different, I guess."

"We'll be back though," I added. "I want to live here anyways, not in Hana."

"And I want to live here too." Ua added, "Well... I want to live here when the war ends and there is peace."

Silence fell over us. The crackling fire cast shadows on the grass, and smoke stretched up to the night sky. I glanced at the stars, wondering where Ali'i was now, and thinking about all the details we needed to work out. Would I have to overcome my desire to kill the king, in order to be with Ali'i? He said he'd step down from his position, but would it be that simple?

Ua suddenly gasped. "My father is here," she said, and we all stood.

Ua's father was a large man, with dark hair that ran down his back. He looked different from Ua in many ways, just as my father looked different from me. He was dark, while she had lighter color features: light brown hair, eyes, and skin.

"Aloha father," Ua said, opening the gate so he could enter. Though I didn't know Ua's father well, I was pleased he knew where to find Ua. He didn't seem to know much about her, but at least he knew that we were best friends and he could find her here.

"Aloha uncle," Melika and I said, each of us kissing his cheek. I studied his body language, immediately feeling my heart seize up.

"Aloha," he said, then looked down, shaking his head. Ua froze in place. I quickly placed my arm around her, while Melika grabbed her hand.

"What is it?" I asked, when Ua started trembling, her eyes wide.

"I asked Oponui. I negotiated. But..." He looked away

and made a face. "He said that the offer from the chief is greater. So..."

Ua stood straighter, her voice thin. "Thank you for asking, father."

He nodded, offering no hugs, no words of comfort. Instead, he looked at me, Melika, then his daughter again. "There's a man in the valley who asked for your hand."

Melika suppressed a gasp by covering her mouth. Ua's father eyed her, but continued. "He's a good man. A farmer. He's a little older, but he's well off. I agreed that you would marry him."

Silence.

I wanted to punch Ua's father in the face. He didn't care one bit for his daughter. She was a commodity, just like Melika and I to Oponui. While he didn't care for Ua, I cared for her. She was my best friend, and I wanted her to be happy. How could I be happy with Ali'i while knowing that my best friend didn't get her happily ever after?

Ua nodded, and I noticed that she squeezed Melika's hand tight. "Thank you, father."

"What if she doesn't want to get married to that man?" I blurted, unable to contain myself.

"Ka'ala—" Ua gave me a look. But I wouldn't stand by and let my friend's future burn to pieces. Not if there was something we could do about it.

"It is expected of her... and of you, when your father chooses your mate," Ua's father said, his voice stern, as if he were scolding me. "You know your place, Ka'ala. Your father has given you too many liberties in this forsaken hut." He looked behind me to the large home I'd built. "And I don't know what you do, but you will not be a bad influence on my daughter."

"She should have a choice in who she marries—it's her

future—"

"Ka'ala, you would do best to respect your elders," he cut in, his eyebrows deeply creased. "One day *you* will be given to someone else in marriage. You will have to make it work, understand?"

I wanted to fight back, but both Melika and Ua gave me the eye, saying it wasn't worth the fight. It had never been. The older men would never listen to us.

I drew in a breath and nodded. "'Ae, I understand."

"Good. And you should watch that tongue of yours." He paused before tipping his head. "Good night ladies."

"Good night," Melika and Ua said at the same time. I said nothing, unable to contain my anger. This was so unfair. So. Horribly. Unfair.

Both Oponui and Ua's father were so stubborn and so uncaring. We stood in silence until the large man disappeared down the path, then Ua let out a stifled sob.

"Ua!" Melika and I immediately hugged her.

"There's got to be another way!" Melika exclaimed over and over, while Ua broke into tears.

"Shh, that's enough, Melika," I said, not wanting to give Ua any false hope.

But why shouldn't she hope? What if she and Kona ran off together? They could move to the Big Island, start a new life there. They could even move to O'ahu or somewhere else... this couldn't be over, could it?

They both seemed to give up so easily. Kona accepted his fate to marry the chief's daughter. But Ua fought. Maybe Kona needed to fight for his love too.

"I'll be fine," Ua said, wiping her tears. I grabbed a clean kapa from inside the hut and handed it to her. She dabbed her eyes and blew her nose. "It's not like this hasn't happened before, right?"

As much as I wanted to laugh, it wasn't funny. None of this was funny. It wasn't right.

That night, we went to sleep in defeat. In our world, we seemed to have no control, unless we did things undercover, like the sanctuary operations.

Though I hated to think that Ua might have to run away with Kona, I started to think it might be the best thing. They could leave this place.

When I opened my mouth to say it though, the words didn't come out. I needed to give Ua her time and space to grieve. Melika and I could figure out operations here. Prince Kekoa could find another person to give the refugees passage to Lanai until Kona and Ua returned from their elopement.

Meanwhile, I wondered where Ali'i was, and if he'd ever come tell me what my father said. Fear passed through me that maybe he didn't want me anymore... but it was quickly replaced with my adoration of him. I did love Ali'i, and he wasn't trying to inflict this anxiety on me. There had to be a reason why I'd waited so long for an answer, right?

THE NEXT MORNING, the three of us moved in silence, making kapa, and airing out the hut. A gentle Lanai breeze wafted through, making it a pleasant, cool day. As I worked in the back of the hut, cleaning around the bushes and pruning the tall, bright orange bird-of-paradise stalks, Melika came running.

"Ali'i is here!"

"He's here?" Ua poked her head around the corner, as she'd started weeding on the other side of the back.

My heart raced. "Alright..."

"Come on, what are you waiting for?" Melika grabbed

my hand and we ran to the front of the hut where, indeed, Ali'i stood. He looked handsome as ever, wearing the yellow cape, his wavy hair pulled halfway up, and his facial hair neatly trimmed.

"Hey..." Shyness overcame me as we hadn't seen each other since we kissed. And I was *definitely* not comfortable kissing him in front of Melika and Ua. They crowded around me, the anticipation building up.

"Hey." A small smile crept up Ali'i's lips and then he nodded to Melika and Ua, acknowledging their presence.

"So did you talk to Oponui?" Melika blurted, grabbing my hand and squeezing it so hard, I had to touch her arm to loosen the grip. Ua placed her arm around my shoulders, like I'd done to her the previous night. Her fingers shook, and I started to feel the anxiety pang my own chest.

What if Ali'i bore similar news to Ua's father?

"'Ae, I talked to him," Ali'i said, hesitating as he stared into my eyes.

"And?" Melika looked like she would burst if he didn't say something soon.

"Ka'ala..." He looked like he wanted to touch me, grab my hand, or something, but Ua and Melika crushed me between them, their nerves getting to me. "Your father said..."

He said what? Come on Ali'i!

"He said that I can't marry you."

"No!" Both Ua and Melika exclaimed it at the same time. My knees went weak, but I blinked up at Ali'i, wondering if I was fighting tears.

"Why not?" Melika was my voice now.

"He said you're already betrothed."

"No she's not!" Ua and Melika looked like they were ready to fight.

"To who?" I asked, wondering if my father had agreed to something without even telling me.

Ali'i frowned. "He said you're betrothed to Mailou—"

Melika groaned while Ua gasped. "She's not!"

"Oponui said that it was agreed upon Mailou's return here. I suppose he never told anyone... or maybe he just decided it, because he didn't want me to marry you."

"Why not?" Ua asked.

"He used to be under my command and... he never liked me. He thought I was too young and inexperienced for my position."

I wanted to fall into Ali'i's arms, to let him hold me, to feel like this wasn't happening. Ua and Melika buzzed around me, saying all the things of how wrong this was, and how Oponui could decide this? It wasn't fair.

Ali'i raised his hands, trying to quiet them. "But there is one way I can win Ka'ala's hand."

I could hardly keep my eyes on him, as I struggled to not let any emotions show. I'd always been reserved, hard to read. And now, well, this was awful. My father always got his way. Mailou always got his way too.

"I asked to challenge Mailou."

Ua nodded firmly. "An honorable move, captain."

"He's going to crush you!" Melika cried out, moaning and covering her face with her hands.

"The winner of the fight gets Ka'ala." Ali'i gently lifted my chin so I could look at him. With his contact, Ua and Melika stepped back, giving us some space.

"How does one win?" I asked, my core feeling weak, my body so shaky I wasn't sure I could stand still.

"We fight to the death."

I didn't doubt Ali'i's abilities. We'd easily fought one another the other night, and I saw his skill, speed, and agility. But... what *if* he failed? I couldn't–no, I didn't want to–imagine him getting crushed by Mailou.

Ua had a practical head in the moment I needed it. "Mailou is a bone crusher," she said, then placed her hand on my shoulder. "But he is slow. He lacks speed and has no form with weapons."

"Because he doesn't need weapons," Melika said, her voice whiney and panicked. I *felt* panicked. As I looked up at Ali'i, he gently pulled me into his arms. I fell into him, stiff and frozen.

"I'll be alright," Ali'i said, trying to reassure not only me, but Melika. She went off about Mailou's old wives, and how he crushed their bones, tossing them into the ocean. She reminded us that Mailou and other creed members once did dirty, evil business for elites on Lanai or other islands.

"He's a murderer–"

"Melika," Ua said, giving her a look. She folded her arms. "When is your duel? And are you allowed to use weapons?"

"No weapons..." Ali'i paused before saying, "And no rules either." My stomach dropped. In *hakoko,* wrestling, and *moko*, boxing, there were strict rules so that neither person in the duel received fatal injuries.

Ali'i didn't lie. This challenge really was to the death.

"When is the event?"

"In two days time." Ali'i rubbed my arm, but I still couldn't look up at him. I just wanted him to hold me forever, and to think that none of this was real.

Ali'i and Mailou are going to fight... to the death.

"There has to be another way," Melika said, stealing the words from my mouth. She grabbed my hand again, probably more for her own comfort than mine.

"I attempted to ask if there were alternate solutions, but

Oponui said I was a coward if I couldn't face Mailou. He thinks I'll get killed."

"But you won't," Ua said, sounding confident as ever. She had more confidence in Ali'i than I did. He was skilled, but Melika was right: Mailou was huge. He had the size, brawn, and build to squash anyone in his path.

But I'd always felt I could take him on if I needed to, so why shouldn't Ali'i?

"Ka'ala..." Ali'i lifted my chin so I had to look at him. "Are you alright?"

I shook my head, still trying to fight tears.

"Come on," Ua said, pulling Melika away, giving us some privacy. They went around to the back, but I had no doubt Melika would be peeking.

"I'm..." I started shaking and Ali'i kissed my forehead.

"What is it?"

"I'm nervous... worried."

"Ka'ala..." He stroked my cheek. "I've fought in plenty of battles. I've been trained by grandmasters in many arts of war, including hand to hand combat and the art of lua. I'll be fine." At this, he leaned down and we kissed. His lips felt so good, and I wished we didn't have to deal with all the hardships. Why couldn't we just be together?

No. My father, Oponui, had to go and make a decision that I was betrothed to Mailou. He probably made it up on the spot and went to talk to Mailou after telling Ali'i the lie.

"I promise I'll be fine." He kissed me again and then I fell into his embrace, wanting to stay there forever. I bit my lower lip to keep from crying, but a few tears escaped.

I don't want Ali'i to die. I really didn't. *And he won't. He promised he wouldn't.*

"I won't see you until the challenge though," he said, gently pulling away and then wiping my tears.

"Why not?"

He hesitated before saying. "The king will be here, either tomorrow or the following day."

"For the investigations?"

Ali'i nodded and continued stroking my arm. "Your secret is safe with me."

"I know." We hugged again, but I couldn't help the emotions from swirling inside.

King Hua of Hana will be here. This is my chance. Though I still worried about Ali'i and the upcoming challenge, my mind couldn't get over the fact that the very man who caused so much heartache, war, and bloodshed would be here. Again.

This is my chance... I hated that I worried more about King Hua's presence on the island than Ali'i's duel coming up. But Ali'i promised he'd be fine, so I could focus on figuring out the king.

And I had to do it behind Ali'i's back, because he said he would protect the king.

What am I doing? After all this time, was I *still* lying to Ali'i?

Because there is no winning here. He was loyal to the king, and would step down honorably so he could marry me and live on Lanai. Yet I didn't want him to know that, deep down, I still wanted to kill the king.

I was the only person fit for the job. I had been trained to protect people, and if that meant killing King Hua, then so be it.

As Ali'i and I held each other for a moment, I no longer focused on the captain's upcoming duel. Instead, I planned out how I could figure out the king's secrets and silence him, ending these bloody, unjust wars against Kohala.

CHAPTER EIGHTEEN

*A*ll of Lanai was apprised of King Hua's arrival. Many of us donated lei, food, and other goods to the local chief as gifts for the king. It was the usual custom of respect, showing King Hua of Hana that the people of Lanai were friendly and welcoming of him... even if many of us felt far from it.

A hawk arrived that morning and perched on the gate, warning us of Kona's arrival later that night. While Melika, Ua, and I were swamped with preparations for the new set of refugees, I ensured we went to watch the king arrive in his canoe. Melika and Ua didn't argue, as their curiosity peaked as much as my own.

What was the king doing here? How would Aliʻi handle the situation?

I, specifically, wanted to go. I needed to see the king again, to evaluate his condition. Was there a chance he'd be wounded? Feeble? Weak? Old in age?

Once we reached the crowd of people, Ua separated from Melika and I, just in case King Hua saw us together and had some kind of flashback.

The sound of the *pū*, the conch shell, rang through the air, and the king's large canoe, manned by experienced sailors, pulled onto the shore.

Ali'i and the two red-caped servants stood in the water, prepared to greet the king first. I felt a presence nearby and grabbed Melika's hand, pulling us deeper into the crowd.

"What is it?" she whispered.

"Mailou."

He stood on the outskirts of the crowd, observing. I met his eyes and, instead of glaring, like he usually did, a wicked grin spread across his face. My stomach knotted, because he thought he'd won. Mailou had all the confidence in his battle against Ali'i, but he doubted the captain's abilities.

Do I doubt his abilities? I didn't want to, but seeing Mailou's gigantic size, once more, made my heart patter in nervousness.

Melika squeezed my hand, as if thinking the same as myself: Mailou was huge, but we had to trust the captain's skill, strength, and speed.

As the chief of Lanai chanted, welcoming King Hua, I studied the men on board.

The king looks healthier than ever. If anything, he seemed brawnier and taller. Unlike Ali'i, the servants, sailors, and other guards who bore every kind of scar, the king had nothing. No scars. No injuries. No deformities. How could every one of those under him have been wounded in war, but not the king? Did he even go to battle?

He does...

I heard he led his armies, but not all the time. Prince Kekoa and the captains usually led men to war. Yet... how could King Hua look so flawless?

He had dark brown skin, black eyes, and dark hair.

Everything about him was dark, including his countenance. An eerie feeling surrounded his being, like he had been in the dark for so long, he no longer exuded any light.

Melika let out a little sigh and I glanced at her. She rolled her eyes, mouthing, *No Prince Kekoa*.

She was right. Prince Kekoa did not come. Otherwise, he would have been standing behind the king, a red and yellow cape around his shoulders. I secretly wished the prince *did* come. Perhaps he'd have answers and share them with me concerning the king's secret to health, longevity, and invincibility.

While Prince Kekoa did not stand behind his father, another man did. He was tall, with long white hair running down his back. From the rich feathered attire, bone and woven hair jewelry adorning his body, and the staff he carried, I assumed the man was one of the king's high priests.

Every ali'i had a kahuna to counsel with, so this didn't surprise me.

Similar to King Hua's energy, the high priest had no light in his eyes. He looked down his nose at all those around him, and when he chanted, his voice sounded as if it came from the darkest corners of the islands.

"He gives me the creeps," Melika whispered. I gave her the look, not wanting to draw attention from the other Lanai residents around us. I spotted Ua at the other end of the crowd, her arms folded as she stared at the king.

"Do we know his name?" I asked, so only she could hear. Melika shook her head. After all the chanting finished, the king stepped off the boat, the water going up to his ankles. He shook Ali'i's hand then they touched one another's foreheads.

How can Aliʻi bear to touch that man's hand? Those hands were guilty with so much blood on it. The captain then greeted the high priest in the same manner. King Hua looked up to the crowd of people and waved. I made sure to move a little, so the person's head in front of me blocked the king's view of me. Ua, on the other end, did the same, looking down, as if fixing her kihei.

The people waved and then the king and high priest walked with Aliʻi to greet the Lanai chief. There was not much left to see here for me.

The king and his high priest are here. He's brought about twelve soldiers. Kekoa didn't come.

I looked back to make sure Mailou left, which he did, then Melika and I made our way onto the path. Ua waited a while before joining us.

"What do you think?" she asked as she caught up. The path back was empty, as the people were occupied in watching the king of Hana.

"He looks just as he did the last time we saw him," I said, realizing that not even his hair had aged.

"No wounds. No battle scars. Yet he's strong and muscular as before." Ua shook her head. "I don't understand."

"I don't either." We exchanged looks full of frustration. How would we kill the king?

"I don't know about you guys, but the high priest scares me more than the king," Melika said, rubbing her arms.

"Me too." Ua shuddered. "Do you think the kahuna has something to do with the king's strength?"

I'd heard of magic before. In fact, rumors spread that Mailou had fled Waialua under the threat of being turned to stone by menehune. Menehune, dwarf men, could do magic. Some kahuna could do magic.

But could King Hua's kahuna do magic?

Ua changed the subject to the list of tasks we needed to complete before Kona's arrival that evening. Not once did she mention his name, but Melika, keen as ever, finally said, "Do you want to be at the hut when Kona comes?"

Silence.

We hadn't talked much about Kona and Ua since the night her father bore the news. We didn't even talk about the old farmer Ua was betrothed to marry. Melika said no words about weddings. Even when Oponui came by, just a few days ago, to tell us what we were in charge of for Kona's wedding, we said nothing of the matter.

My heart still ached for Ua, because she had tried. She went to her own father, a man she hardly knew, and asked for his help to marry Kona.

But it failed.

And now she was supposed to marry an old man in a few week's time.

"I want to be there," she said. "Actually... Melika, you and Ka'ala should go tonight. It's best if Ka'ala and I aren't seen together." We especially couldn't be seen together by the king of Hana. Who knew if he'd be lurking around tonight?

"Really?" Melika's eyes sparkled. She'd never gone in the night to help pick up refugees from Kona. I hesitated, knowing that Melika had never been the stealthiest.

Don't doubt her, I thought, reminding myself that I'd been fifteen when I started this whole thing... alone. Melika had also helped take the children to safety, so she was more than capable of bringing refugees to the sanctuary.

"She's right. You should come with me tonight, Melika."

My sister's hands balled into fists and she punched the air. "Yes! I won't let you down!"

"We know you won't." Ua smiled, but it looked weak. I gave her a sympathetic look, wondering what plans she had in mind. Was she still hoping to be with Kona? I secretly hoped she did, because Ua deserved her happily-ever-after.

And if she did hope to be with Kona, what lengths would they go?

While Ua probably thought of what she'd say or do when she saw Kona that night, I thought of King Hua. What was Captain Ali'i telling him now? Was it convincing, or would Hua tear down every house until he found me?

No doubt the king would find out about Ali'i's duel with Mailou. Then he might have to meet me, the woman Ali'i wanted to marry. Would he recognize me then?

As we prepared the beds and food for the night, I couldn't help but feel guilt sink inside my stomach. This whole time I thought about King Hua. Nothing else could seem more important.

But Ali'i is going to fight Mailou, and I should be worried and thinking about him. Why did I feel so conflicted inside?

Because I'm also going behind Ali'i's back. Oh. Right. But I never told him I would *stop* my pursuit of killing King Hua, so I wasn't really lying to him. And besides, he didn't need to know about my secret investigations.

But relationships with secrets are already off to a bad start, I thought. No, no, no. I felt justified in my actions. Nobody, but me, could do this deed. My sanctuary wasn't enough. Housing refugees wasn't enough. I had to get to the root of the problem, because nobody else was able to.

I was finally able to silence my guilt and focus, once more, on getting answers. That night, as Melika and I snuck off to get the newest refugees, I planned to speak with my brother. He had fought in the wars, and had probably heard rumors about the king.

I'd start there. And if Kona didn't have the answers I needed, then maybe, just maybe, I could somehow get them out of Aliʻi. I pushed down the guilt that he needed to focus on the duel, and, instead, reminded myself that this was for the safety of everyone. No more sanctuary. No more refugees. No more war.

MELIKA DID WONDERFULLY. She kept her eyes and ears open for any signs of danger, any signs of being followed. We exchanged no words, as we communicated with each other through eye contact and body language. Normally she struggled to understand her role, and had to ask clarifying questions, but not tonight.

As we hid in the bushes, watching Kona's canoe pull onto shore, I couldn't help but feel a surge of pride within. Melika had grown so much, and now here she was, crouching next to me, ready as ever for anything that came our way.

But was this enough for her to run the sanctuary by herself? What if Ua and Kona ran away? And what if Aliʻi and I had to move to Hana for a time? Would Melika be able to do everything? I'd done it alone for a year or two, with only help from Prince Kekoa and Ua, before Melika and Kona joined, so it was possible. But... could Melika handle all that pressure?

As Kona's canoe stopped, Melika glanced at me, as if asking, "Now?"

I studied the area around us, then pointed to myself first. Melika nodded, and held the knife in her hand, waiting, as I sprinted down the shore, stepped into the water, and hid behind the boat. Kona moved about on top, and my anxiety rose high.

What if he brought another baby? Or more children? Could we house such young ones, undetected, again?

"Hey Ka'ala," he said, peeking over the side of the boat. "I've got eight today."

"Eight?"

"Four women, and four men. Some of the men are wounded."

Whew... Although I was glad to have saved the children, I wasn't sure if we could do that again, especially with Hua on the island. His guards and servants would be keeping careful watch of any suspicious activity, and if Captain Ali'i couldn't keep them away, they might figure out the sanctuary.

"I'll take two men and two women—let me take the most wounded and feeble. Melika will take the others."

"Melika?" Kona frowned, as Ua usually came with me. But he didn't argue, and, instead, helped a young, wounded soldier, and some elderly people step down the back of the canoe.

The wounded soldier wore his arm in a cast, and most of his face was wrapped, except his nose, meaning he bore a bad injury to his face. My heart went out to him. The elderly did their best to help guide the warrior, as he couldn't see a thing, anyways.

"I'm 'Iwa," I told the four. "You're safe with me, as long as you follow my lead and directions." They nodded, and we went on our way. Melika darted past me, taking her turn at the back of the boat.

My palms went sweaty as I studied the trees and path ahead. This was incredibly dangerous.

But it's worth it. It was *always* worth it. Saving these

people's lives was a service I could do to help in these awful wars. Yet... it wasn't enough. I had to *stop* these wars. As I looked at the wounded soldier, the scars lining his young body, I couldn't help but feel sorry for him. He didn't ask for this. None of us did.

I'd get us out of this mess, no matter the cost.

CHAPTER NINETEEN

*A*s Ua got the refugees settled in the back room, I anxiously awaited Melika's arrival. All the worst case scenarios went through my head.

What if someone stopped her? What if *the king* stopped her? Did Melika know alternate routes, in case she suspected something? Did she know it was alright to stop and hide with the refugees, if needed?

The night wore on, the geckos chirping and the stars shining above. Finally, Melika's dark head appeared along the path, the arm of another wounded soldier across her shoulders. She brought two more wounded soldiers, and more elderly people.

Eight. We had housed up to ten people before, and, since they were adults and capable of caring for themselves, it wouldn't be too hard.

I hurried to open the gate and help the wounded soldiers inside. Kona, no doubt, would be here soon too. I squeezed Melika's arm, smiling at her accomplishment.

She grinned back, probably as proud of herself as I felt.

Once I helped everyone inside, I kept watch on the

porch. The smell of food wafted from within, as Ua prepared leaf plates in the front room. Meanwhile, Melika, in the back room, got the refugees situated and told them all the details: who we were, how long they'd be here, the rules, where to sleep, where to relieve themselves, what to do in certain situations and emergencies, and so forth. She spoke so quietly, I heard nothing from her.

Ua paused in her preparations to squeeze my arm. "A lot of refugees today, huh?" she whispered and nodded, pleased that we, especially Melika, brought them all safely. Her expression changed from pleased to longing.

Ua handed me the plate she'd been holding then rushed to the gate. I watched as she threw her arms around Kona's neck and kissed him. He embraced her right back, and I wished they could be together.

And they can... we'll think of something.

I also thought of my own relationship with Aliʻi. I missed him, but he was busy, and we had our duties to perform.

The guilt gnawed at my stomach once more: *You should tell him the truth.* But if I did, he'd try to convince me otherwise.

Ua and Kona held each other and I realized I stood there, invading their privacy. I excused myself by finishing up the plates of food and taking them to the refugees. When I went into the back, I grimaced at the sight of the wounded soldier's face. The wrap was now off, and the older men and women sat on either side of him, tending to a large gash across his face. It looked awful, gorey, and unnatural.

My heart, once again, broke in two for these people. All the emotions ran through me as Melika tended to each person, her tone caring, no judgment or disgust in her voice as she cared for the refugees.

As I served the food, I couldn't help but justify my cause again: it's better that King Hua died, than this many people have to suffer. Aliʻi would just have to understand that.

THE FOLLOWING DAY, Ua's voice came from the porch as she stepped on all the loud squeaks and planks. Melika and I tended to the refugees, especially the ones with wounds. The warrior with the gash across his face had a raging fever, so everyone did what they could to keep him comfortable, cool, and drinking water.

"Someone's here," I said to Melika, quietly, then motioned for everyone to be ready to dash out of there and hide, if needed. I slid the bedroom door open and stepped out, finding Ua on the porch, speaking to Oponui.

Kona had left late last night, and returned to our parent's home. So what did Oponui want?

Ua kept her voice loud, which was warning enough for me that our visitor was someone we *didn't* want seeing the refugees.

"Father," I said, stepping onto the porch and tipping my head.

"The duel is today," he said, and a wicked grin spread across his face.

My heart skipped a beat. I had completely forgotten about the duel. How could I be so uncaring about Aliʻi, the man I wanted to marry?

"I expect you to be there, Kaʻala." Oponui folded his arms. "And bring a lei for the winner, which we all know will be Mailou."

Ua made a face, and I kept my own expression uninterested.

"I'll bring a lei," I said. "Anything else?"

"'Ae. Kona's wedding will be in a week's time. I need you to prepare and make all the lei and decorations. Send Melika down in three day's time to help prepare the food."

I hated being bossed around by my father.

"Of course."

Oponui smiled at Ua, as if knowing that he had gotten his way yet again. Her father had offered Ua to Kona, but Oponui refused.

"The challenge begins in an hour's time," he said, pointing to the sun as he walked away. "See you soon."

When he disappeared down the path, Ua rolled her eyes. "He loves being in control."

I nodded.

"Are you worried?" She asked, studying me but finding no answers.

"About Ali'i?"

"Of course I mean Ali'i. Unless you were thinking about something else." She rubbed her arms. "The closer it gets, the more nervous I feel for him. Mailou is terrifying."

"He's a warrior, he'll be fine." But I *was* getting worried. The anxiety I felt though, wasn't only for Ali'i, but about studying the king. No doubt King Hua would be there. Would there be an opportunity, or even the slightest possibility, to attack him?

"Ka'ala," Melika came onto the porch, her expression fraught with worry.

"What's wrong?" Both Ua and I asked at the same time, each of us grabbing one of her arms.

"I think he needs medicine. His fever is raging really hot."

Oh no. The Kohala warrior did look pretty bad, and I sent a silent prayer to the heavens. We had sick refugees and deeply wounded warriors stay with us in the past, but they always made it. Though we had no deaths of refugees in the past, I still worried for the warrior's health.

"I'll get it," Ua said. "Ka'ala, you need to go to the challenge, and we need to stay separated anyways. Don't want Hua to see us together."

I nodded.

"What did father want?" Melika asked before heading back inside.

"I need to bring a lei to the duel in an hour, and Kona is getting married in a week's time," I said. "So father needs our help for preparations."

"Oh." Melika looked from me to Ua. "Did it go alright with Kona last night?"

Ua blushed when she met my eyes, because I'd seen her embrace Kona. I shrugged, and regretted not asking her about how it all went sooner. How could everyone be so focused on the present, while I worried about King Hua? I should have asked my best friend how it all went.

I'm losing it. I forgot about the duel, and failed to care about my best friend's situation.

Ua bit her lower lip and rubbed her arm. "We're thinking of running away."

"Ua!" Melika and I exclaimed at the same time.

"You've been keeping that inside all day?" I asked, both annoyed and delighted.

"I'm sorry, but... we have so much to work out. What about this sanctuary? Kona's position? If Kona doesn't marry honorably, will the king dismiss him?" Ua sighed and put a hand on her forehead. "And there are other bigger problems to worry about right now—Ali'i's duel, the wounded warrior..."

"But you have to do it," Melika cut in. She opened her

mouth to say more, but stopped short, glancing at me. "I mean... right, Kaʻala?"

I thought about the sanctuary, the refugees, and, of course, Hua.

It's up to me. If I killed Hua, I wouldn't have to worry about Ua's absence at the sanctuary... because there would be no sanctuary. The wars would be over. People could live in peace. There'd be no more wounded soldiers, no more refugees.

"She's right. You have to do it," I said, a half lie, because she wouldn't actually need to run away in the end. A smile formed on Ua's face and she hugged us both.

"I'll let you know what we decide," she said. "I'm not going to let all of this hard work go to waste."

But you won't let it go to waste, I thought. Because I'd kill King Hua, and she could live in bliss with Kona. My father wouldn't approve of their elopement and marriage elsewhere, but at least we wouldn't have to do all these underground operations.

"I better get that medicine," she said, wiping a tear from her eye.

"And you better make the lei—" Melika started.

"And get to that duel." Ua finished. "Aliʻi loves you so much, Kaʻala."

"It's so romantic he's fighting for you," Melika said, smiling. I didn't feel like returning the smile. Battling and fighting were not romantic. There was nothing romantic about taking another person's life, even someone as disgusting and evil as Mailou.

"I'll be back quick," Ua said, "And Melika you go to the challenge with Kaʻala as soon as I get back, alright?"

We all nodded in agreement, hugged and kissed each

other's cheeks, and went to work. As I hurried to make a lei of ti leaves, my stomach tightened.

Ali'i is going to fight Mailou. And Hua will be at the duel. Would I find out answers on how to kill King Hua... or, was there a possibility I'd have the chance to kill King Hua?

THE EARLY EVENING sun shone on the dueling grounds, a large field of grass in the middle of the valley. Almost all the islanders had come to watch, which made me wish Melika were at my side. They stared at me as I approached, and pointed to where I could sit and watch the duel.

My palms were sweaty as I noticed that my father, Oponui, sat not far from King Hua, his high priest, and the local Lanai chiefs. Oponui beckoned for me to sit next to him, which I did, but not until I bowed to the king.

He smiled. "Ah, so you are Ka'ala, the flower of Lanai. No woman, but you, has caught my captain's eye." His eyes went from my face, down my body, and I felt sick to my stomach. "You are, indeed, beautiful."

From the look on his face, King Hua did not recognize me. I bowed and then leaned forward to kiss his cheek. He stroked my arm with his hand and it made my skin crawl.

Creep. Memories of the night Ua and I led him into the dark resurfaced. He was up to no good when it came to women, even women who were already in relationships.

He winked when I stepped back, and I wanted to vomit. Was he... *flirting* with me?

Disgusting. I nodded to the high priest, who ignored me, then sat by my father. All of us sat on a stand, above the commoners, for a better view. But I didn't want a better view. This whole thing was barbaric.

"Where's Melika?" Oponui asked, trying to keep a scowl from forming.

"She took too long to get ready, so I left without her."

"Ah." My father didn't seem annoyed by this, and, actually, chuckled, as if understanding. I wondered if he was hoping to show her off to someone here.

"Liha is here," he said, nudging me and pointing out the chief and his lovely daughter. "Where's Kona?"

"He said he'll be by a little later."

I doubted it. Kona would probably stop by the hut and discuss plans with Ua, while everyone was occupied.

From the crowd came Aliʻi, and I had to fan myself. He was completely bare on top, with a skirt down to his knees. His hair was pulled back, and he looked handsome as ever.

Mailou came forward too, and the nervousness came right back to me. He, too, was bare chested, and the bulk and brawn of his body were so big, I looked away. Tattoos of the shark and other birds of prey covered his arms and chest.

Please be alright Aliʻi. The captain met my eyes and nodded, as if to assure me. But what if things went wrong? What if Mailou cheated (if that were even possible)?

"Citizens of Lanai," King Hua started. "We are here to witness the duel of Mailou, the bone crusher, and Kaaialiʻi, the greatest captain of Hana—"

The greatest captain? That was a huge statement, especially coming from the king. Aliʻi avoided my eyes when I glanced at him. If he was "the greatest captain," then what did that mean for our future? Hua wouldn't want to lose his best man...

Which once again means... Hua must die.

Instead of looking at the two contenders, I watched Hua. The king wore a red and yellow feathered cape. He had no weapons on him, nor did the high priest. What warrior went around without a weapon?

Because the king is no warrior. He bore no battle scars, no wounds. If anything, the king looked as if he'd never seen a day of war in his life. What was his secret to invincibility? He continued his speech, making me feel utterly uncomfortable as he went on and on about my "beauty."

Oponui positively beamed, even though he'd called me "too freckled" and "ugly" many times before.

"May the strongest man win Kaʻala's love!" King Hua finished. I hugged my arms, hating his words. Aliʻi already had my love, right?

The crowd cheered, rallied by the king's speech, and then went silent. These sorts of things never happened on this island, at least not for a long time. The creed would do challenges, duels, and tournaments, but the people of Lanai were smarter than to get involved with the giant creed members.

My heart pounded and I clutched the ti leaf lei in my hand.

Come on, Aliʻi.

The two men circled one another. Mailou laughed and spit on the ground. "I'll crush your bones, young man! Your limbs are like a tender cane," he said. "I'll kill you with one hand."

I had to close my eyes for a moment, thinking that this wasn't real. Who could be so violent?

Aliʻi smirked. "You'll need both hands." I wanted to cover my face now. Why were we doing this again? I didn't ask for a duel.

But Oponui did. He truly did not like Aliʻi.

"You break women's bones, not men's bones," Aliʻi said, and the crowd murmured and gasped, the superstition being said in a public place. "You talk as if you're brave, but you're just a coward."

Before Mailou had a chance to reply, King Hua said, "Fight!"

The old bounty hunter ran towards the captain, hands extended, as if to choke him. I squeezed the ti leaf lei so tight, the juices started running between my fingers. A hand touched my arm and I was startled to see Melika sit next to me.

Ali'i pretended to be surprised by Mailou's sudden movement, but he had plans of his own. The captain moved his arms upward, breaking Mailou's attempt to choke him. Then he side stepped to the left and used his right foot to trip the bone breaker.

Good move. It was the same technique I'd used when Mailou attempted to hurt me on the cliff.

Mailou fell to the ground. The thud resounded with an "oof" from the crowd. Swift as ever, Ali'i jumped on Mailou's back, grabbed the bounty hunter's right arm, and snapped the elbow.

I had to look away now, as the people of Lanai went crazy. They cheered, scoffed, and screamed at the violence.

I forced myself to look back as Mailou stood, glancing at his broken, dangling right arm. Hatred burned in his eyes as he, once again, rushed towards Ali'i. The captain delivered a hard punch to the man's chin, which sent him falling to the ground once more. With the bone breaker on the ground, Ali'i broke Mailou's left arm, the same way he'd broken the right.

"I can't..." I said, inhaling sharply and looking away. Melika was fixed on the fight, her mouth gaping open.

Mailou screamed in a rage and bent his head, running towards Ali'i. The screams and shouts of the crowd muffled out all the sounds. Everything seemed to move in slow motion.

Aliʻi easily tripped Mailou, then grabbed his hair as the bounty hunter fell to the ground. I closed my eyes as I heard the loud snapping sound through the chaos.

Melika screamed and stood, cheering, along with the rest of the people, but I couldn't open my eyes. Oponui cursed beneath his breath, but kept his composure, as I knew he would. He was always more concerned with how he looked to others.

"We have a winner!" King Hua announced.

I opened my eyes to see Aliʻi standing in the circle, head down, staring at the fallen body of Mailou. He'd snapped the man's back, which killed him. Though the people cheered, relieved to no longer have creed members lurking around, Aliʻi's shoulders sunk.

He doesn't want to kill... He had told me himself that he didn't feel worthy of me, because of the lives he took. Here was one more man he killed with his own bare hands.

King Hua went down to the arena, grabbing Aliʻi's hand and raising it. The people cheered even louder.

I should have been looking at Aliʻi, but my attention went to Hua. Was now a good moment to kill him? And why didn't Aliʻi do it—he was right there. He could snap the king's neck or back, just as he did to Mailou...

"Kaʻala, go to Aliʻi!" Melika exclaimed, but I sat there, frozen.

So the king and the captain came to me. My knuckles were white as I stood and finally looked into Aliʻi's eyes. They were filled with every emotion: longing, guilt, pain. As much as I wanted to hug him, I was confused.

King Hua is right here, unaware. And I had a knife

hidden in the fold of my skirt. Could I grab it out and kill the king while he was distracted?

"Oponui, we have a winner," King Hua said, patting Ali'i's back like a proud father would his son.

"'Ae." Oponui took a steadying breath. "You've won her," he said. "She will be your wife, Captain." He bowed his head and motioned for me to step forward. "Take her with you, wherever you go."

Before Ali'i could embrace me, a *pū* sounded, silencing the crowd and the commotion. We all turned to see a group of the king's soldiers running towards us.

"Your majesty!" They bowed to the king. One of the soldiers stood, sweat lining his brow. "We've just spotted a canoe full of warriors from Kohala."

The people gasped and began speculating aloud.

"Silence!" Hua said, his focus on the soldiers below us, his back facing me.

Now, Ka'ala... Now... I reached for the knife hidden below my belt, ever so slowly. Anyone would think I was just holding my skirt.

"How many?" asked the king.

"At least twelve."

"What are they doing here?"

"There are a few who are wounded, but some of them look fresh. We have a feeling they're assassins, come here to kill you, your majesty."

"What are you waiting for? Get them!" King Hua's face turned red with anger. He was about to follow the soldiers, then stopped to congratulate Ali'i first. He clapped Ali'i's shoulder.

"Congratulations, captain. Take a moment with your love, but come as soon as you can," he said, then ran off.

My moment is gone... I watched the king hurrying after

the soldiers. The high priest, too, trailed behind the company.

"Kaʻala, give Aliʻi the lei." Melika's voice brought me back. How long had I been staring at the king running off?

I looked up at Aliʻi and guilt overcame me. He did this, all of this, for me. The captain truly loved me. I put the lei over his neck and paused before embracing him.

He studied my face, trying to read me, and I think he did. His eyebrows creased, and he looked hurt... hurt that I was so focused on the king, and not even celebrating or showing gratitude that we were now able to marry.

"Aliʻi..." I couldn't stand looking at the pain, because it made me feel even more guilty. To dispel it, I wrapped my arms around his neck and kissed him.

The crowd cheered. Aliʻi kissed me back, but there was something different this time. A huge secret wedged between us, and I knew, sooner or later, we'd have to face it.

But, hopefully, when we faced it, Hua would be long dead, so Aliʻi could do nothing about it.

CHAPTER TWENTY

"What are we going to do?" Melika paced back and forth on the porch, wringing her hands in worry. Not only did our refugee's fever seem to be getting worse, and he started shaking, but Oponui said that Kona's wedding, and mine and Ali'i's wedding would be held on the same day. That meant we'd be married in only two days.

Having two weddings in one was my father's way of being cheap, of not recognizing Ali'i's status, and, instead, putting him on the same level as the local chief whose daughter Kona was supposed to marry. I was sure Ali'i didn't care though, as he would just want to get married and move on.

The sound of crickets filled the air outside as I stood in the door frame. Ua sat on the edge of the porch, staring at the stars, her eyes wide. While everyone went to the fight earlier, sure enough Kona visited Ua. They decided to run away and elope... but when?

"I can't leave you guys," Ua said earlier. "I mean, we'll go to Hana and continue the operations, but I can't leave you *now*. Not when Ka'ala is supposed to get married, and when Hua is on the island, and when there are *more* men somewhere on this island that we need to hide."

She spoke of the Kohala warriors who landed on the shores, of course. After searching the entire day, nobody could find them. The king and his warriors, as well as the people of Lanai saw no trace of the warriors, except their canoes on the shore. It was as if their tracks disappeared.

I squeezed my eyes shut for a moment, trying to process everything. Why did it all have to happen at once? Why couldn't things be simple?

I should've just stabbed King Hua right then and there... Guilt panged my chest. I'd been so slow, so cowardly.

No, I was anxious. I secretly worried that Ali'i might stop me. Since we embraced after the duel, he left to catch up with the king and search for the Kohala warriors. The hurt in his eyes lingered with me. Would he still want to marry me?

Do I even want to marry him? I could think of nothing but King Hua. Where was he now? Did they find the Kohala warriors? If they did, they'd brutally murder every one of them. I heard of the ways King Hua tortured his prisoners of war. The refugee in our house was a prime example of it. Not only did he have a large gash across his face, Melika and the others found out he'd endured much worse torture, like having his limbs dislocated and relocated, or some of his toes cut off.

I winced at the thought and swallowed hard. *King Hua must die.* Ali'i had to understand that. But since he swore an oath to protect the king, I had to do this behind his back–as much as possible. Though I knew he could read me, and see my intention. He'd said it before, and he probably would've said it again: *I know an intent when I see it.*

So how can I marry someone who won't stop the island's

most evil person? Didn't Ali'i see how wicked King Hua truly was? Or did he choose to be a coward and turn a blind eye? I sighed quietly to myself, trying to block out the confused emotions swirling within. I could focus on mine and Ali'i's relationship later.

"We need to find the warriors," I said, speaking up for the first time that evening. Melika paused and nodded, grateful to have any sort of direction. She'd been worried the entire day, as Ua and I went about our business, quieter than usual.

"I agree," Ua said, standing and raising her chin. "We'll provide them a safe place."

"And possibly help them in their mission," I said, remembering the words of King Hua's warrior: *We have a feeling they're assassins, come here to kill you, your majesty.*

That meant the Kohala warriors and I were on the same team. A new idea crossed my mind: perhaps King Hua couldn't be killed by a woman, which is why I couldn't stab him years ago. What about a warrior, or, even more dangerous, an assassin? No doubt the warriors from Kohala were all men, so was there a chance that King Hua's secret was to be killed by a man?

Ua tipped her head, understanding my thoughts, and I nodded, envisioning the memory of us duping the king years ago.

"Melika should stay here, just in case," I said, knowing that Ua was my best ally in this plot. Not only was she an excellent actress, but she helped me lure the king away last time. She was the only person I knew who could help me get him in a vulnerable position.

"But you two aren't supposed to be seen together." I'd never seen Melika this anxious before. She kept looking towards the path, as if worried someone might overhear our plans or show up unannounced.

"We won't," Ua said.

"Let's go," I said, stepping off the porch and feeling for my knife. I was sick of these games, sick of the king. We'd find those warriors and get their help to assassinate King Hua, once and for all.

"Wait!" Melika said, running after me. "Ka'ala... I don't know what you're planning or thinking but... please be careful." My sister's care for me made my heart ache for a second.

"I will. I promise. Keep watch, and don't let anyone inside the hut."

She nodded. We kissed one another's cheeks, then Ua and I ran along the path, ready to find the Kohala warriors and either offer them a place of refuge, or assist them in their plans.

KNOWING that Mailou wouldn't stalk my every move was... different. Ever since the encounter with him and his buddies years ago, I knew I had to watch my back.

And now... well, I didn't have to worry about that. Ua and I moved with ease, checking the town. Ua went through town, while I walked around the outskirts. The canoes that the Kohala warriors used were guarded by some of King Hua's men.

As I walked along the shore, I felt a presence behind me and checked my back.

"Ali'i..." I ran into his arms and hugged him, feeling the swirl of emotions again: confusion, anger, secrets, love, fear...

"What are you doing? It's late." He looked down at me,

searching my face for answers. I stared at my feet, knowing that he'd read me, just like he always did.

"I could ask the same of you..."

"We found the warriors, and we're setting up traps to catch them all."

My heart sank. So they knew where the Kohala men were after all.

"And then what will you do when you catch them?"

"The king wants to take them back to Hana as sacrifices."

"Ali'i..." I groaned to myself, aching to get his help in this plight but knowing that it would be an eternal wedge between us.

"Ka'ala, you can't kill him. He's invincible." He attempted to lift my chin but I pulled away and focused on my feet again.

"He's not—"

"Look at me, please." The pain in his voice stabbed me with guilt. What was happening between Ali'i and I? I thought we were perfect for each other, and now... we were on completely opposite teams. Or maybe that was the case all along, and I was trying to force something that was never meant to be.

"Ka'ala, do you even want to get married?" At that, I did look up at him, my heart pounding inside my chest.

Do I?

Ali'i gently tucked a loose piece of hair from my face. "I don't want to force you into anything and..." He sighed. "You didn't seem to care that I won the duel. If anything, you seem more interested in the king—"

"No, no..." I cut him off. I was *not* interested in the king. Not ever! He was disgusting and I hated him so much, I wanted to do anything to kill him. Maybe even...

No, Ka'ala... My thoughts warred with each other.

Use Ali'i. He seems to know the king's secret.

Don't use Ali'i. You would never manipulate someone you love.

But what if I don't love him?

Did I even love Ali'i? I thought of the kindness and gentleness he always showed me. He even went so far to get rid of Mailou, the man who followed my shadows, in order to win my hand. Ali'i truly was a man of any woman's dreams, and I... well, I was obsessed with wanting to end King Hua's life. He was the reason for so much heartache, including the one we faced now.

If I kill King Hua, then Ali'i and I can live in peace. That was true. Our children would not have to grow up in war. There would be no more sanctuary, no more refugees. Hana would no longer sacrifice people for the king's wars against Kohala.

I have to do this... for the good of all Hawaii. Kona's words came to my mind, the one he spoke after delivering the children. "Don't take on the world when you're already doing what you can to make it better."

But I wasn't doing enough. King Hua was the root of all the problems, the worm eating at the core of everything good.

If I had to keep this secret from Ali'i, I'd do it. And after all was said and done, I could be completely honest with him. But, for now, I put on my best acting face.

My insides tightened as I stroked his face, then stood on the tips of my toes and kissed him.

"I do want to marry you–I'm sorry I've been distracted."

Ali'i held me for a long moment, and I began to worry that he was reconsidering. I kissed his cheek and pulled away.

You're terrible, Ka'ala. I was, and I knew it. I was no better than the girl, Noni, that the captain once wanted to marry. He looked into my eyes and I allowed him to.

Don't waver.

After a moment, which seemed to last an eternity, he gently kissed me. The sweetness in which he did it made me want to melt.

You're not being honest with him. I couldn't. I had every reason not to. If I had to use Ali'i for one big purpose, to save the people of Hana, Kohala, and other islanders who had to help in this war, then so be it.

"I love you, Ka'ala." His words stabbed my heart, and I swallowed hard before hugging him and saying, "I love you too."

But love wasn't secretive. Love didn't lie.

I'm doing this for the people.

"You should head back. It's late and I don't want you anywhere near town when those warriors come."

"Why?"

Ali'i looked towards the ocean. "The king is very angry right now. I'm just hoping I can calm him before he does something to one of the warriors."

"Like what?"

"It's too gruesome to say." He stroked my arm. "I saw Ua walking through town and figured you'd be close by. Will you head back to your hut with her? I just want to make sure you're safe."

"I am safe, especially with Mailou gone." I interlaced my fingers in the captain's, loving and hating it.

You're playing his heart. That is cruel. And mean. You're not like this, Ka'ala.

It's to end these wars.

The corner of Ali'i's lip turned up as he squeezed my

hand. It was nice having his hand to hold. "Promise you'll head back?"

"As soon as I find Ua, 'ae."

He kissed my forehead. "I probably won't see you until the wedding."

"Alright."

"Can't wait." He winked and my whole body warmed.

"Same."

Liar.

I hurried off before I accidentally revealed the battle within myself. Ali'i didn't need to know about it. He didn't need to know anything, especially the fact that I planned on using him for answers... again. Because if the Kohala warriors were going to get caught tonight, which I had no doubt they would, then it was up to me... again.

It was always up to me. Perhaps I tried to get someone else to do the deed, but I had the power to find the answers. Ali'i seemed to know something that I didn't. He even said, "He (the king) is invincible." But how? The captain knew the truth, and I'd find out, even if it meant pretending to be deeply in love with and marrying him.

But do I love him? Not enough to tell him the truth, apparently.

There's no way around it.

I hid along the forest path, waiting for Ua. When she appeared, water lined her eyes.

"What's wrong?" I asked, squeezing her arm.

"They've captured all of them, and they're going to sacrifice them in Hana." Ua's compassion was a big reason she was one of my greatest allies. I took a deep breath.

"I didn't know they'd capture them so fast. I just talked to Ali'i."

"Will he stop them?"

I shook my head and Ua rolled her eyes, looking away. I wanted to defend Ali'i, but I could say nothing. Everything showed us that he wasn't on our side.

"I saw Kona. King Hua is going to attend your wedding. He plans to leave the following morning with the warriors." She shook her head. "We can't let them leave."

"We won't. We'll figure something out."

"But what about me and Kona?" Ua smoothed her hair back, but it fell in front of her face once more. I didn't know *how* to save the warriors, especially since the king and his whole entourage of guards and soldiers would be escorting them. But I *especially* didn't know how to save the warriors without Kona, Ua, and Melika's help.

I learned to rely on them, after years of their help with the sanctuary.

Once more, the thought of deceiving Ali'i for information on the king entered my mind.

That's it... I'd have to find a way, on our wedding night, to get the information from Ali'i. Then I could sneak out, kill the king myself, and it would end all of this. It would make Prince Kekoa the king of Hana immediately, and he would put a swift end to the war. The warriors wouldn't be taken as sacrifices back to Hana. The refugees could return safely home. We could openly find help for the warrior, suffering from King Hua's torture, back at the hut.

This time, I squeezed Ua's arm with confidence. "Don't fear Ua."

She wiped a tear and nodded, always trusting me.

"I have a plan."

CHAPTER TWENTY-ONE

"*W*here is my son?" Oponui's face raged red as Melika and I hurried about the house, making last minute preparations for the wedding. Some distant family members stopped by, helping pick up the food and decorations, and taking them to the festival area.

"Maybe you should go look for him," Melika said, impatient with his whining. Kona was supposed to grab some mats from a neighbor. He left earlier... and still hadn't returned.

The evening sky painted colors of pink and purple above, meaning it was soon time for the wedding festivities.

It's all going as planned.

Oponui yelled so loudly, I couldn't understand what he said, then he stormed out. Our mother, Kalani, was gone, having been escorted to the wedding site by an aunt of ours. She couldn't help us get ready, nor could she prepare any of the food or decorations. Not only was she clumsy and things were hard for her to do, but she kept forgetting her tasks.

It was better that she wasn't around while we prepared things.

"Finally," Melika said, rolling her eyes. "Hold still, Kaʻala. Your hair is already getting frizzy."

"Oh let it be—" But she grabbed a hold of the strands and began twirling them with her fingers.

"You look so lovely."

"I don't feel it," I muttered. Anxiety panged my chest. My siblings, Ua, and I were playing a very, *very* dangerous game tonight. Just the fact of Kona missing was already making my father lose his head.

But it wasn't my father I worried about. It was Aliʻi, and playing this trickery all night, convincing him that I was so deeply in love, and hoping that I'd get the answers I needed.

All of my anxiety was for good reason. Because tonight, I would stab the king through the heart. There was no other solution, no other alternative. It was tonight, or never.

The Kohala warrior's lives depended on it. Many relationships depended on it. The whole ending of the war depended on it.

"Aliʻi won't be able to take his eyes off you."

"Oh stop please."

"You're shaking like a leaf." Melika frowned. I didn't usually show my emotions. I quickly pulled myself together and gently moved her hands.

"I'm fine."

"Just one more strand—"

"That's enough." I stood and smoothed out the thick paʻu skirts. I wore my hair down, something I never did, because of the island heat. I desperately wanted to pull it back, feeling like it hindered my sense of hearing and eyesight. A lei poʻo, made of ferns, ti leaves, and white orchids, sat on my head.

Some older women from town made my wedding attire, thick white kapa skirts with tribal prints along the edges.

Melika made my head piece, as well as the lei and greenery around my neck, wrists, and ankles. Everything felt heavy, and I longed to change out of this, pull my hair up, and get to work.

I secured the knife beneath the inside belt of the skirt and faced Melika.

"Am I presentable enough?"

"More than enough," she said, grinning. But there was nothing to grin about. She sighed. "I know you're nervous. I know. I know the plans, but... come on, it's your wedding."

"What if Oponui figures it out–"

"*Nobody* will figure anything out, alright?" Melika said, standing and holding my arms. "Everyone is expecting festivities, a celebration, a wedding. There will be dancing, food, drinks... everyone will have no idea. Let's just follow the plan, and it'll go smoothly."

I swallowed hard. Right. Follow the plan, the plan that I made.

The "what if's" ran through my head: What if Ua and Melika got caught? What if Kona was found out tonight? What if Ali'i saw through me and refused to share any answers? What if someone snuck into my hut and found the refugees, because nobody was keeping watch–besides one of the not-wounded Kohala warriors, but still...

"Ka'ala, focus."

"You're right." I never knew how much I needed my sister's strength until then. I embraced her, and took a few deep breaths.

"Tonight, history will be made," Melika said, smiling. "Legends will be born."

I couldn't help but laugh. "You're full of it."

"At least I'm full of something." We broke into giggles,

partly from our nervousness and our own giddiness about a wedding.

Tonight wouldn't only be about my wedding, but about Kona and Ua's wedding. They'd elope after tonight, and father would not be able to say anything about it.

I fixed Melika's own lei poʻo on top of her dark hair, then took her hand and we walked together to the celebration site.

ALIʻI STOOD and stared at me as I approached. He looked handsome as ever, his hair cleaned and pulled back. He wore a thick white kihei, with tribal prints to match mine, across his chest.

The festivities and food had already been distributed, as King Hua took charge. Oponui finally appeared, late, having no luck in finding Kona.

The lower chief and his daughter, Liha, gave each other perplexed looks. Sooner or later everyone would realize Kona was gone, and that he wasn't coming to the wedding. But, for now, Melika reassured our father she'd seen Kona hurrying to the family hut to get ready.

I glanced at Oponui apologizing to the other bride and her father, saying Kona wanted to look his best. He shared some elaborate lie about what Kona had been up to earlier that day—something about serving someone, so he'd be late.

"You look..." Aliʻi smiled, returning my attention to him. "You look beautiful, as always." But there was more than just admiration in his eyes, and I had to look away, feeling myself falling into whatever emotions swirled beneath the surface.

"Thank you."

As we sat, he took my hand and leaned in. "I've never

seen you with your hair down before." He felt so warm, and I had to keep reminding myself to stick to the plan, stick to the purpose.

"Do you like it?" I asked, now meeting his eyes.

"I love it." At that, he touched a strand. Guilt panged my chest once more. Ali'i really was happy to be getting married, while all I could think about was the plan, Hua, finding answers. Would this night ever end?

King Hua sat at the head of the circle of food. Neighbors and family members served the king, other chiefs, and us, while everyone else had to get their own food. Kona's bride looked about, anxious, and I felt sorry for her. She had no idea that Kona had no intention of marrying her.

Meanwhile, I wasn't used to all this attention. It had been so long since I'd seen many of my aunts, uncles, and cousins. They crowded around, congratulating Ali'i on his win, telling me how lucky I was, and kissing our cheeks. They doted on me, telling me how beautiful I was, and how much I'd grown.

"Look at all those cute freckles!" my aunts said. It was strange to hear so many of my family members commenting on my freckles, when they all used to say it wasn't normal to have that many.

"What have you been up to?" Family members asked me. I had to fight my cheeks and ears from turning red as I lied, saying I'd been making lei, and living quietly in the woods.

They believed it, but they'd also quickly get over it because I turned the attention to Ali'i, the hero. My family doted on him and said they were sorry his family couldn't attend (as they were in Hana).

Another wave of guilt overcame me... I knew nothing about Ali'i's family. Was I so far removed from him that I didn't care to know about his childhood, his parents, or if he had any siblings?

I kept glancing at Ua, wondering if she noticed anything. She sat not far from the king, keeping a keen eye on his mood, the guards, and the high priest. Melika, meanwhile, entertained guests and cousins and others, though I could tell she kept a careful eye out for any signs of danger, any disturbances.

The festivities seemed to last forever. A local kahuna placed a long green lei around mine and Ali'i's necks, symbolizing our union. As the moon hovered above us, the local chief finally stood and cursed Oponui. The festivities came to an abrupt halt, and Hua, who was busy eating and drinking, looked alarmed. It was the first reaction he'd given the entire night, and it made me realize he wasn't as drunk as I hoped he would be.

"Your son is not coming—you cannot lie forever Oponui!"

I sat straight, noticing Melika and Ua had done the same, their hands reaching to their sides by instinct.

"He is on his way—he is just late!"

"If you lie one more time, I will have your tongue cut off and burned!" The chief stormed out. His daughter wiped her eyes and hurried after him.

My heart sank for her. She hadn't asked for any of this. Maybe she had even tried to look forward to her wedding, as this was the lot of us women.

But Ua and Kona were in love, and why would anyone try to separate them?

An awkward silence filled the area, and my attention returned to King Hua. He waved his hand, as if dismissing the drama.

"Play the music!"

The drums and chanting continued, and the king's eyes lingered on Melika. A smug look filled his face.

Oh no you don't...

Family members hurried to dance, trying to bring the livelihood back. But everyone knew that the *mana,* the energy of the event, had turned sour. The local chief's daughter had been duped... big time.

Oponui stormed away, and two of his brothers hurried after to calm him down.

"WHERE IS KONA?" Ali'i whispered, gently taking my hand.

"I don't know." I refused to look the captain in the eyes, afraid that I might give away too much. With Oponui gone, the king made his way to Melika, sitting next to her and saying something. My heart pumped and it took all my strength to keep from jumping up and stabbing him right then and there. I didn't yet know if I *could* stab him, as last time something prevented me from doing it. Would that happen again? I had no idea. But I so desperately wanted to spare my sister of the disgusting, perverted looks he gave her.

She's so young. He's a creep.

Melika glanced at me, the look so brief that anyone else would have missed it. But she meant to tell me she was alright. She returned her attention to the king, pretending to look flattered. She was as good an actress as Ua.

Meanwhile, Ua had perked up, her entire being as rigid and tense as mine as she tried not to stare at the interaction between Melika and the king. Melika was as much Ua's younger sister as my own.

"Ka'ala..." Ali'i placed his hand on my back, and this

time I did look at him. "Melika will be alright. She's not a fool, and she can take care of herself."

"She's only fifteen," I said, my tone venomous. I regretted speaking, forgetting that everything about me was uptight and tense.

"I can draw the king's attention away. He's drunk, and should retire."

Was this a clue? I tried to relax, but ended up feeling more awkward than before.

"You're right. She can take care of herself."

We didn't exchange any other words until Ali'i announced we were going to retire. We went around the circle, telling everyone good night. The strong, earthy smell of kava reeked on the party-goer's breaths, and people picked at the remains of the food while gossiping. I hated late night events like this, wishing everyone would just go home. There was nothing good that came after a long night of drinking, partying, and gossiping.

"Thank you for attending, your majesty," I said to King Hua as I kissed his cheek, resisting the urge to grab my knife out. He leaned on Melika's arm and she stiffened, but he was too drunk to see. She gave me the eye, once again reassuring me that everything was going as planned.

It really was going well, maybe even better than planned. Everything now rested on me...

Ua also gave me the same look as Melika: *This is going well, Ka'ala. It's your turn now...*

I took Ali'i's hand and squeezed it as we made our way to the wedding hut. Taking silent, deep breaths, I prayed that my charm and wit would get me the answers I needed from Ali'i. Because I didn't know what I'd do if Ali'i wouldn't cooperate.

CHAPTER TWENTY-TWO

*M*y heart started beating fast as Aliʻi opened the flap and let me in first. This was the place where newlyweds were expected to consummate their marriage. There were several of these huts around the island, and Kona would have been expected to take his bride to another down the path from this one.

"You've been quiet. Is everything alright?" Aliʻi faced me and started taking the leis off my neck. Relief overwhelmed my physical senses to have the weight gone, and to feel the air on my skin again. He removed the lei poʻo, and I immediately pulled my hair up.

"I guess I'm a little nervous. Not used to all the attention either."

"Same."

Instead of standing there awkwardly, I took off Aliʻi's leis, then made my way to the bowls of water. I washed my face, trying to keep my hands from shaking.

What should I ask? Without being suspicious?

"Aliʻi, I never asked you about your family... where are they?" I wiped my face, neck, arms, shoulders, and hands with the clean kapa cloth. I felt dirty from the people kissing my cheeks and embracing me. Being able to clean and refresh myself eased some of the anxiety building up within.

"My parents are in Hana. They're very old and wouldn't have been able to make the journey here anyway."

"And siblings?"

"I had three older brothers..." He went quiet, and my heart sank as I realized why he didn't keep talking about them. They must have been killed in the wars.

"I'm so sorry..."

"I am too." He wiped himself off then slipped the kihei over his neck, leaving him bare chested. "I'm sure they're resting in peace now. It's just too bad they had to die so young. None of them were married though, at least."

He now stood there, studying me. I removed my kihei and pa'u skirts, leaving the white wraparound dress on, and used a lauhala fan to cool myself off.

"I can't believe it."

I tried to relax and let out a laugh, but there was no laughter. I was tense as ever. "Can't believe what?"

"You're my wife." At that, he pulled me into his arms and I melted into his chest. He had so many scars from battle, and when I looked at his face, the one on his right side was as prominent as ever. How did he look so handsome with the slight disfiguration? Was it possible that it made him look even more attractive?

The captain stared at me in such a way that made my insides tighten. I was now Ali'i's wife. We were expected to consummate the marriage, and he was a man. There was no doubt he wanted this...

He leaned down and kissed me.

An internal battle began with me.

This feels good, said my body, my lips, and my heart.

Focus... you're taking too long to get the answers... Melika and Ua can't keep the king occupied all night... My plans kicked back in, reminding me of my purpose.

What would it feel like to go beyond kissing? Was it possible that my body could rule out the logic in my mind? That would be dangerous.

You don't even love Ali'i, and you're just using him. So get it over with...

"Ka'ala, you're shaking." Ali'i pulled away and held my arms. "What's wrong?"

Oh no. Now he'd figure me out.

Think of something...

"I'm just nervous..."

"About what?"

I shrugged. "I just don't know if I can relax and..." I blushed, "Get into it right now, especially knowing that Melika was being creeped on by the king."

"Ka'ala..." He rubbed my arms. "We can go out now and check on her. I can escort the king to his hut..."

"No, no. I know she's capable of taking care of herself. She's only fifteen, but she's wise enough. I..." How could I twist this conversation around? "What if he forces himself on her though? I'm just worried about that."

"We can go right now," Ali'i said, already taking my hand. "You're right. We shouldn't leave the drunk king alone, especially if nobody has the courage to stop him."

"But what will you do?" I asked, holding him back and now pulling him close. Guilt panged my chest. I was trying to coax answers from him. Would he be able to tell?

"The captains and high priests are the only highest in rank that have a right to stop the king, especially if he's going to do something that is not fit for his status." Ali'i frowned. "Sleeping with his wives is one thing... but being promiscuous is not allowed, especially for ali'i."

"You know that he tried to seduce Ua and I," I said, trying to keep my voice even. "Ali'i, if we didn't have that horribly fermented kava, he might have forced himself on either of us."

"I know."

Silence.

"Can you live with that knowledge? He's on the loose, right now—"

"And you're right. We need to get Melika to safety."

"But what about other young women? We can't just *hide* every young woman on Lanai or Hana." I spoke so quickly that Ali'i tensed. A shadow crossed over his face, and the ickiest feeling ran through my body.

He knows what I'm up to...

"Ka'ala..." He took a sharp breath, as if not believing what he saw and heard. I felt like the dirtiest person on the whole earth. I married this man, hoping to seduce and coax answers out of him. Not only was I failing horribly, but he read my plans, my *intent.*

"You didn't want to marry me for me..." He pulled away from me, an iciness growing between us. "I killed that bounty hunter... for you. I am resigning from my position... for you. I want to move here... for you..." His chest rose and fell as his breaths shortened.

"I know and..." The words got stuck on my tongue. *I love you.* I couldn't say them because I'd be lying. Love didn't hide things. Love didn't manipulate, even if it was for the greatest cause in the world.

I ached to explain it all, to tell him that my motives were right and good, and he was just confused... but no words escaped my mouth.

"Ka'ala, you really married me to find out how to kill King Hua?" Hearing him say the words out loud sent chills down my spine. How could he read me, when nobody else could?

"I didn't have any other options." At this, I stepped forward and took his hand. But he shook his head and moved back. "You have to understand," I said. "You're loyal to him, and you're close to him. You know more than anyone else. Ali'i, we *have* to end these wars."

"You're doing more than enough."

"It's not enough. It's never enough. We have to destroy the root of the problem, and that is Hua." At this, desperation filled my chest.

"Help me," I said, trying to stop my body from shaking.

"I can't." He held the bridge of his nose. "I swore an oath of loyalty–"

"An oath that you can break–"

"Ka'ala, you don't understand." He whirled around, looking angry. My mind flashed back to the moment he watched Mailou and said he could kill the bounty hunter, easily. The killing look wasn't directed at me, but... felt more of a hatred for himself.

"Ali'i..."

"You didn't want to marry me. You don't *love* me." He shook his head, like he was absolutely disgusted with himself. I just wanted to hug him. *I* did this to him. "You want answers, fine," he said. "When I swore an oath of loyalty, the high priest put a spell on me, alright? I have to protect the king when I'm around him, even with my own life." Ali'i clenched his fist. "And every man who is recruited has this spell placed on him, understand?"

Things started falling into place.

"My brothers... all three of them were captains. They

were each killed in battle while defending the king." Ali'i pointed to the scar on his face. "This is because of that spell. I jumped in to protect the king, and almost suffered the same fate as my brothers." He sighed and rubbed his face. "It's one of the reasons he's invincible."

My heart ached for all the men who joined the wars, who had a spell placed on them by the high priest. They had to throw themselves in harm's way to protect the king. How awful!

"Did they know the spell was placed on them?"

"They have no choice but to comply."

I stepped forward to embrace Ali'i, but he only stepped back again. My heart ached.

"Another reason he's invincible is that the high priest has placed dozens, if not hundreds, of wards of protection on the king. He won't be harmed by any weapon, any hand, nothing... at this point, only a god can kill him."

"He's not a god," I said, feeling both angry and weak at the same time. My hatred for King Hua flared hotter and hotter the more Ali'i shared. "So he can't be killed?"

"Not with all those spells, no."

"What about the high priest?"

Ali'i let out a sigh and shrugged. "I've heard that spells have to be undone, not just broken. So I don't know if killing the high priest breaks the spells... I don't know. The man with him now is not the highest priest in Hana. He's a lesser priest, wanting to advance in rank and be known as the highest priest."

I thought of the gods around Maui, but none were friendly nor involved with the people. The only gods who seemed awake and moving about were Pele, goddess of Kilauea volcano on the Big Island, and Kamapua'a, the pig god, who wandered, always steering clear of Pele. Neither of them would care to help, so that option wasn't going to work.

"Does the high priest put wards on himself?"

Aliʻi looked angry, impatient, and sad as ever, his shoulders slumped. He didn't even look at me as he shrugged. "I don't know. I assume he does, but... you never know."

My mind raced as new plans took form.

I have to kill the high priest. He had spells cast on multiple, maybe even hundreds, of people: Hua, Aliʻi, other captains, and the soldiers.

"Kaʻala..." Aliʻi now stepped towards me, but made no move to touch me. "I love you... but it's clear that you have no intention of loving me–"

"Aliʻi–"

He held up his hand, not wanting to be interrupted. "I should have watched and paid attention to the warning signs. You had every reason to lure me in, and you did it. Now you have what you wanted. So what do you plan to do? Kill me, now that you have the answers?"

My heart ached. "It's not that I don't love you... I do. I just..." I couldn't breathe. "I'm sorry, Aliʻi. I didn't want to hurt you. I didn't want to use you. There was just no other way–"

"You don't have to kill the king–"

"I do. I must. And if you try to stop me, well..." I rubbed my forehead, trying to think. "I'll do what I have to..."

"I *do* have to stop you, Kaʻala, especially if I follow you." The captain shook his head and smiled, but it was bitter. "I seriously thought we'd start a life together, that we could be happy together. I'm such a fool."

"We still can..." Even as I said the words, they felt wrong. I'd lied to him, and used him. "I'm sorry... I already said it–"

"No amount of apologizing will fix this. We were doomed from the start, and I should have known."

Anger welled up in me once more.

"You're stubborn," I said. "I don't believe you can be bound by magic, only. Just because someone put a spell on you, doesn't mean you can't fight it."

"How do you know? You've never had magic placed on you."

"We're wasting time," I said, thinking about Ua and, especially, Melika, with King Hua. Did they lure him to the secret spot by now? Were they alright? "I'm sorry we're married and we aren't in love—there *was* something between us, and it felt right." I hesitated. "I'm sorry to have made it all feel so wrong."

Before I could continue arguing more with Ali'i, I headed towards the door. I had no time to waste. The high priest was out there, somewhere, with his deep, dark magic. Those spells needed to be broken, and the king needed a knife stabbed through his heart.

As I passed Ali'i, he grabbed my hand. "I can't let you go, Ka'ala. This isn't you."

Just great... I didn't want to fight Ali'i, not after what happened last time. He was skilled. I was too, but it might take time to somehow bind him up in cords to prevent him from following me.

"Well then break your spell so you can help me." I tried to pull my hand free, but realized Ali'i was not playing or teasing. His eyes were dark, like all the anger, sadness, and disappointment I caused him had finally settled and he realized our fate: we wouldn't work out, because we both fought for different sides all along.

"Ali'i—"

"I'm sorry. I can't let you do this. The king is in invincible. You could get yourself killed."

"You can't stop me—"

At that I moved my wrist up, breaking his grasp with my other hand. As I lowered myself to trip Ali'i, he lifted me by waist, and threw me over his shoulder.

"Put me down!"

"I can't let you go..."

"Ali'i!"

Instead of carrying me out, he placed me on the bed. Before I could leap up, he pinned me down.

"Give it up, Ka'ala, please—"

"I can't, and you know I can't!" At this, tears began streaming down my cheeks. Why did this have to be so complicated? My heart ached. I wanted Ali'i—I wanted him badly, but he felt so far from me.

Before I knew what was happening, Ali'i leaned in and kissed me. I kissed him back, desperately wanting us to work out, wishing things weren't this way. I stopped resisting the battle within myself and wrapped my arms around his neck. The new and alarming sensations from his touch and kisses made me dizzy and hot with excitement.

I love Ali'i. How can I fight him? I couldn't.

"Ka'ala! Captain Kaiaali'i!"

We immediately broke apart from each other, our faces rosy with heat.

"Oponui?" I frowned at the flap door and Ali'i grabbed his knife while approaching the door. My whole body tingled, feeling anger, embarrassment, and desire all at the same time.

"We're coming in!" Oponui opened the flap and Ali'i got into a ready stance, as if defending me.

"What are you doing, barging in? This is a private

space," Ali'i said. I thought Ali'i was mad earlier, but this was definitely a different level of his anger. This was the "consummation" hut after all, so it should be kept *very* private.

"You're under arrest!" my father said, pointing at Ali'i. He glanced at me on the bed. I quickly stood, smoothing my messy hair back.

"What are you talking about?" I asked, stepping towards Ali'i, feeling more dizzy and confused than ever.

Two of the king's guards and the high priest entered the hut, making it hotter and cramped.

"We've found evidence that you cheated in the duel against Mailou," Oponui said, holding up a small gourd. He motioned to the high priest. "The high priest has even confirmed that using this is considered cheating—"

I frowned. It was the small gourd of healing stuff Ali'i gave to me. I used it to help baby Keola's fever, and it worked like a charm.

Why didn't we use that for the wounded warrior? Once again, my obsession with killing King Hua had clouded my view of what mattered most.

"You *searched* through my personal belongings?" Ali'i asked, and even I felt the uncomfortable, intrusiveness that my father had imposed on both of us.

"Your win against Mailou was *too* easy," my father said. "And I've found out why. The high priest has confirmed it."

Ali'i looked from Oponui to the high priest.

"You use that for everything," he said, but the high priest shook his head.

"It's obvious you used this before the duel."

Ali'i frowned. "That's ridiculous. I had no reason to use it." The muscles on his body tensed as Oponui stepped forward, grabbed my wrist, and pulled me towards him.

"Get away from this cowardly filth," my father said, his grip so tight, I fought to yank my arm free of him.

"It's not cheating. Everyone who has served in the war has used this at some point," Ali'i said.

"But it's not to be used before a duel."

"I didn't use it before the duel," Ali'i replied, then eyed me standing next to my father. The ocean between us formed again, and guilt overcame me. I longed to stand by him, but felt too embarrassed and guilty to do so.

I almost lost myself in Ali'i... just a few minutes ago, he'd been kissing me passionately, and I'd returned the gift. And now I was behind my father, while the high priest and guards were ready to pounce on Ali'i.

My father opened the gourd, showing that some of it had been used. Little did he know that the small portion was used on a refugee in my sanctuary...

"Turn yourself in honorably," the high priest said, then studied me. He moved past Ali'i, checked the bed, then nodded at Oponui. "We made it in time. The marriage has not been consummated."

I felt like I'd throw up. Our privacy had been invaded, and everything was falling apart.

A smirk spread across my father's face. "Good. Then the marriage is officially canceled." He pointed his long finger of scorn at Ali'i once more. "You've cheated, and you do not deserve my daughter. Come on, Ka'ala. This man is going to prison."

Oponui grabbed my wrist again and pulled me out. Anger and fear overcame me. This wasn't right. My father set this up, because he was angry that Mailou lost. He was probably even more angry that Kona didn't show up to his own wedding earlier.

"Let me go!" I started to fight, and Ali'i came to aid me. The guards and high priest pulled him back.

He was much stronger, and I quickly got out of my father's grasp. But before I reached Ali'i, the high priest stuck something to his nose, and the captain fell, unconscious. The guards grabbed him before he hit the ground, and horror overcame me.

"What did you do?" I ran to Ali'i, placing my hand on his cheek and gently shaking his shoulder. He still breathed, but couldn't be woken. "Ali'i—"

"Come on, that's enough." As my father, once again, pulled me away, I resisted. But my efforts were in vain as the high priest put something—the same thing he probably poisoned Ali'i with—to my nose and everything went dark.

CHAPTER TWENTY-THREE

*M*y limbs were frozen to me. As awareness heightened my senses, I blinked at the dark ground.

The poor lighting indicated late night, and from my awkward position of staring at the ground, I was slung over someone's shoulder. The person struggled to carry me, but he had persistence.

Oponui.

The sound of crashing waves caught my attention.

Where are we?

A cool night breeze wafted through the area, carrying the smell of the salty brine. We had to be by Kaumalapaau harbor and the cliffs beside it. Was my father going to toss me over the cliff? That would be a waste of a daughter, and he seemed happy to have "canceled" mine and Ali'i's marriage. Perhaps he had other plans in mind.

The more I thought about it, though, the more I wanted to roll my eyes. My marriage to the captain was not canceled, no matter how much my father wanted it to be. King Hua would have the final say, not the high priest. No doubt King Hua loved Ali'i like a son and would side with him.

In my mind, we were still married.

I thought of the way the captain kissed and touched me, and my body warmed.

What have I done? I tried to get answers from Ali'i, but he read right through me. He figured out my plot, and he wouldn't let me kill the king. But, instead of either of us following through with our plans, our attraction and desire for each other won... only for a moment. What would have happened if my father didn't interrupt? Would I have loved Ali'i, or followed through with my plans?

If I followed through with my plans, I would have found a way to bind Ali'i, so he couldn't follow me. I had no intention of killing him. The high priest and King Hua were my targets.

Ali'i... My heart ached for him. Was he alright?

What time was it? How much time had passed since my father and the high priest came to the hut and drugged us? If the night was still young, maybe I had time to get to the high priest and kill him. Then I'd find Melika, Ua, and the king... if they were able to hold him off this long.

If it was late enough, they probably escaped from him, knowing that I had failed. They would have found Kona, and aided him in freeing the Kohala warriors.

Then Kona and Ua would run away, while I had to trust that Melika could return safely to the hut on her own...

My neck tingled and I could barely turn my head to glance at the sky. The moon shone above, and my heart sank. It must have been hours since my father took me from Ali'i's arms.

Ali'i's arms... Why did I keep thinking about him, and wanting him so badly? The feelings I had for him were real, right? I told him I ruined it, and made us feel wrong but... when we kissed and let ourselves get lost in each other, it felt right.

I can't think about him right now... No doubt the high priest and guards bound and took him somewhere, until he could talk to King Hua. With him bound somewhere else, he was one less worry for me. One less obstacle stopping me from getting to the king.

He is bound by a spell. Ali'i couldn't help it, but... could he? I didn't believe in magic, and hardly heard of people on Lanai doing it, besides the crazy old kahuna. So... if someone didn't believe in magic, did it lose its power? Why couldn't Ali'i see it the way I did?

Oponui tripped and my stomach crushed against his shoulder. I moaned and he growled.

"Shut it, Ka'ala..."

"Where are you taking me?" My voice came out groggy, slow, and slurred.

"Where you deserve to go."

"Where?"

"You'll see." His voice, full of hatred and venom, told me it would not be a pleasant place. I never thought my father was vengeful, but I remembered that Oponui *knew* Ali'i from the past.

He had been under Ali'i's command during the wars, and he didn't like to listen. Ali'i said Oponui was even punished for not listening...

Perhaps this is my father's way of getting revenge on the captain...

"I'd let you see your mother," he said, breaking the silence after a moment. "But she won't remember you anyways."

A pang struck my chest, followed by a moment of panic. "What do you mean?"

"You'll see."

I couldn't have hated Oponui more than I did then. Why did he have to be like this? He was always so concerned with his looks, and now... well. He was taking matters into his own hands.

"Where's Aliʻi?" Again, I couldn't seem to control my voice. It sounded sick and distant.

"The high priest will put him in prison until King Hua makes a decision. He cheated though, and it's obvious that he did."

"He did not—"

"Mailou should have won... easily."

We started descending a cliff edge, and my stomach tightened at the height. It's not that I was afraid of heights, but what if Oponui tripped, or if he dropped me? I, or we, would plunge into the swirling water far below.

My father had never been the athletic type, and it now showed. The strong smell of his sweat filled the air, along with his constant curses—on me, Aliʻi, the rocks, the cliff, and so forth.

Finally, we stopped along the ledge and he put me down. I collapsed to the earth, unable to move.

Come on, body... My joints felt lifeless, and no muscle or body part responded to my pleas.

"What happened to me?" I asked, only able to move my eyes and look about slowly. Oponui looked over the cliff edge, hands on his knees as he caught his breath.

"The high priest... it's a sleeping scent. Knocks people out. You'll feel your limbs soon."

I groaned, annoyed as ever. "Where's Melika?"

"Why does it matter? The king seemed interested in

her. I wouldn't be angry if she was to become another of his wives."

I wanted to say something, to express my anger, but I knew it would do nothing. My father cared only for himself, and that was that.

He sat by the top of my head, so I couldn't see him. From the sound of it, he munched on something and drank water from his gourd.

"We'll wait for a moment, until the tide is right."

I sighed. Though he didn't have his youthfulness and athleticism anymore, Oponui was a skilled diver and spear fisher. He knew the ocean well, and even found incredible underwater places around Lanai. Many inexperienced divers and spearfishers went to my father to learn and ask questions about where to hunt squid in the dark places and how to dive for big fish in deeper waters. Oponui knew secret cave entrances and it was rumored he slept in many of them because he knew the tides and waters so well, he had the timing exactly right to enter and exit the dangerous caves.

Keawe, Ua's brother—who was married and a farmer (the only reason he was allowed to stay home from the wars)—was one of those people who used to frequent our home, asking Oponui all kinds of questions.

My father sometimes shared information, but mostly kept things to himself. It didn't deter the islanders from asking him questions though. Oponui's unpredictable moods probably kept them coming back for more, as they hoped to catch him in a good mood, when words came freely. Though my father sometimes shared secrets with others, he never taught anything to his children.

And, most likely, his secrets would die with him.

"What are we waiting for then?" I asked, starting to feel

the uncomfortable hardness of the cliff rocks under me. It was good, meaning that my senses were returning. As soon as they did, I'd run off, away from my father.

I thought of my new plans: Once my body got its strength back, I could run as fast as I could to the high priest. Kill him. Find King Hua. Kill him. Then free Ali'i and the Kohala warriors. The war would be over.

"We're at Spouting Cave."

I grimaced, my plans shattering in a split second.

No. Anywhere but Spouting Cave. The place was a nightmare. It was a cave with an underwater entrance. A person could find access to the cave only at certain times, and only from a certain place. Many had died trying to find the entrance.

It was said that inside Spouting Cave were large black crabs, so dark and aggressive, that killing one and bringing back a claw won someone high prestige.

My father had a black crab's claw hanging in his hut, and I shuddered. It was the largest pincher I'd ever seen.

I'm so far... Oponui had truly gone great lengths to bring me here, hiking along the cliffs and beaches.

"Why?" I groaned as I tried to move my arms, and they did... but ever so slowly. Every part of me felt sluggish, like I ran a hundred miles and collapsed at the end.

"That captain does not deserve you. He deserves no one, and he will pay for what he did."

"He did... nothing to you." I sat up, my back feeling all out of place from the way my father carried me for hours. Mostly my ribs and stomach hurt from crashing against his shoulder.

"He's young, inexperienced, immature. I would've rather died than been under *his* command." Oponui sneered in disgust and spit off the edge of the cliff. He grabbed the back of my dress, in case I couldn't hold myself up, and would fall forward, into the water below.

We weren't so high up now. In fact, if I fell off, I'd probably be fine. I sized up my escape, but felt more and more hopeless. My body was not doing what I needed it to do.

And just sitting up made me feel more tired than I'd ever felt in my life. What sort of drug was this?

"Not only am I sick of these wars, but to be told what to do, and by someone so inferior..." Oponui shook his head. In a way, I did feel bad for him.

The wars *were* terrible, and nobody wanted to fight in them. Then to have a captain who was young, handsome, and well-liked... that must have miffed Oponui to his core.

I wished I could tell my father the plan of ending the wars by killing the king, but Oponui had no courage. He would rather play it safe, and be on the ali'i's good side, in case it raised his own status.

We sat in silence, listening to the waves break against the side of the cliff. I watched the way the moon glittered on the ocean horizon, and it reminded me of 'Eleu and her grandfather, sailing away with the children and the baby.

I sure hoped they were alright.

"The tide is up. We can jump in now." Oponui took my wrist and helped me stand on shaky legs. Everything about my body felt off.

Before I could protest, he jumped off, dragging me with him.

Wind rushed past my ears, and my stomach leaped clear to my throat. As we hit the water, a combination of cold and warm surrounded me.

The ocean...

I surfaced, coughing and choking as water had rushed up my nose. Immediately, the waves tossed us to and fro, and I realized I couldn't move my body fast enough to stay afloat.

Oponui, still holding my wrist, pulled me towards him. "Get on my back."

"I'm not a little–"

"Now!"

I did so, knowing that if I didn't, I'd probably drown. If only I weren't in this broken physical state. I could swim away, run away, follow through with my plans...

Oponui swam for a while, until we passed under the cliff. Darkness encircled us.

"Hold your breath."

I listened to my father, taking a deep breath, and took my own deep breath, then we went under. He swam for a moment, but not long enough that I became uncomfortable. I could hold my breath for a long time if I wanted.

When we surfaced, a dank, cold air nipped at our noses. I shivered, looking around.

Light barely reflected off the surface of the water, and when it caught hold of the cave around us, everything looked green, black, and ghostly.

"Where are we?"

"Spouting Cave, I told you." Oponui stood and placed me on the hard, black rocks. I hugged myself, my teeth chattering against each other.

My father sat to catch his breath, and I drew my legs in, noticing something slithering in the water.

Eel... I shuddered. I never liked eel, but it told me I was not alone. In the darkness of the cave hid those black crabs too.

The thundering sound of the waves against the outside of the cave was a continuous groan.

"You're going to leave me here?" I asked, and Oponui nodded, not looking at me.

"To die?"

Silence. For a moment, I thought my father pitied me, and felt sorry for bringing me here. What father would bring his daughter to a chilly ocean cave, and leave her to starve (or get eaten) to death?

My strength slowly returned, despite being cold, and I now spoke in a normal tone and speed. "You don't have to do this. We can go back..."

Oponui caught his breath and then finally eyed me. "The only condition you will go back is if you promise to marry the chief of Olowalu, in the valley of Palawai. And not only that, but you must let that low captain see you in the chief's embrace—"

"Father!" I'd never thought him to be so low, so jealous.

"That is what you must promise, and we will leave."

So Oponui wanted me to marry the old chief of Olowalu. Furthermore, he wanted me to embrace this old man *in front* of Aliʻi.

Oponui is spiteful, jealous, petty... I wanted to say all the things but I shook in anger.

"No, I'm not going to do that."

"Either love the chief of Olowalu, or die here."

In other words, my father would never want me and Aliʻi to be together. But I loved Aliʻi.

Wait... I do? Yes. I truly did love him. Nobody made me feel safe, protected, and loved like he did. And though we had *so* much to figure out, I would never want to embrace another man... not after Aliʻi.

"I'd rather die here than be free based on your monstrous conditions."

Oponui stood and folded his arms. "Fine. Then you'll

stay here... until either I come back, or the chief of Olowalu comes to take you to Maui." He stepped into the water, and I stood to follow, though my body ached in protest.

"You will stay where you are, Kaʻala. Don't try to escape, especially without my help."

"I don't need your help."

Oponui smiled, but bitterness filled it. "If you try to escape on your own, your body will crash into the rocks." He chuckled and it made my skin crawl. How could my father be so heartless? "And you will be food for the sharks."

With that warning, my father dove into the water and disappeared completely. I stepped into the water, trying to see where he'd gone, but everything looked black. Perhaps in the daylight I'd be able to see how to get out of here.

Spouting Cave also had a sort of column that we swam through to get here, so my father was right about the tides. All the conditions had to be right to get into this cave.

Something moved in the water and I quickly got out. My skin tingled as I made out the form of a stingray, gliding along the edge of the water, then disappearing below.

I hugged my arms and looked around, hating that I could see nothing. My surroundings felt as dark and bleak as I felt.

"I'll get out of here, I will," I whispered to myself, then remained silent. The echoes of my whisper sounded like ghosts conversing.

Shuddering again, I held my knees and tried to think of the next step. Should I try to exit the cave now, and follow my father?

Though strength had returned to my body, it still was not the same. I probably wouldn't be quick enough to swim through the column in one breath.

Perhaps I'll wait til morning... But that ruined *all* my plans.

My plans are over. Perhaps I had truly failed in my attempt to kill the king, and I was stuck here. Realization began sinking in.

No... I really *was* stuck here. I had no idea how to get out, couldn't see, and I didn't even have the strength.

Not yet.

My siblings and Ua were on their own. Ali'i was on his own. And I... Well, I was *definitely* on my own. I buried my head in my hands, trying to think of a solution, but I knew there was none.

I was stuck here, until my strength returned, or my father or the chief of Olowalu came to get me.

CHAPTER TWENTY-FOUR

*D*arkness settled around me, a thickness that made it difficult to breathe.

I can't see anything.

The moon must have passed over the cave, because now there were no bits of light reflecting on the surface of the water. I trembled, hating how muggy, wet, and chilled I felt. My dress was plastered to my body, and I was glad nobody could see me like this. I should have left my pa'u skirts and kihei on, instead of undressing down to my wraparound dress earlier. Wet strands of hair stuck to my face and neck, and I swiped them away, but the darkness remained.

Because the cave was so clammy, cold, and wet, I didn't know if I'd dry off. The sticky salt water, mixed with the cold, gloomy air made me feel dirty.

Or maybe I felt dirty because of what I did to Ali'i. I loved him, then used him, then loved him again...

What have I done?

If I hadn't married Ali'i, I wouldn't be here. Could I have gotten the answers out of him without going to such great lengths?

My heart ached. But... I *wanted* to marry Aliʻi. I loved him. He was everything I ever wanted in a husband: kind, compassionate, protective, attractive. Aliʻi did everything for me. He fought for me, literally.

I groaned, and the echoes bouncing around the cave made me jump. The roars from crashing waves outside the cave continued, but they didn't sound as eerie as my own voice. I resigned to stay quiet once more, the hair on my skin standing on end as the groan continued to echo.

I'm stuck.

That meant I really had no options. Should I wait for my father? What if he didn't come back until... who knew when?

Ua said that the king would take the warriors back to Hana in the morning. What if the situation with Aliʻi stalled the king from his departure?

I have to get out of here... My mind tortured me with thoughts of Melika and the king, Ua, Kona, the refugees, the Kohala warriors, and, of course, Aliʻi. All of them were in danger, *right now*. Perhaps Aliʻi was just in prison, but if King Hua believed Oponui and the high priest, would he have Aliʻi killed? Surely he wouldn't kill the "greatest of all" his captains, right?

But as for my siblings and Ua... they were all depending on me. Did they figure out that the plan fell through? Did they manage to set the Kohala warriors free? Was Melika, especially, alright?

Please protect her, I begged the gods, hoping that the king didn't touch or hurt my sister. She was smart, and an excellent warrior... but the king was also invincible.

I have to think of a new plan. Right. I had no time to waste... except, I couldn't see anything, and my limbs were not at their full capacity and strength just yet.

As soon as I get better, I'll have to take the risk... I looked in the direction my father disappeared earlier. I didn't know all the perfect conditions of leaving this cave, but... I couldn't just let my siblings and Ua risk their lives out there.

We all have to take risks. Though my father threatened me, saying that I'd get dashed by the rocks should I try to escape, I would not fear. I had to get out of this place, as soon as morning came. Hopefully, by then, my strength would return.

I tried opening and closing my fists, but even that rendered me exhausted. A light splash in the water caused me to jump.

It's just the stingray.

I held the bridge of my nose, calming myself down. This cave was starting to spook me, but I would be alright.

The image of the black crab's pincher, the one my father hung in our family hut, came to mind and I shook my head. *Don't think about that.* But it had been so big, unearthly, and like something from the darkest places of the earth.

Just focus on the new plan. When morning came, I'd have a little more light to get myself out of here. I'd also, hopefully, be able to see where the eel and stingray were, so I could avoid them. Once I got out of the cave, I'd have to climb the cliff edge and run across the island.

Just the thought of the physical exertion to do all of it made me dizzy.

I'm exhausted. Earlier, when Ali'i and I had gone to the hut together, I knew I was absolutely fatigued. All of the feeling came back: *I could sleep right now.*

And maybe I should sleep. There was no sense in staying awake, trying to pretend that the morning would come sooner than I hoped. I would need my strength to get out of here anyway.

I sat up against one of the cave walls, then rested my head back. Nothing felt comfortable, but perhaps I was tired enough to knock out, no matter what.

I focused on the sound of the waves crashing against the side of the spouting cave. The roaring sounded like monsters from the deep, and offered no comfort or peace. I closed my eyes, but found no sleep. Perhaps this cave was cursed, long ago. But that didn't bother me so much as the time passing by, my siblings, lover, and others in danger.

Because if I didn't get my strength back, I might be stuck here forever. That was a curse in itself.

Heaviness fell over my eyelids, finally. My dreams were replays of the events that happened recently: Aliʻi fighting Mailou, bringing the refugees to the sanctuary with Melika, watching the king of Hana, kissing and loving Aliʻi...

My dreams lingered on Aliʻi, the protection and love he offered, the possibility of a happy marriage and family, the future we could have had.

That we still can have, if I kill the king. Memories surfaced of the opportunities I could have stabbed the king: after the duel, during the wedding...

Why didn't I?

Because I wasn't sure if it would work. I tried stabbing him before, years ago, and it didn't work. Come to find out it didn't work because of the king's many enchantments.

The high priest must die. I wish I could tell Melika, Ua, and Kona everything. Perhaps they could help me. But did they have the same fire and anger as I did, the same burning hatred for King Hua?

Ua probably did, but my siblings were focused on the

sanctuary and the refugees. Should I have continued to focus on that?

But there's so much more I can do. And so much more I was capable of.

A new dream washed over me, one where Ali'i kissed me. His lips were warm, while I felt so cold. He said he wished we had worked out, and then I watched as he walked away.

I called after him, but he didn't turn around, not once.

I hurt him.

I woke up, realizing that I had, indeed, called out Ali'i's name. It bounced around the cave, haunting my mind.

I covered my ears and squeezed my eyes shut. It was just a dream. If I killed King Hua, everything would work out like it should. Ali'i and I could be together...

SLEEP CAME AND WENT. I dozed off, only to be awakened by the sound of the pounding waves or the occasional splash of the stingray. Time felt like it stood still, as there were no changes in the cave lighting.

Something rubbed against my leg, but, in my half-awake state, I didn't think something was *really* there. That is, until a stinging sensation ripped across my left calf. I screamed as I jumped up, looking for whatever had hurt me. And how did it hurt me?

Darkness.

I felt my leg, a warm substance greeting my hand.

I'm bleeding...

A clicking sounded by my feet, and it bounced off the walls. Another clicking sound came from behind. My hair stood on end.

The black crabs. I couldn't see anything. I swiped the

area around me and my fingers brushed against hard, skinny legs. The black pincher, the one my father was so proud to hang in his hut, came to mind once more.

The pincher had to be the size of my foot, and, no doubt these crabs could shred me to pieces if they wanted. In my delirious state, I forgot that whatever crab had been behind me now brushed against my calves. I screamed and kicked the air, not knowing where anything was, but afraid for my life.

"Get away, all of you!" My foot kicked against something, and it splashed into the water. I definitely got one of the crabs. Another few splashes followed, and, to more of my astonishment and horror, I realized that the stingray must have swallowed the crab.

My hand swiped another black crab behind me, and silence ensued.

I let out a whooshing breath and felt my aching muscles. Was Aliʻi feeling this exhausted and sore too, after being drugged?

Aliʻi... Every time I thought of him, my heart hurt. Would we work out?

Once I kill Hua, ʻae.

I swiped back my sticky, salty hair then felt my leg once more. The crab had pinched my calf, and it was bleeding, actively bleeding. I ripped the bottom part of my dress then sat to wrap the wound.

As if the silence had been too much, the clicking noise started again.

A chill ran down my spine as more clicking noises joined in.

The black crabs... Were they getting their revenge on me for feeding one of their own to the stingray? I wished I had my knife with me, or something, anything... But all I had were my bare hands and feet.

The clicking noises blurred as the sounds echoed off the walls, making it impossible to locate where they might be.

Something clipped my ankle and I screamed. Did my father know that I might get attacked by these crabs? He probably didn't even care, and this was not the time to think about it.

I kicked something behind me, only to wince when something pinched my toe. These crabs were ready to attack, and I had no choice but to fight.

This would be a long night, but the battle for my life in this cave had begun.

THE CRABS ATTACKED, and I did all I could to keep them at bay. They pinched any part of me that they could. When I reached my hand out to swipe away wherever it was in the darkness, one of the pinchers clamped on my wrist. Luckily I got it off, otherwise it might have cut off my whole hand.

I screamed in a panic as I defended myself. The fact that I fought blindly scared me, as I never knew where my hand or foot would go, what it would hit, or if I'd lose a finger or limb in the process.

The night wore on, and the crabs continued to pester me with their clicking noises and attempts to pinch and snap at me.

After a while of screaming, punching, and kicking the air, I realized that they had stopped. The clicking noises ceased, and the cave became silent again, save my exasperated breaths and the roaring of the waves outside.

"Is that all you've got?" I asked, my voice coming back to taunt me. A gasp escaped me as I realized that tiny flecks of light sparkled on the surface of the water. The light came from the column my father must have dove under.

Could I follow that light and get myself out of here? What about the stingray, or the eel? They wouldn't hurt me, would they? They didn't eat people, after all.

I would have been more comfortable with a shark swimming in the cave pool, instead of the eerie creatures. At least sharks had the decency to mind their own business, whereas the eel and stingray seemed overly interested in whatever splashed into the water.

The light wasn't enough to illuminate anything in the cave, but enough to spark some hope in me. As I stepped towards the water's edge, the stingray surfaced and swam close to me, as if warning me not to cross my boundaries.

"I need to get out of here," I said, desperation panging my chest.

I sat, staring at the water, but listening all the while for the black crabs. Perhaps it was morning, and they didn't come out until the night. It still felt like night in here though. How could anyone survive here without any light?

I had nothing to make a light either, else I would have done so long ago.

I touched the surface of the water, aching for the light to grow stronger so I could see my way out of here.

What time was it? How long had I been fighting those crabs? Were Melika, Ua, and Kona alright? Was Ali'i alright, and was he thinking about me?

The sound of a distant pū, a conch shell, aroused me from my melancholy. It sounded far, but it should sound far because *I* was far, deep in the Spouting Cave. I looked up at the cave ceiling, finding nothing but darkness. Somehow the noise penetrated through.

The shell sounded again, and my heart might have

stopped. It was no ordinary pū, but that of royalty. It meant that royalty was either coming into Lanai, or leaving the island.

It can't be... If it was royalty leaving Lanai, that meant King Hua and his high priest were taking the Kohala warriors back to Hana. That meant the king would be gone, and I'd lose my chance to kill him, unless I went to Hana myself.

"No..." I splashed my fist in the water. "No!" My own anger reverberated across the walls.

Then another thought came to mind. *Where's Ali'i? Where are my siblings and Ua?* If Hua was leaving with the warriors, what happened to everyone? Did they get captured, or worse, found out?

"No..." The anger turned to despair. "No..."

I did this to all of them. I let them *all* down. Kona's words came to my mind again, reminding me that I couldn't do *everything.* I had been so obsessed with killing King Hua, I let everything else fade to the background.

First of all, I was selfish, not satisfied with my sanctuary, feeling like I had to do MORE. But I did enough, and Kona was right. I had helped dozens of refugees find safety and healing. I had helped children and even an infant!

Second, I had the best crew in the world: my helpful brother, brave sister, compassionate best friend, kind Prince Kekoa, clever 'Eleu, her master wayfinding grandfather Naula, and, of course, my sweetheart Ali'i. He was cursed, bound to do something he didn't want to do, but he protected me. He made it so the king no longer searched for me or Ua. He protected me from Mailou.

I had been so busy protecting and serving others, I didn't know how much it meant for someone to protect *me.* And I threw it away, took it for granted.

Because I wanted more. I thought of the training Ua and I did under her grandfather, a master at fighting. "You are trained to protect," he told us, "Not to kill." The motto had stayed with me forever... until I became obsessed with, what I saw as, the greater good.

I thought I'd be justified in killing King Hua.

But I had been doing plenty already. Maybe I cut off my options too soon. Perhaps I had to find a way to use my sanctuary to build and empower people to voice their opinions against the king. Perhaps I could've raised my own secret army and then taken matters into my own hands, forcing the king to step down.

But I had forgotten who I was, all because of the injustice I saw around me.

I was doing enough, and I lost so much of myself by focusing on one thing. I let my friends and relationships slip through the cracks. I recalled not even knowing if Ali'i had a family–not even knowing until our wedding night! Or when my best friend–*my best friend*–was tortured because she didn't know what to do about her relationship with Kona. Should she run away, or stay and protect the sanctuary?

How could I have been so heartless?

How could I have been so distracted?

I am doing enough. The sanctuary was my part, my contribution. I couldn't change *everything,* but I could start with where I was.

My heart ached as I thought of all that I'd lost now: my relationships, my loved ones. Perhaps when someone realized they were going to die, was when they realized what mattered most in life.

I'm that person. I wished I had taken advantage of the love and goodness of the people around me, instead of hyper-focusing on one task that I thought would change the world.

I was doing enough for everyone, but I didn't need to do everything.

And now I lost Ali‘i. Surely he was gone now, either traveling back to Hana with the king, or being punished for "cheating," though I doubted the king would consider Oponui's scam.

"Ali‘i..." I sniffed, realizing that tears began to stream down my cheeks. "I'm so sorry..." He was wonderful, the man of my dreams, and I used him.

It was better I was here, unable to torture him anymore. He was so good, *too* good for me. I buried my head in my arms and cried.

I cried because I was defeated: there was no way out of here, and all the plans I'd ever made had failed. If only I'd cared more for my loved ones, instead of pining after something that didn't even align with my standards, then I wouldn't be here.

But I was a fool, and now everyone paid the price for my poor choices.

CHAPTER TWENTY-FIVE

*M*y broken sobs echoed throughout the cave. I didn't usually cry, because I had become accustomed to masking my emotions. It was easier that way, because Melika, Ua, the refugees, and others looked to me as their source of strength.

But I let them all down. I was *never* someone people should look up to.

My cries made the cave feel spookier and darker than anything I'd ever endured. It was as if the cave enjoyed teasing me, making known to myself, over and over again, that I had let everyone down. I lost the love of my life, and I was going to die here... a failure. Alone.

The stingray passed by the surface of the water again, eyeing me out. Was it thinking about eating me? No doubt it had crunched on the shells and sucked the flesh of the black crabs I kicked in earlier.

I sniffed and wiped my eyes, realizing that dry blood caked my wrist.

"What the–" I tried to see my injuries in the tiny inklings of light coming from the column, but couldn't make anything out. I resorted to feeling my injuries and winced at the gashes and cuts that laced my fingers, hands, arms, legs, ankles, feet, and toes.

I deserve this. I shouldn't have tried to do more than I was called to do. I had been doing more than enough, and my contributions of saving people from this war were enough.

I sat in the silence for a long while, my stomach growling, my body trembling from my sobs and the cold air. The light flecks on the surface of the water seemed to stay the same for a while, and I decided that it was probably all the light that would come through.

Thoughts of my family, the refugees, and especially Aliʻi came to mind. Perhaps I let them all down last night. But... what if there was a way to save them all? Maybe Aliʻi wouldn't want me back, especially after last night, but I was still alive. I could make things right, and ensure that my siblings, Ua, Aliʻi, the refugees, and the Kohala warriors were safe from the king.

I was trained to protect, not to kill. I would do what I could to make sure those I loved, and those who were innocent, would have the safety they needed.

Straightening out, I looked at the light on the water with purpose.

I need to get out of here. Though I felt the lowest I'd ever been in my life, I knew that sitting around wouldn't help my siblings or those in danger.

I eased my foot into the water, keeping an eye out for the dark form of the stingray. It hovered close by, but made no movement to come towards me.

"Will you show me the way out?" I asked, my voice bouncing around.

The stingray turned and swam deeper, disappearing. I frowned.

"Fine. Be that way. No more crabs for you." At least it wouldn't bother me—or I hoped it wouldn't. The eel was somewhere in these waters, but I couldn't worry about it. The eel wouldn't attack me unless I threatened it, or so I'd been told.

But the black crabs... Crabs had never been known to hurt humans, so I had my doubts about the eel. Perhaps this cave made the animals behave as monsters.

The salty water burned my open wounds, but, at the same time, the iciness of the temperature numbed the hurt. With my whole body under the water, I made my way towards the underwater column. The light was still ever faint, making it hard to know *where* the column was. But I couldn't be deterred.

I can do this. I'd done hard things before, and I wouldn't give up now. I would get out of here and do what I could to protect the people I loved.

As I reached the edge of the pool, and my hands touched the black cave wall, I tried to make out the column.

"It's here somewhere," I muttered, hoping that when I dove under, I'd be able to feel my way out. Much to my annoyance, the light coming through didn't focus on one column or hole. Instead it was sporadic, making it difficult to discern where the underwater cave entrance and exit was located.

I'll just explore and feel it out, I thought. I dove under, feeling the wall with my hand and finding a large sideways column. My heart leaped. This had to be the exit. However, as I dove deeper, I found another sideways column.

Which one is it? I tried to remember how deep my

father swam the previous night. Had there been much pressure in my ears? I wished I paid more attention, but I'd been unwell, my body still fighting whatever thing I'd been drugged with.

I had no choice but to try them both. If anything, I could always pull myself out the other way, right?

I don't know. I'd heard of people getting stuck in underwater cave entrances, because they ran out of breath. They couldn't go forward, but they couldn't go back, and so they drowned.

I shuddered.

I'm still alive, I reminded myself. Though this place was dead, or like a place of death, *I* was still breathing. I held onto the side of the cave wall, gathering my courage. Every inch of my body hurt, but I thought of my loved ones.

I'm going to get out of here.

I took a deep breath and dove under, choosing to try out the upper column first. I used my hands to feel the column around me, and propel me forward.

I hadn't gone far when a gush of water pushed me back into the cave. I surfaced and drew in the air.

What? What happened?

Then a thought came to mind. Perhaps it was the tide and time of day. The water pushed *into* the cave, instead of out. So when did it push out?

Or perhaps I needed to try the lower column.

I took another deep breath and dove deep. Pressure built up in my ears as I swam into the lower column. It was much smaller, leaving me to think that this might not be it. The opening last night had been large enough for me to be on my father's back. I didn't remember getting any cuts or hitting my head or body on anything.

Get out of there... My instincts screamed at me. This was *not* the entrance. But I was slow to pull myself back, and something seized my wrist. I yanked my hand away while punching something muscled and slimy with my other hand.

This is the eel's home. And I'd threatened it by coming inside. It wouldn't have attacked me, but because I blocked its way out, it needed to do something.

The eel released its bite on my arm and retreated while I also pulled myself out and surfaced. My left wrist stung and I pulled myself out of the water, trying to see the damage.

I slammed my good hand on the water surface, frustrated.

"Let me out!" I screamed to nothing and no one in particular. Warmth seeped around the bite, meaning I was probably bleeding, so I ripped another piece of my dress and wrapped the wound.

Determination overcame me once more. At least I knew where the underwater entrance and exit was. All I had to do was get through, somehow.

I wasn't sure how much time had passed. The light flecks on the water still gave no indication to the hour of day. But I had a feeling it might be evening soon. The hunger in my stomach, combined with my aching body and bleeding injuries, made me feel somewhat nauseous. But I had to get out of here.

I let myself into the pool of water once more and swam to the entrance.

It was now or never. After taking a big breath, I dove in and swam as hard and fast as I could. Memories of

Ali'i, approaching on his surfboard to aid me, came to mind.

He was so caring... The way he listened to me, believed me, and did something about Mailou made my heart melt. Nobody had ever done anything about Mailou, believing it was just something that didn't bother me as much as it did. But Ali'i saw right through me.

The water didn't push me back, like it did earlier, giving me a flicker of hope that I'd chosen the right timing to swim through. However, I reached a wall. No, not a wall... the column split into two. One went right and one went left.

Panic rose in me.

I'm running out of air. Which one should I take?

Before I could decide, a current of water rushed against me. Since I floated in the middle of the water, holding on to nothing, it was easy to get smashed against the side of the column entrance. Pain ripped across my back and neck, no doubt the reef and rock had sliced through something.

I turned around in haste, panicking for air. I needed to get back inside and get another breath, then decide which way to go from there.

Another current pulled me back as I swam towards the cave. *Oh no...* My lungs started tightening, my heart racing for air. I kicked, fighting the current, and grabbed rocks protruding from the side of the cave to push myself towards the cave.

The cold rush of water told me I could surface, and I did, gasping for air. I pulled myself onto the ground and coughed water. Tears fell once more as I held myself and cried.

"I'm so sorry Ali'i... I'm sorry Ua, Melika, Kona..." My voice repeated itself, like a sad song. But though I was sad and scared, I was not going to stop trying to get out of here.

. . .

I DON'T KNOW how many times I tried to swim out, but no matter which route I took to get out, I realized it was like a maze. I would come back to the cave, breathless, with new lacerations and gashes crossing my body. The current continued to toss me like a leaf in the wind. It slammed me against the reefy side of the column entrance, pushed me back into the cave, or lured me towards dead ends.

I finally slumped on the cave floor, too tired to sit up or even cry. My father was right. I wouldn't get out of here, not without getting smashed to pieces.

THE CLICKING NOISES STARTED AGAIN, which told me it might be night again. But the black crabs didn't come and attack me like they did the previous night. Instead, they moved around me, mostly by the water's edge. What were they doing?

After a while, my curiosity got to the best of me and I moved, cautiously, to get a better look. Though it was still pitch black, I could make out a strange, ever quiet, sound of... slurping? I touched the ground next to me, finding it warm.

Shuddering, I let out a breath. It was my blood. I was bleeding, and the blood trickled down the cave.

And the crabs are drinking my blood.

Spooked, I secluded myself away from them. This place *had* to be cursed, and perhaps, if I did die of the loss of blood or starvation here, the crabs would feed off me.

The overwhelming sensation came over me that I really might die here. I had no energy to escape anymore. Being thrashed about, with little to no air, and barely making it back into the cave, left me exhausted. I hadn't eaten anything, and my wounds, especially the lacerations, would not stop bleeding.

I buried my head in my knees and wanted to cry more, but no tears came.

CHAPTER TWENTY-SIX

A large splash of water awoke me from a restless slumber. A black crab had been licking my leg, but I had no energy to push it away.

"Who's there?" I tried to sit up, but exhaustion wore at me.

"Have you learned your lesson?"

My stomach tightened. My father had come to humble me.

"I'm dying," I said, feeling no need to answer his question. "You got what you wanted."

"You're not here to die... only if you accept the chief's hand. It's not that complicated, Ka'ala." I couldn't see my father, but I could feel the irritation and impatience in his voice. "Choose now, or stay here and die."

"I'd rather die than betray Ali'i."

Oponui laughed. "He might have gotten away with King Hua, but he won't ever get away with the sins he's committed against me."

I sat up, realizing my father probably knew everything that went on outside of here.

Ali'i is safe then... King Hua didn't believe that Ali'i cheated against Mailou. Of course the king would side with the captain. So where was Ali'i now? My heart yearned to ask questions, but, as it was my father I dealt with, I had to choose every word carefully.

"Did the king cancel the marriage?"

"'No, but that doesn't stop the chief of Olowalu from wanting you."

"Why does he want me so bad?"

"He's heard of you. You are the flower of Lanai, after all."

I shuddered at the name. I'd been called it several times in my life before, but I didn't know that the title reached the ears of men looking for wives.

"Where is Ali'i?"

"He's going to leave the island."

My heart might have stopped beating. "You're lying." My father would make something like that up.

"He is leaving. You didn't show enough interest in him, so you're not worth looking for." Had my father observed the way I acted around Ali'i? I blushed with shame, thinking that my disinterest in Ali'i *for* Ali'i had been so clear, even to others.

I didn't want to give up though, especially when I had so much to make right.

"He is not leaving. He's looking for me right now, I just know it." I paused. "Maybe he followed you here." At that, I raised my voice. "Ali'i! I'm here! Ali'i, I'm here in the Spouting Cave!"

"Silence you fool!" From the sound, Oponui got out of the water and approached, though I doubted he could see me.

"He did not follow, and even if he did, he'll drown trying to find the entrance."

"Where's Melika? You didn't even let me say goodbye to her, or Kona."

"They wouldn't want to say goodbye to you anyways–"

"Where are they?" I growled.

"That's no way to speak to your father."

I wanted to throw something at him, but I remained silent.

"The king has eyes for Melika and has privately offered me a handsome wage to take her to Hana. He says she will make a fine maid for one of his wives."

I gasped. "Father!"

"This is a wonderful opportunity for her. She will probably meet and marry someone of higher rank in Hana."

"She's only fifteen! How dare you sell her!" I wanted to stand, but I couldn't move, my aching body so tired from hunger and the effort I took trying to escape earlier.

"I didn't sell her–"

"You took a wage in exchange for your daughter." I needed to get out of here. Now. There was *no* way Melika was going with the king to Hana.

"Did the king leave yet?"

"No. There was some trouble the night of the wedding. Some of the Kohala warriors escaped from the prison, so it's stalling their return trip."

For the first time, hope came into my heart. So Kona was able to save a few of the warriors–not all of them, but enough to give them some extra time. But I heard the conch shell blown, meaning...

"Did another ali'i come to Lanai?"

"'Ae. You probably heard the blowing of the shell. It echoed all throughout the island. Prince Kekoa is here."

My heart leaped even more with hope. Another person to help us! Prince Kekoa, King Hua's son, was on our side. He was the one responsible for getting the refugees to Kona for safety. Perhaps between him, Ua, Kona, and Melika, they'd be able to get the Kohala warriors free. And who knew? Maybe 'Eleu was on the island too. If she was, she could take all the refugees, and the warriors out of there.

"Where's Kona?" I changed the subject.

"Your brother has disappeared. I haven't seen him since the wedding day." My father muttered something to himself then added, "He will be severely punished for what he has done. The chief has called off the betrothal for his daughter."

More hope! That meant Kona was truly free to marry Ua.

I was glad my father couldn't see the gleeful look on my face. One more question remained. "So when will the king leave the island?"

"Why does this concern you, daughter?" The term *daughter* sounded annoyed and rather bitter.

"Because I'm going to die here. It'd be nice to know what's going on outside before I die, and to know that my siblings are safe."

"Melika is—"

"Not if you sell her to the king. You know he indulges in debauchery and gives beautiful wives and young women to his favorite companions."

Silence.

"You would sell your daughter—her innocence, her dignity—for wages?" I wanted to spit in disgust, but I left the question in the air. It echoed off the walls, and I was grateful for it for once. The echoes made the question ominous, as if to awaken my father to morality and to the role he should have in protecting his children.

"I have no more use or time to talk to you." The sound of water meant Oponui had stepped back in. Should I follow? What if I couldn't keep up, and I drowned in the column?

No, I have to try.

"Melika deserves a better life," I said. "As do I."

"This is your last chance, Ka'ala." He ignored my words completely. "Either agree to marry the chief of Olowalu, or stay here and die."

Could I lie and say, *Sure I'll marry the chief?* Just to get out of here?

I hesitated.

"Swear it on your life, and I'll take you out." Of course Oponui would make me do something so drastic.

I remained quiet for a stretching amount of time. "No. I won't swear to marry that chief. I'm already married to the man I love."

"A man who has no love for you," Oponui sneered. "Fine. Die here." He didn't say goodbye, but dove into the water.

Without hesitating, I rushed into the water, every muscle and bone protesting. The crabs that had surrounded me, inched away in surprise at my sudden movement. I dove in, trying to see my father's figure, but darkness enveloped me.

It's night. I found the column and reached my hands out, hoping to touch my father's foot. I felt the rush of water from the kicks he made and I followed. When we reached the part of the column that split into two, a current thrashed me against the side of the cave. It was so unexpected, because everything had gone smoothly following my father up until this point, that I gasped for air.

Panic overwhelmed me once more. I didn't know which way my father took because the water pushed me. I couldn't see anything, and I was running out of air.

I turned around and swam as fast as I could out of the column. When the icy water brushed my skin, I surfaced and coughed for air.

Slamming the water with my fist, I let out a cry. Once again, I couldn't get out.

CHAPTER TWENTY-SEVEN

*A*fter a few more futile efforts to escape, I lay on the rocks, wondering if these were my last breaths of life. It felt like it. Every breath came out painfully shallow and hoarse. My stomach tightened with hunger, and I'd lost so much blood from trying to escape, and trying to defend myself, that I wasn't surprised when consciousness began to fade in and out.

I caught myself thinking about Aliʻi, my siblings, or Ua, and then everything would fade away, meaning I was passing out. Between passing in and out of consciousness, I sent out silent pleas for help to Aliʻi.

I still love you, I thought, wondering if he felt the same as me. Because if Oponui was right, then Aliʻi would be long gone by now. But if he wasn't, and if I had a second chance, I would make everything–*everything,* from caring more about my siblings and Ua, to being grateful for the sanctuary I created, and especially loving Aliʻi with no lies or secrets–right.

· · ·

THE SOUND of muffled voices awoke me. The slurping noises of the crabs continued to echo off the cave walls, along with the roaring of the outside waves. I'd become so accustomed to the darkness, I wondered what light even looked like anymore.

I tried to blink, but every part of me felt crusty, sticky, and cold. Did I die? Was I hearing the voices of those on the other side?

No sooner had I decided that maybe I, indeed, had died, then a big splash sounded in the cave, followed by someone taking a gulp of air.

It's not Oponui. It sounded too young. Another splash sounded, followed by a girl taking a deep breath.

My heart leaped out of my chest. *It can't be...*

"Ka'ala, are you here?" Ali'i's voice was full of panic and alarm.

"She's here, I know it." Ua's voice.

Another splash, with someone taking a deep breath. "Move aside, the king is coming. We've got less than five minutes to get out." It had been a while since I'd heard this voice. It sounded similar to Ua's voice, but in a masculine way. It had to be Keawe, her brother, who used to stop by my family's hut and ask questions of Oponui.

Another splash and gulp of air followed. *The king is coming,* Keawe had said. My hair stood on end. King Hua was here.

"Ka'ala—" I could hear Ali'i's wet footsteps as he searched the cave. Ua and Keawe must have been searching too, because they kept hitting things or stubbing their toes as they walked about.

"I'm—" My voice came out softer than a whisper.

"Ka'ala!" Strong arms found me, pulling me into an embrace. I wanted to cry, but no tears came out. Ali'i was breathless, his heart hammering so fast and hard, I could feel it beating out his chest. I embraced him back, and in that exchange, felt the silent love that was between us.

A light slowly lit up the cave, and I gasped to see King Hua holding an orb. Everything that had been dark was now apparent. The cave had several nooks and holes for the black crabs to hide, and the black cave walls looked even more ominous. Green mildew-like forms grew over the rocks.

"We need to go," Keawe said, stepping back into the water. "Before the tide turns."

I had been standing, but my legs gave way. Ali'i caught me, scooping me into his strong arms. I had no strength to hold my own weight, and my head and arms dangled as if I were dead.

"Ka'ala..." Ua took my hand, tears in her eyes.

"She's dead." King Hua said. "And if she's not, she will be soon. No sense waiting around for her to die. We must go."

Ali'i hesitated.

"She's not fit to swim through these caverns. Leave her be," the king finished.

Based on Ua's tears, even she believed I was dead. When Ali'i continued to stand there, staring at me, his eyes wide, his heart pounding, I tried to move, but no part of my body would cooperate. Consciousness faded in and out. Perhaps I was dying.

"You need..." My emotions swelled within me. "Save yourself, Ali'i..."

"She speaks as a ghost. Come, captain, there are plenty of other women to wed." The king's voice grew impatient. "You can marry this one here. She's from Lanai and looks similar enough to Ka'ala. Come, we must go."

I could feel Ua's resentment against the king at that moment, but she kissed my hand and stepped into the water.

"We really need to go, or our chances won't open until... at least two days' time." Keawe stated the facts, increasing the urgency that they needed to get out of there.

My heart ached for Ali'i. If I was going to die anyway, I didn't want him dying here with me. He deserved to live a full life.

"Go–" I said to him, but, as if realizing something, he turned to the king.

"I'm not leaving her."

A tense silence filled the cavern long after Ali'i's words finished echoing.

"You... will disobey me?" The king was obviously not accustomed to being turned down, and especially by one of his finest captains.

"I've served you for years, and I have obeyed every one of your orders. But I can't leave Ka'ala. I love no one more than I love her. I'm not leaving."

"Then you will throw your life away for a girl?" King Hua's face twisted in confusion.

"'Ae. I have served you faithfully, but my service ends here." Ali'i sat, still cradling me in his arms.

I tried to turn my head and look at the king, Ua, and Keawe, but I could only focus on Ali'i. He looked so handsome, yet exhausted.

"We must go," Keawe cut in. "Now or never."

"Goodbye Ka'ala." Ua's voice was thick with tears. "And Ali'i. May you both rest in peace." She took a deep breath and followed Keawe out.

The king lingered behind, staring at us for a moment, still not believing that his captain would choose a girl over his own life. The king was right though—there were *plenty* of beautiful women that Aliʻi could marry. But the captain's choice was made.

"Very well." The king's tone surprised me. Part of it was full of emotion, something he never exhibited. Was there, possibly, someone feeling under the barbaric face he put up?

The king took a deep breath and dove under the water, taking the light with him.

Darkness encompassed us and Aliʻi pulled me closer to him, kissing my face and taking slow, deep breaths.

"Kaʻala..."

"I'm so... sorry." I struggled to speak.

"Shh... Save your energy."

"We can't get out."

"Let's not talk about it. Let's just enjoy being together." He shuddered. "I looked everywhere for you. I'm sorry I didn't find you sooner." Hearing his voice, feeling his warmth, and being encompassed in his arms filled me with gratitude and hope. His love gave me a boost.

Aliʻi would do anything for me... I love him.

"I love you Kaʻala." It was as if Aliʻi read my thoughts. He kissed me on the lips, and I used whatever strength I could muster to kiss him back. The captain pulled away too soon, adjusting so I sat on the ground next to him. I rested my head against his arm, but he gently pushed me away.

A pang struck my chest. Did he decide he didn't want me?

"Just rest. Ua and Keawe snuck food, water, and kapa in here. I just have to find it."

My heart welled up in more gratitude. Even if Ua believed I had died, she didn't abandon me, or leave me with nothing. So that's what she and Keawe were doing, walking around the cave? They probably *were* trying to find me, but also snuck in some food and drink.

"It's so hard to see—ouch!" Ali'i went silent for a moment, and my breath caught.

"Are you alright?"

"'Ae." Anger filled his tone.

"Ali'i?"

"I'm sorry. I'm just... I could kill Oponui."

"Ali'i..."

"I know. Please rest."

I obeyed, knowing that I shouldn't exert myself by talking. Already my heart beats felt fainter and fainter. After a while, the captain pulled me into his lap, and my head rested on his warm chest.

"Can you drink?"

Water sounded amazing. I nodded, and though he couldn't see, he could feel my movement against him. A gourd was placed to my lips and I drank slowly. I didn't realize how parched I felt because the other injuries on my body felt worse. But as the water went down my throat, a soothing energy ran through me.

"Here..." Something salty was placed on my lips and I took a bite.

Aku. Sun-dried fish. Luckily it wasn't too hard to chew, and, slowly but surely, Ali'i fed me more food: some sweet potato, haupia, poi, and fish.

With each bite, more energy returned to me. When I finished, I wrapped my arms around Ali'i, while he wrapped his arms around me, and we said nothing.

We didn't need to say anything, as the captain's actions spoke louder than any words. He loved me. He was here. And we would either die or live together.

There was no place I would ever want to be, but in his arms. *I love you Ali'i. I will do anything for you. Anything.*

After a while of soaking in each other's company, the fact that we were both alive and *together,* Ali'i cleared his throat. "We still have time."

"Time for what?"

"Time to save the Kohala warriors."

I sat up, realizing that much of my strength had returned. I still felt tired, but well enough to hold myself up.

"Kekoa is here on Lanai. He's stalling time while Kona figures out a way to free the warriors. Ua and I have been searching for you. It took a lot of convincing to get your siblings to stay at their posts, instead of blowing their covers and looking for you." I could see it in my head: Melika and Kona, my brother and sister, aching to find me, but also wanting to tend to their duties. They were right to trust Ali'i, and, perhaps they knew that Ali'i coming to find me was exactly what I needed. I could have peace of mind knowing that Kona worked to free the warriors, while Melika tended to the sanctuary.

"How long has it been since the wedding?"

"Two days." I shivered. If Ali'i had come any later, I probably would have died of dehydration and starvation without even realizing it. "It took long enough to get the answer from Oponui. Luckily Ua's brother, Keawe, knew exactly where the Spouting Cave was." He kissed my forehead. "I know you're wounded, so my first priority is getting you out of here and tending to your wounds."

"And then?"

"And then we need to get to those warriors."

"Is Melika alright?"

"'Ae. She's been up at the sanctuary. Ua said one of the warriors is in bad condition." These little tidbits of information said more than Ali'i meant them to say. First of all, Melika was taking charge. I should have trusted and believed she would, because she was more than capable. Second, *Ua,* of all people, who once seemed dismissive and untrusting of Ali'i, told the captain about the warrior's condition at the sanctuary. That meant she trusted him, and knew he shared our secret. No doubt Kona, Kekoa, and Melika also trusted him too.

That meant Ali'i was a part of our crew. I stroked his chest, loving him, his presence, the fact that we were on the same team. Why did it take a near-death experience for me to realize this?

"I'm thinking that if we can get out, everyone will think we're dead. So we need to just stay hidden, help free the warriors, and get some of the other refugees—especially that wounded one—out of here."

"Right." I loved hearing Ali'i's plans to save the people. It made my heart feel all mushy, like I couldn't stop gushing about everything he said or did.

"Ka'ala?"

"Mmhm?" I snuggled into him, feeling deliriously happy, yet anxious. Many questions remained. How would we get out of here? What if someone saw us?

It was weird to think that the island of Lanai thought me and Ali'i dead. But, in a way, it started making sense. If they thought we were dead, we could move about as we pleased. Ali'i had no obligation to King Hua. But what about the sanctuary?

Melika will take care of it...

Perhaps, after the war, we could return to Lanai.

Or maybe never at all. Ali'i and I could sail to another island and start fresh, both of us. We'd be nothing more than a superstition, of lovers who died in Spouting Cave. I would miss my siblings though, dearly.

Ali'i chuckled, and I felt warm all over at the sound of it. "You alright?"

"Now that you're here, 'ae." I kissed his cheek.

"I know, but we can't celebrate yet. Not until we're out of here." He stroked my arm, but I could tell he was extra cautious, due to the wounds across my body.

"Right." I wiped my eyes and tried to focus. "What did Keawe say about getting out?"

"The current won't work in our favor for at least two days. There are only a few windows of time that make it possible to come in and out of the cave."

I sighed. "That's too long."

"I know, especially since the king is heading back to town at this moment. If Kekoa and Kona haven't freed the warriors by now, then they'll need our help."

"Why?"

"The warriors are surrounded by at least a dozen of the king's soldiers. Not to mention all the men are severely tied up. Their canoes have been burned, and so they'll need to steal other canoes on Lanai to get out of here."

"Alright..." I could picture it all in my head. Kekoa and Kona, waiting for the opportune moment to get the warriors free. Or, they could be devising a plan, like distracting the guards while one of them snuck into the group of prisoners. I trusted both of them, but it would be vastly easier to have more than just two of them at work.

"With the king's enchanted torch, I was actually studying the cave. There are no holes, and no way out... except the entrance," Ali'i continued. I admired his keenness on not only trying to find me, but studying the cave.

"I've tried swimming it. It's impossible without knowing where to go."

"It was hard even following Keawe in here..."

"Wait." I said, clarity now coming over me. The lack of food and water, as well as my open wounds and fatigue, had exhausted me. But with Ali'i here, and having had some sustenance, I started to feel more like myself, despite my broken body. "The king... what was that light he had?"

"It was an enchanted light. I don't know where he got it, but it was made by the mermaids. It's what they use to light up their kingdoms in the deep sea."

"A mermaid light?" I started breathing fast and the captain sat up, alarmed.

"What's wrong?"

"A mermaid—of course!" I wanted to hit my head against the side of the cave for my stupidity. Why hadn't I thought of mermaids sooner? I had been so overwhelmed by my grief, and so determined to get out alone, when all I had to do was ask for help!

"Ka'ala?" Anxiety coated Ali'i's voice, as he couldn't see my expression or know that I was shaking from excitement and hope, not fear.

"I know how we're going to get out of here," I said. "I have a friend, and she owes me a favor..."

CHAPTER TWENTY-EIGHT

"Moana!" My voice echoed off the cave walls, and the once quiet pool of water in the cave began to lap against the rocky sides. No doubt the ocean had heard the call and now sent the message to the mermaid.

"Who's that?" Ali'i asked, shifting as I sat up so we weren't so cuddly against each other when the mermaid came. The last thing I wanted to do was make her uncomfortable. She was the only mermaid I'd ever spoken to, and I couldn't mess this up. Not when this was, quite possibly, our only way out.

"Remember the day you first saw me?"

"I'll never forget it." I could feel Ali'i smiling in the darkness. "You're the most beautiful woman I've ever seen. I couldn't help but stare."

The sweetness of his words made me want to melt, but I composed myself. "Thanks... I'd gone to see the fishermen along the reefs, but they weren't there. Instead, I found a mermaid stuck in a net."

Ali'i remained silent, and I wish I could've read his

facial expression, but, of course, the cave was darker than night.

"I helped her out, and she said to call her if I ever found myself needing help."

"Perhaps we are in the favor of the gods after all." Aliʻi kissed my forehead, then pulled away as a light came from the underwater cave entrance.

My heart pounded against my chest. This was our chance! The light grew until it came over the surface, illuminating the cave. It was much brighter than the king's orb of light, and cast a warm, golden glow on everything.

Golden-brown, sun-kissed hair floated around the shoulders of the teal-eyed mermaid. She took in the surroundings then focused on us. A look of amusement crossed her face.

"Kaʻala, I didn't expect for you to be here."

"Nor did I," I said, trying to stand. Aliʻi helped me, and we made our way to the water's edge.

Moana let the orb of light float on the water and folded her tanned arms. "What did those humans do this time?"

"My father put me in here," I said. "Everyone thinks I'm dead."

"And you look close to it." She had a silvery voice, strong like the waves, yet deep and melodic like the song of the sea. "Is this your lover?"

"My husband, Aliʻi." It felt weird to say the word, but it was true. The captain and I were married.

"That's sweet. So... I'm assuming you want help getting out of here?" Moana looked around. "The crabs are whispering to each other. They're saying you both won't last long here."

I exchanged looks with Aliʻi, and we must have thought

the same thing: mermaids could hear the sea critters talking? Fascinating.

Moana swam to the edge of the pool as I approached. "They're already making plans to feast on your flesh." Now she made a face. "I don't know if you can get out of here with all those wounds, protector girl. You're going to need some healing salve."

"I don't have any, and I don't have much time. My siblings and friends need my help."

"Does this have to do with all those burning canoes?"

"'Ae. A bunch of Kohala warriors have been taken prisoners," Ali'i said, as I was nearly out of breath from talking and getting to the water's edge at the same time.

"I see." Moana made a face. "You'd think after all these years the wars would be over..."

"But our priority is getting out of here first," I said, though I wondered if she'd be willing to help us free the Kohala warriors. "Can you help us?"

"Of course." She nodded to me. "You saved my life, and I'll save yours."

"Thank you."

"So here's what you need to know. The currents are very strong right now, and they're pushing into the cave, the opposite direction of where we need to go." She played with her glass-looking orb of light, tossing it into the air and catching it. The brightness of it made me dizzy. "I'm used to swimming against the current. In fact, I'm one of the strongest swimmers around but..." She eyed me. "Swimming against the current means that it might take a little longer to get out of here. So you'll have to hold your breath longer. Think you can do that?"

"I don't have much of a choice."

Ali'i's hand slipped around my waist, steadying me as I

sat and put my legs into the water. The salty water bit my wounds, causing a stinging, then numbing, sensation.

"I think I should take him out of here first," Moana said, pointing to Ali'i. "The waves are really choppy against the cliff, and you might not have the strength to pull yourself out."

Moana had a point, and I didn't argue. Ali'i looked worried, and I understood. Why would he want to leave me behind, alone, once more? But Moana was absolutely right. Once I surfaced outside of this cave, I probably wouldn't have strength to swim, much less to pull myself onto the cliff side.

"Sounds like a plan?" she asked.

I nodded. "It's perfect. We just really need to get out of here."

"It's quite dismal in here," Moana said, rubbing her arms. "Already the cave walls are speaking of you, as though you're dead."

"We're not dead," Ali'i said, then kissed my forehead. "Not yet at least." He took my hand. "Are you going to be alright?"

I nodded, my eagerness to leave overwhelming everything else. We were *so* close. I'd felt utterly hopeless over the last few days, thinking I couldn't get out of here. But there had been hope: Ali'i, Moana, my siblings, Ua, and Prince Kekoa. They were all working, in some way, to save me and others. I had more help and support than I ever realized.

"You won't be separated for too long," Moana reassured us. Ali'i got into the water and Moana took his hands. "Hold on tight, understand?"

He looked at me, then her, and nodded. I could tell he wasn't completely comfortable—and nor was I. Mermaids had such a sketchy reputation, we had no reason to trust them. But I had no other choice. Moana was my only option now, and I had saved her life before...

"Take a deep, long breath. Ready?"

Once again, he nodded. I watched them, grateful that Moana would leave her light behind so I could see. The two descended under the water and disappeared.

I reached for the orb and held it as I waited, my heart pounding. Would Aliʻi be able to hold his breath? Would I?

I studied the orb, fascinated by the hard, clear outer shell of it. The light inside was too bright to stare at for long, but I did notice that there seemed to be water in the inside and... fish?

Glowing fish. I'd never seen anything like it. The orb was a fish bowl, with a tiny hole at the top. Two tiny golden fish swam within, and I marveled. What other magical wonders did the underwater mermaid world hold?

The golden glowing fish kept me distracted and my anxiety down until there was a splash, and the rainbow tail of Moana peeked up behind her. She grinned. "It was a success. He's out on the cliff waiting for you now. Are you ready?"

"ʻAe." Relief flooded through me. Aliʻi was out of here, and I would be too.

"Like the light?"

"It's fascinating, ʻae. King Hua had one."

"He stole it from some mermaids in Lahaina. That's where most of the mermaids live, anyway."

"And you live there too?" I got into the water and felt Moana's strong grip on my arm to keep me from sinking.

"I live in Kaʻanapali."

"What are you doing all the way out here?"

"Visiting with the whales. They're my favorite."

"Do you speak to them?" I thought of how she heard the crabs communicating with each other.

"I try..." She made a face, as though she said too much, then continued. "I love hearing about their travels. One day I'd like to go north with them, experience their migration and the waters up there." She paused at the cave entrance. "Anyway, I need you to take the biggest breath of your life, understand? Don't think about holding your breath, just focus on something else, something pleasant."

"Alright."

Moana raised an eyebrow, as if not believing me. "Are you alright holding the light?"

"ʻAe."

The mermaid took both my arms with a firm grip. "Let's go."

I did take a deep breath, knowing if I didn't, I could possibly drown. As we went underwater, I focused my thoughts on Aliʻi. I could see him, waiting on the cliff side, ready to help me. We were so close to getting out of here, a narrow escape from death.

I knew that the mermaid and I moved fast, because the water rushed all around me. Moana pushed against the current, made a few crazy turns, and kept going. My body, already tired from overexertion, began to collapse on itself. I needed air.

The pressure around me began to lessen, and I knew we were getting close to the surface. But the desperation for air was strong.

Air... My body panicked and everything went black.

"Kaʻala!"

I coughed and choked on water, then felt strong arms holding me.

"Thank goodness..." Ali'i's voice sounded strained for a moment, and my heart welled with emotion. Did he think I had died?

A relieved sigh came from the mermaid, and I knew we made it out. I opened my eyes, looking up at the starry night sky. I wanted to cry, never taking a view like this for granted again. We sat on the edge of a cliff, the waves brushing up against the sides. Moana sat on the cliff too, her tail part way in the water.

"Well that's sweet," she said, getting ready to leave.

"Wait–" I pulled away from Ali'i, but still held his hand. "Thank you, Moana."

She nodded, her long hair plastered to her body. "Already I hear the chants and songs about your death."

I listened, hearing nothing but the wind and the beating of the waves.

"They're telling stories about you on Lanai, the two lovers who died in the Spouting Cave." Moana blinked and looked at the swirling waters. "They're calling it the Spouting Cave of Ka'ala."

I marveled, while Ali'i squeezed my hand. Everyone thought me dead. And I'd have to keep it that way, especially if we were to complete our last task.

"Good luck out there," I said as the mermaid eased into the water. "I mean, with the whales and stuff. I hope you get to migrate with them at least once."

She smiled and nodded. "I do too. We will probably never see one another again, Ka'ala of Lanai." She tipped her head. "But I wish the best of luck to you both." With that, she dove into the water, the last sight of her being the rainbow tail.

"That was different," Ali'i said, then pulled me into his arms. "But I'm grateful. Your goodness, once again, has saved us."

I remained quiet, realizing that my commitment to *protect* people had saved us. Meanwhile, when I lost my vision of my motto, I lost everything. I wasn't meant to kill, and that also included killing King Hua.

I took a few deep breaths, then met Ali'i's eyes. "We need to get to town as soon as we can."

"'Ae. Do you think you can hold onto my back?"

I wasn't completely sure, but we had no other options. I climbed onto Ali'i's back, feeling rather shy, after all we'd been through. I remembered our intimate kiss before Oponui barged in on us, and my cheeks warmed.

Ali'i must have noticed, because he glanced at me. "Everything alright?" He started climbing the cliff side, and my heart, once again, felt mushy with gratitude. But our plight wasn't over yet. My siblings and the prisoners needed my help.

"Just thinking..."

"About?"

"About us."

"What about us?" He smiled as he climbed, and my stomach lurched at how high we were, with nothing to hold us if we fell. But I trusted him. Completely. He wouldn't let us fall.

"Our future... our past."

"I don't want to forget our past," the captain said as we reached the top and he slid over, breathing fast as he caught his breath. "But I do want to keep moving forward."

"Me too. No more secrets."

"No more." He held my hand as we started walking towards town. We had a ways to go, but, filled with determination, we kept a brisk pace. I couldn't help but feel the lightness in my step.

I'm alive. Ali'i is here. We're in love.

"Where will we go?" I asked.

"Everyone thinks we're dead..." Ali'i shrugged. "So where do you want to go?"

"I don't want to leave Melika, or the sanctuary but..." I grew quiet, knowing that Melika would be fine without me.

"If King Hua finds out I survived, he'll want me in his service again." Ali'i shook his head. "I think everything happens for a reason. Since everyone thinks we're dead, we are free, you know?"

"But the wars, the people..." My voice trailed off.

Melika will be fine. I had to trust that, and she proved to me, time and time again, that she was responsible enough.

"I know you've worked hard to build your sanctuary," Ali'i said, "But you have to protect yourself too. If your father finds out you're alive, he might as well kill you himself. And if he finds out I'm alive, he will probably stop at nothing to kill me."

Though a part of my heart ached, thinking that I would leave all of this behind—the life I knew—another part of me looked forward with anticipation.

I'm not alone. I would have Ali'i. We could start a new life somewhere else, and leave this behind. Of course I'd want to see my siblings, but I'd have to return undercover. It wasn't like I'd done undercover operations for years...

I chuckled and Ali'i glanced at me, puzzled.

"You're right. We need to help as much as we can tonight, and then leave."

"We'll find a place to call home." The captain squeezed my hand and I stopped him on the path, pulling him close.

"Home is where *you* are, Ali'i."

He grinned and kissed me, then we continued in a happy silence.

My FREEDOM, and the food Aliʻi gave me, had offered some strength, but I could feel it waning as we got close to town. For a while, Aliʻi carried me, but I insisted on walking.

Every bone and muscle protested, but I pushed myself. It would be worth it.

"If everything has gone as planned, Melika will still be at the sanctuary, while Kekoa is in town, and Kona is in his hiding place. Ua should also be at the sanctuary by now. She, her brother, and the king had a group of fine warriors and seamen on the canoe, so I imagine they're back by now."

Excitement filled me as we approached the sanctuary. Melika, keeping watch on the porch, covered her mouth to keep from screaming. She ran straight to me, embracing me so tightly, I thought I would suffocate.

"You're alive," she breathed, tears streaming down her cheeks.

I held my sister, forever grateful for her. "I'm alive, and we're going to get this all figured out."

"Do you have a plan?" Melika asked as she wiped her face.

"No," I said, taking one of Aliʻi's and Melika's hands in my own. "But together, we can all come up with one."

CHAPTER TWENTY-NINE

*P*erspiration lined my brow and the heavy breaths coming from my chest didn't pass Ua. She gently took my arm.

"Are you sure about this?" she asked, sweat beginning to form on her own forehead. The breeze had died down since we started to carry out the plans we all made together, leaving the night hot and muggy.

"I don't trust anyone more in this world than you guys."

Her look softened and she squeezed my arm. "Thanks Ka'ala. I'm so glad you're alright. We really thought we'd lost you back there."

"If it weren't for you, I wouldn't be here." I smiled at her, but the tension rose inside of me. We were far from celebrating, for the night was still young. And those warriors couldn't free themselves. Not to mention, Kona and Ua needed to have their marriage confirmed by Prince Kekoa, an ali'i, before they could sail off together.

There was much to do tonight, but I wanted to appreciate every moment. Ua was right. I had almost died in that cave. If Ali'i didn't find out the location from my father, and if Ua hadn't asked her brother for help in getting inside the cave, I might have died from starvation and thirst.

We crouched behind a large fern bush, listening to the noises coming from the king's camp. A group of Hana warriors sat around a large fire. From the sound of their slurred voices and loud laughter, they were obviously drunk.

King Hua sat at the head of the circle, his arm around a young woman's shoulder. I recognized her as someone from the island, but I didn't personally know her. She was not drunk, and looked most uncomfortable. The girl kept looking around in desperation, and I wondered if she was a random young woman, picked (or maybe even kidnapped) from the town, who wanted nothing to do with this.

Or maybe her father sold her off to Hua. My stomach tightened at the thought of Melika being sold to King Hua. I wouldn't let it happen, and committed to speak with Kekoa about it as soon as I could.

But first, the prisoners...

Ua made a face. "He probably doesn't need us to distract him..."

"He seems bored with her though..."

The king kept coaxing the young woman, but she withdrew, her eyes wide in terror. My heart went out to her.

Memories rushed back, from the night when we tricked the king. Ua and I had only been sixteen years old, and Ua played her part well. She acted drunk and sat next to the king, giggling and looking up at him through her lashes. Since he was truly drunk, it was easy for him to take the bait.

Ua led him away from the safety and security of his

warriors. None of them even followed, probably used to the king participating in debauchery and promiscuity. And that's when I tried to stab him.

Not this time, Ka'ala. I was beyond that. We weren't here to kill him, but to distract him, giving Ali'i, Prince Kekoa, and Kona time to free the warriors and get them all out of here, unsuspected.

The prince sat in the circle, as expected. He and Kona came to the sanctuary a little after Ali'i and I arrived. Pride rose in my chest for the initiative and courage my siblings and friends had taken to gather and make plans, even if they weren't sure of my survival.

The sanctuary will be fine without me. It would.

The prince wore a perpetual somber look on his face, and I couldn't blame him. He had been born to the wicked king, and he could do nothing about it. He had tried to convince his father to end the war, but he bore a terrible scar for his effort.

He stared at the fire, his green eyes reflecting the flames. Kekoa occasionally glanced at the king, the darkness of the forest around him, or the warriors.

They were all getting quite drunk, and the prince continued to motion to the servants, bribing them to bring out more kava. Since the warriors and soldiers didn't often receive this much kava, they heartily partook. The king did too, but showed obvious signs of annoyance at the young woman.

He took her hand and kissed it, and it seemed that she had to muster every fiber of her being to not pull her hand away. The king then played with her dark hair, and leaned in to kiss her cheek.

"That's enough," I said, and Ua grabbed my hand before I stepped out.

"I'll distract him," she said.

"He's going to recognize you."

"Of course he is. I was the one who brought us to the cave—" Ua started to say.

"No, I mean from last time."

The drums and drunken laughter covered our whispers as we remained in the darkness, hidden from view.

Ua shook her head. "He won't. It's been years. We've grown."

"Ua..."

"We have no choice. I feel as sick and sad for that girl as you do."

My best friend and I looked back at the young woman, who grew more and more uncomfortable with the king's advances.

"We have to do something. And with the king distracted, it will give Kekoa an opportunity to slip out, unnoticed."

Right. Kekoa hadn't left yet, but he needed to. Ali'i and Kona were hidden near the prisoners, waiting until Kekoa arrived. The prince would bring kava to the guards protecting the prisoners, and invite them to join the fire.

"You have to be convincing though," Melika had said in the planning session earlier, delighted to have finally met Kekoa in person, though he showed no romantic interest in her (as he shouldn't, since she was only fifteen). "You'll have to really convince them to join you, because I doubt they'd easily leave their post."

"I'll be able to manage," the prince had replied, his voice even and low.

"Will you follow me?" Ua asked, already crouching and moving to get closer to the king.

"'Ae, of course." I would never let my friend down. She

303

had trusted me this far, and I usually trusted her. But this was risky.

My heart pumped in anticipation as Ua stepped from the darkness and joined the circle. The prince did no more than glance at her, and then continued his distant, distracted gaze into the fire.

Ua sat next to the king and took his arm, which only encouraged him. Immediately, his attention shifted from the poor innocent young lady, to Ua.

My best friend was beautiful, and charming, but she was also poorly dressed and wore modest attire, making her look nothing like the other girl. The other girl had to have some sort of higher class because of the fine kapa she wore.

The look of relief on the girl's face eased my fears for a moment.

But now the girl and I watched as Ua openly flirted with the king. His eyes gazed on her in the disgusting way they did years ago.

Kekoa slipped into the darkness with gourds of kava in hand. Not one of the guards or soldiers noticed.

Ua pulled the king's hand, beckoning him to follow her.

The young woman gave Ua a warning look, but if only the girl knew what Ua and I were capable of... she shouldn't be worried.

Don't get too confident. Anything could happen. Last time Ua and I easily stole the king away–away from the safety of his guards and soldiers. This time things could have changed.

We hadn't discussed this at all, and Ua still didn't know I'd discarded my previous plans to kill Hua.

Perhaps Ua hasn't. The fierce look in her eyes, of determination and anger, told me that maybe she intended on drawing him away so we could kill him.

But I'm not going to kill the king... I'm a protector, not a killer... I had learned in the cave, right?

I moved in the darkness, alarmed by how quickly Ua drew the king away into the forest. He was drunk as ever, stumbling and cursing as she pulled him into the forest.

"I'll show you a secret place," I heard her say, and my stomach tightened even more. The entire moment felt strange, because this had happened once before.

But things never happened the same twice... or did they?

Maybe this really is our chance... a chance to end the war, to end the tyranny, and to restore peace throughout the islands... I glanced at the ocean sparkling under the moonlight, hoping that Kekoa, Ali‘i, and Kona were freeing the prisoners now.

But if we killed the king, none of their actions would be necessary.

Ua pulled the king into a clearing and he fell to the ground, sick as a dog from too much kava. He vomited into the bushes, then took the gourd from Ua's hand and took a deep swing of it. Ua watched him, clearly disgusted. I could tell she must have stolen one of the gourds of kava, and put something in it to strengthen the hallucinating effects.

The king fell to the ground, laughing, unable to pull himself up.

"Oh come on," she said, the irritation clear on her face. "You disgusting, wicked man..."

"Ua..." I whispered, but didn't want to reveal myself too soon. We could have been followed, but, as far as I'd been watching, nobody had come after the king and Ua.

Not yet.

Ua looked around the clearing, and, once satisfied that only I watched, took the gourd and knocked it expertly at the side of the king's head. Both drunk and knocked out, he went silent.

It felt like air escaped me.

This is it... we could try killing the king again.

My best friend didn't wait for me and, instead, pulled ropes from her bag, dragging the king's body into the darkness and binding him.

Help her. But I was frozen in place. I had decided not to kill the king, and that my priorities and loyalties to others were more important.

But we have the opportunity... right now. Could we try stabbing him again?

Not without the high priest.

As if on cue, a figure crouched in the bushes, and I ran straight towards him. He would not surprise attack my best friend, not while I had something to say about it.

I tripped the man. Before he could stand back up, I grabbed his hands, jumped on his back, and placed my knife to the back of his neck.

"Don't move," I said, and my heart pounded. It was the high priest.

Ua moved in the darkness, though the high priest couldn't see her. He didn't see either of us, unless he saw my face.

"What is the king's secret to invincibility?" I asked, and when the high priest remained quiet, I pressed the knife against his skin.

He whimpered, and I realized he was afraid. Deathly afraid. *I could kill him right now.* Because if Ali'i was right, the high priest put spells and wards of protection on King Hua. The high priest also put spells on the warriors and soldiers, making them protect the king at all costs.

This had to stop.

But I made a commitment to Ali'i. I remembered who I was...

My best friend paused to watch, probably wondering if she should intervene.

"Tell me now," I said, quiet enough that nobody could hear. The island breeze picked up, causing a chill to run down my sweaty spine.

"It's the spells."

"How do you break the spells?"

"They can't be broken..."

"There's always a way to undo a spell–tell me now," I ordered, pressing his hands against his back, but keeping the knife in place. I didn't want to knick his skin, no matter how much I hated the man. He let out a little cry, and I could sense the anxiety pounding his chest.

"Only the gods can decide–"

"Hurry up or this knife will go straight through your neck." My voice didn't sound like my own, and it shocked me. It sounded demonic, venomous...

This is not me. I was not a killer, but a protector.

"Only I can undo them," he blurted.

"How?"

"Time. Magic."

"Can I just kill you to undo them?"

Silence, then, "No, no, no... it's impossible."

"He's lying." Ua's voice came from the darkness. "Kill him, and then let's kill the king."

Sweat coated my arms and my hands shook.

Ua is right. We could end this right now... But I wasn't a killer. I'd never been one, and never wanted to be one. That had become clear to me in the darkest moment of my life, when I thought I would die in the cave. When Ua and I trained under her grandfather, he told us, specifically, that our skills were to protect people, not kill.

But these are wicked men. We could end the war.

"I'll do it." Ua intervened, stepping forward, knife glistening in her hand. I could see the buildup of hatred in her eyes, the many years we saved refugees, listened to their stories, and risked our own lives for others.

For so long I thought the anger against Hua had only consumed me. But obviously it had taken its toll on my best friend.

I can't let her do this—she's not a murderer either. Though it was unfair, and though she had to do things unconventionally, like eloping with Kona, she would have to live with someone else's blood on her hands. This wasn't her.

And it wasn't me.

She raised her knife to stab the high priest, but I let go of him to grab her hand.

"Wait—" I started, and she met my eyes, alarmed and... angry.

The high priest took his opportunity to escape, scrambling away from me and mumbling strange words under his breath.

"He's casting a spell!" Ua said, running towards him.

I couldn't let her kill him. This was not my best friend. This was hatred, years of it, boiling over until she forgot herself. She had let it consume her, just as I had.

"Stop!" I rammed into her before she could stab the high priest, and he fell over, covering his head.

Frustration welled up in Ua as she slammed her hand on the ground, about to yell at me. She had never done this before, never had a temper, never even raised her voice.

And she had especially never gotten angry at me. Surely we had both been consumed by our demons at some point. And I would not let her regret her actions.

Instead of fighting my best friend, I ran towards the high priest. The amazed look in his eyes as he recognized me made my insides squirm.

Someone knows we're alive. Well, he knew *I* was alive.

"You were in the cave..." the high priest muttered. "Dead... the king mourned your death, and the captain's..."

"Well I'm back from the dead," I said, grabbing his hands and lashing them together with rope. He didn't resist, but only stared in pure terror, like he really was seeing a ghost. "I'm not going to kill you," I said.

Ua grumbled from the darkness and the high priest started shaking. Did he really think I was dead? He was spooked to his core.

"But I have conditions. You have to swear that you never saw me."

"'Ae..." He started shaking even more violently, his eyes wide.

"And you have to stop putting the spells on the king."

"I can't do that."

At his words, I put the knife to his throat. "Swear you'll remove all his spells of invincibility, and you will never cast another again... on him, on his soldiers, or the warriors."

I pressed the cold stone against his skin and the apple on his throat bobbed as he swallowed hard.

"I..."

"Swear it all, or I'll kill you." This felt more like me. I could threaten, but I wouldn't actually kill him. The look in his eyes told me that he was beyond terrified, and he would agree.

"I..." he sucked in short breaths. "I swear it."

"Swear what?"

"I never saw you. And I'll take off the spells... And I will never cast another spell on the king."

"Or his warriors–" I started.

"Or his warriors or soldiers or any of his men," he stuttered.

In the black forest behind the high priest, Ua folded her arms and lifted her chin, pleased with my actions. We'd probably have a long talk about it later though.

"You swear it on your life?"

"I would rather die than tell a lie." His breath came out foul and rotten, and he looked sick. It was strange to see him like this, in his most vulnerable state.

"Good. You can tend to your king, but if you should *ever* break your oath, I will find you."

He shuddered, and my heart rested knowing that he was too scared to ever do such a thing. He had truly been spooked to the deepest fiber of his being. Why he was spooked didn't make sense to me–perhaps he really thought he'd seen a ghost, or perhaps his life had never been at the hands of someone so young...

When I let him go, he fell to his knees, scurrying away like an animal. He looked back at me, his eyes still possessed like he saw something from the other side, then he stood and ran away.

A stillness overcame me.

I didn't kill him. Because I was a protector. A hand sat on my shoulder and I turned to face Ua. In the moonlight, her eyes watered.

"Ka'ala..."

"I know." I didn't let her finish, but I understood every-thing. I understood completely each emotion she went through, and the hatred and resentment she held for the king and the wars.

But it was never enough to take a life. We were protectors of our people in Lanai, of the people of Hawaii. Though our skills made it possible for us to cause harm, we were not killers.

"Thank you," she said, and we hugged. I loved my best friend, and my heart welled in gratitude for her goodness and service throughout the years.

I would truly miss her, but it gave me comfort that she would have Kona, her sweetheart. We didn't need to talk about it, because we had a common understanding.

"Do you think the guys got the warriors out?" I asked.

"I don't know, but if they did, we should help Melika get those refugees out."

Right. Melika was on her own tonight, getting the wounded Kohala warriors out of the sanctuary and to the shoreline, with the hope that Kona, Ali'i, and Kekoa had freed the warriors.

We intended for the Kohala warriors to sail home that very night, but there was no sense in sending them away without their wounded back at the sanctuary. The wounded would get the help and attention they needed back in their homes at Kohala.

"Let's hurry," I said, and started to run. But before I did, Ua hesitated.

"What about the king?"

We both looked back to the edge of the clearing, where he lay on the ground, vomit all over his chin and kihei.

"Ugh." I touched the bridge of my nose.

"We'll leave him... for old time's sake?" Ua asked, a smile now emerging on her face, the darkness and hatred that once consumed her completely vanished. I smiled back, grateful that we both worked through our own dark nights.

"'Ae, for old time's sake." We ran through the forest, towards the sanctuary, and neither of us looked back.

CHAPTER THIRTY

S ilence filled the sanctuary as Ua and I stepped onto the creaking porch and inside. There was nobody on watch, and nobody within, meaning that all the refugees had decided to flee with the Kohala warriors.

I didn't blame them, and I would have made the same choice if I were in their positions. Melika had probably told the refugees that Nai'a would come to get them, but why wait around, when they could flee to safety, away from the hands of King Hua now?

"That's a lot of people for Melika to handle, especially with the wounded," Ua said, already running off the porch and out the gate. I hesitated.

"What's wrong?" Ua stopped outside the gate.

"I just..." I looked at the hut, built years ago, that had housed so many people. It had been a place of safety, a haven from the bloody battles. If Ali'i and I left tonight, I would probably never see it again.

"It's been a good place."

"It has. And we'll take care of it," Ua assured me. Her voice gave me the strength I needed to keep going. I was very weary, exhausted from everything that had happened. But we had to catch up and help Melika.

I took one last look at the sanctuary, and my heart swelled in gratitude. It had been a good time, and had served so many people. My courage grew in this very place, and my dedication to protect served a purpose.

Ua and I ran along the path, keeping an eye out for any signs of Melika and the others. It'd be hard to keep that many people hidden. Perhaps she separated them into groups.

Either way, I hoped she was alright.

Anxiety panged my chest when we found no signs of her along the path. We stopped by several of our hiding places, but there was no trace of her.

"She's getting really good at this," Ua observed.

Why am I so worried? I should have had more faith, like Ua. Melika was doing an excellent job, so excellent that I couldn't even find her trail.

Melika will take care of the sanctuary, the refugees, and she'll be fine. The protective side of me worried, but the other part of me felt peace.

Though I hadn't ended the war, I still did my part to help out. Everything would work out as it should.

"There!" Ua sprinted and I struggled to keep pace. The Kohala warriors helped people onto the king's large canoe. I justified that it wasn't stealing because Prince Kekoa gave them permission. And besides, the king could get back to Hana another way.

As we stepped into the water, Aliʻi wrapped his arm around me and kissed my temple.

"Did we get everyone out?" I asked, my hands sweaty.

"Everyone," Kona said, appearing from the other side of the canoe and hugging me. My heart felt like it would burst.

He then returned to his task of helping an elderly refugee on board.

"Where's Melika?" I looked about, seeing the refugees and the prisoners, but no sign of my sister. Before Aliʻi, or anyone else, could answer, a head popped over the canoe and a bright smile beamed down at me.

"I'm alright Kaʻala. You shouldn't worry so much."

A deep breath of relief escaped me and I reached up to touch her hand. "It was easier than I thought to get everyone out," she said.

"But we have to hurry." Prince Kekoa slipped off the canoe and into the water. "Those guards and the king will awaken from their drunkenness sometime."

"I doubt the king will wake up til morning," Ua said, and we made eye contact, knowing exactly what happened.

Within a matter of minutes, the Kohala warriors and ex-prisoners told us they were ready to depart. The one with the wounded face lay on the canoe, with the other refugees around to tend to him.

"Is he going to be alright?" I asked, and Melika nodded.

"He's doing much better, thanks to Aliʻi's remedy. I stole it from father's hut."

Father. Oponui. He was someone I certainly would not miss.

"Good luck," Prince Kekoa said to the warriors. "May you have safe travels, good health, and bright spirits."

"Mahalo, your highness," said one of the warriors, bowing. "We owe you a great deal." He scanned the group of us as we stood in the water. "All of you."

"Farewell," Melika said, waving. The warriors bowed to her, then Aliʻi, Kona, and Kekoa pushed the canoe out to sea. My heart warmed, knowing that they would be safe, free from the tyranny of the king of Hana.

CHAPTER THIRTY-ONE

*W*e split ways then met up in one of our secret hiding places. I went with Ali'i, holding his hand and feeling grateful the entire time. Kona and Ua went a different path to the hiding place, and Melika seemed all too excited to go with Prince Kekoa.

But I saw that something within her had changed. She didn't look at Prince Kekoa in a way that young teenage girls would. Rather, she admired him, and that mark of maturity made me feel even more confident in her ability to put her duty over emotions.

I still didn't see a future between her and the prince. He was too solemn, and she was too bubbly. But... who knew what the future held?

I let out a quiet sigh as we traversed the forests of Lanai.

It's over. All of it. As a team, we freed the Kohala prisoners, got the refugees to safety, and even managed to convince the high priest to stop his spells and magic.

Now the goodbyes were the last thing to do. My heart vacillated between excited and feeling accomplished, to dreading the goodbye. Would I ever see my siblings again? Or Ua? Or Kekoa?

I knew they'd be able to run the operations without me, but... would this place ever see peace again?

Kekoa and Melika waited at the spot, engaged in a quiet conversation. Melika focused on something in her hands, though it was dark to see. Ua and Kona arrived at the same time that Aliʻi and I did.

"We did it," I said, and hugged my sister. Ua joined while the guys stayed back. I wiped a tear, the pride and accomplishment in my chest a bit much to bear.

"I have something for Ua," Melika said, pulling away. She placed a viney, fern-like haku lei on Ua's head.

"Prince Kekoa said he'll perform the marriage for you both now."

"Oh." Ua's cheeks warmed in the moonlight. She took Kona's hands while Aliʻi, Melika, and I stood back. My heart couldn't take it. This was all so wonderful. And yet so sad. Aliʻi and I were leaving... and I wouldn't see these people for a long time, if ever again.

Prince Kekoa performed the ceremony, his face sober, as usual. His green eyes glistened in the moonlight as he spoke kind words, blessing their marriage. As he spoke, Melika wove more leaves and vines together to form a long, stringy green lei. It wasn't traditionally made, but it would work.

The prince placed it around Ua and Kona, representing that their union was bound.

When he finished, the two kissed, sealing the deal. After we gave them our congratulations, my heart dreaded the next part: goodbyes.

Everyone seemed to feel the dread looming above our heads, the inevitable end.

"Where will you go?" Prince Kekoa asked, the first to address what the rest of us didn't want to.

Ali'i squeezed my hand and looked down at me. "We haven't figured that out yet."

"Kauai is a free land," the prince said, "With great ali'i and plenty of land. Not to mention it's far."

"I've heard wonderful things about Kauai," Melika said, but her voice came out tight. Ua nodded, but her watery eyes revealed her true feelings.

"We'll take care of the refugees and the sanctuary sis," Kona said, stepping forward to hug me. The tears flowed down my cheeks. I would miss my brother.

"And I'll take care of the king," Kekoa said, after I stepped away from my brother. I hugged him, feeling as though Kekoa, too, had been another brother. I pulled away, feeling a strange energy from him.

"Kekoa..."

The prince's eyes held no happiness in them. They never had—he had been raised by a vicious father, one who almost killed him. His mother didn't care for him, and he had never had any hope... until he met Ua and I. I could still remember his eagerness to help us, even when we didn't believe him at first.

I don't want him to feel as Ua and I did.

"You don't have to kill the king."

He hesitated. "It's my responsibility."

"You're doing more than enough."

"But with the high priest undoing every spell that's ever been done, there's a chance that..." He looked away.

"A way to end the wars will present itself," I said, putting a hand on his shoulder. "And you will know what to do when that time comes."

A glimmer of hope ran through the prince's eyes. It happened so quickly, I wasn't sure if I'd even seen it or not.

"Thank you, Ka'ala. Your bravery and wisdom will be greatly missed."

I tipped my head to him, letting him and Ali'i say their goodbyes.

I turned to my sister, her eyes fresh with water. There were no words I could say, so I just hugged her.

You're going to do amazing, Melika. You already have. I'm so proud of you. None of the words came out, and I could only hold her, tears streaming down my cheeks.

"Will we ever see you again?" Melika asked, her voice strangled between sobs.

"I don't know." A hole formed in my heart at the thought of the unknown. I might never see my family again, see their families grow, watch as Melika found her true love, or as Kona and Ua had children... I wouldn't be able to help with the sanctuary, or be able to see the two islands finally have peace with one another.

Yet a string of hope floated around me. *I have Ali'i.* And I trusted these people, even though we'd be miles apart: my siblings, Ua, and Kekoa. One day these wars would end—whether by our playing a part in it or not. But everything we did, and what they would do, was worth it... including my going away.

This probably would have had to happen at some point.

"I trust you Melika," I said, pulling away and holding her hands. Kekoa shifted.

"I have a feeling the king's guards are out now. We should split ways."

I hugged Melika one last time, and Ua joined. We said no words, but we didn't need to. As I stepped back and took Ali'i's hand, a new strength came into me.

I have Aliʻi. It seemed that no matter what, I had him. He had me. Things would work out the way they should.

Perhaps this would be my last glance at my siblings, or perhaps it wouldn't. Though I hated the unknown, I felt peace in my heart.

Things will be alright. They always were, as long as we focused on our purpose, to protect. As Aliʻi pushed his small canoe out to sea, I watched my siblings and friends waving from the shore.

I couldn't help crying again as I waved back. They split up and went their separate ways, as staying around would be dangerous. No doubt the high priest sent guards out, and soldiers went around the island, looking for the prisoners.

King Hua would be furious the following morning, and he would return empty-handed to Hana: no prisoners, no sacrifices, and not even one of his highest captains.

"Are you alright?" Warm hands wrapped around my waist, and a soft kiss was planted on my jaw.

"I'm going to miss them."

"I know." Aliʻi took a slow breath. "I hope one day we can return... in secret." I felt his grin against my cheek. "Undercover, just like your operations."

I couldn't help but smile, still watching the shore. A figure stood on the edge of the cliff and waved one last time: Melika.

She had gone to our spot on the cliff to watch our canoe sail away. That had been the place I accidentally bumped into Captain Naha, and where Aliʻi and I fought. Not only that... It was where I fought all my emotions and let my hatred blind me from my purpose.

But not anymore.

I was with Aliʻi now, his hands around me in a protective and loving way.

I waved one last time to my sister, sending an invisible message of love, comfort, and assurance. Melika would handle the sanctuary phenomenally. Though every part of me ached at the thought of never seeing her again, a peace settled over us.

"Undercover..." I whispered, and held Ali'i's arms.

"Remember that one time we were on that cliff?" he asked.

"I'll never forget it." I turned around to face him, putting my arms around his neck. The moon glistened on him, and the aching in me turned to hope.

We were free, and though the wars weren't over, though my sister would now run the sanctuary, Ali'i and I had a life together. I could be with the man I loved, and there would be nobody to stop me.

"You saved my life," I said, and I didn't just mean in the cave. Ali'i smiled and brushed his lips against mine.

"I'd do it a thousand times over if it meant we'd be together."

I didn't hesitate and kissed him. The canoe skimmed over the waves, taking us towards our freedom and our life together.

CHAPTER THIRTY-TWO

*T*he legend of Ka'ala, the young, beautiful woman who died in the Spouting Cave with her sweetheart, circulated as far as Kauai, where Ali'i and I settled down. Nobody knew it was us though, as Ka'ala was a frequent enough name. The legends made it seem as though the story wasn't real, or it had happened decades ago.

But it had been no more than two years since Ali'i and I fled Lanai. The chiefs in Kauai welcomed us with open arms and we built a home by the beach, my favorite place.

In between work and the mundane of life, Ali'i and I surfed, helped in the community, and sent supplies and resources to aid in the war. I was happy with him, but often found my thoughts wondering about my siblings.

The war against Hana and Kohala eventually ended, and with its end, I longed to return to Lanai, to see my siblings, to know that they were alright. But while life with Ali'i had been wonderful, we had our fair share of trials. Ali'i and I had suffered much loss, and my health hadn't been the same since I was left in the Spouting Cave.

The trauma of it left me more anxious than ever, and I

had suffered from several infections which left me with different sicknesses I'd probably bear for the rest of my life. Perhaps I wouldn't have the energy to leave Kauai and make the journey back to Lanai. And I'd have even less energy to do things undercover.

So I hoped one day Melika, Kona, and Ua would come to find me.

A BRIGHT CRISP morning on Kauai greeted me with its usual cool breeze. The sweet smell of flowers and rain filled the air around mine and Ali'i's home as I picked flowers and sat in the grass. Ali'i had left earlier that morning for a quick surf session, and he now came up the path to our hut.

Our hut was not elaborate—nothing like the one I had Akamu build for the refugees—but it was enough. Two little girls sat on the grass, making lei and chatting.

"Father's home," I said, and they looked up, big smiles on their faces. The girls ran to hug him, and I stood, dusting my skirt off. While Ali'i and I had gone through several misfortunes of our own, we took in the two girls when their own mother passed away. We were not related by blood, but my commitment to protect the innocent never wavered. The girls brought joy into our lives after we suffered too much heartache, pain, and loss of our own.

Ali'i dropped his board, laughed, and scooped them into his arms. "What were you little beauties up to?"

The girls giggled and ached to show him their work. He let them on the ground then beamed at me, putting his hands on my shoulders.

"And what have you been up to this morning?"

I moved a wet piece of hair from his face, feeling the scar on his cheek. The wars, the refugees, the spells, the magic... all of that seemed so long ago. Yet my feelings for Aliʻi remained the same.

He was about to lean in to kiss me, but a bunch of flowers sprouted between us.

"Look!" The girls held up their flower crowns, briefly distracting Aliʻi. I watched him, grateful for the life and family we were creating. It was much different than I imagined, but still beautiful in its own way. When he looked back at me, the kindness in his eyes was apparent.

"You were beautiful on the day I first saw you," he said, and winked. "But each day you become more and more beautiful to me." His words melted my heart, just like they always would. The memory of his double-take when we first encountered each other came to my mind.

He loved me. He always did. I stepped on the tips of my toes to kiss him, and he pulled me close to him. Loving Aliʻi would never get old. The girls giggled and Aliʻi broke away too soon.

"I actually have to tell you something..."

I raised an eyebrow, pressing closer against him.

He kissed my jaw. "I saw an unfamiliar canoe pulling onto the shores."

My heart skipped a beat. "Wait... what?"

"It looks like a canoe built using the skills from Lanai. There was a group of people on board, and..."

"And?" I took Aliʻi's hands, my legs starting to shake.

"I saw a few people that I recognized."

I squeezed Aliʻi's hands so tight, he shook them loose and pulled me into his embrace, one hand holding my head in a protective way. "Deep breaths, love."

I held him, trying to breathe, my excitement deepening. "Is Melika there?"

He rubbed my back. "You'll see. I told them where we

live. They'll come as soon as the inspections on their boat are over."

Overwhelmed by emotion, I let Ali'i hold me up.

"Are you alright Ka'ala?"

"'Ae." It had just been so long, and the wars never seemed to end.

"Are you worried?" The tightness in his voice made me feel anxious, but only for a moment.

"No..." I regained my composure and smoothed my hair back. "I've loved our life together Ali'i. I have missed my family, but I don't want you to ever think our life hasn't been good. It's been wonderful." I drew closer to him. "You've made me the happiest I could ever be, and your protection and love means everything to me."

His look only softened. "But it's also been hard."

"As any life would be, but we're together. We've had each other." I touched his cheek once more. "I am happy."

He moved a loose piece of hair from my face. "I am too. It's my greatest honor to love and protect you."

"And now we get to love and protect these little ones too," I said, smiling at the girls as they continued to make their leis. "I can't wait for Melika and Ua to meet them."

The girls looked up. "You mean aunty Melika and aunty Ua?" Their big smiles showed everything–the stories I shared with them about the sanctuary, the night operations, and more...

"They'll be here soon," I said, memories resurfacing: the children refugees, the infant Keola (who, at this point, would be two years old!), and all the refugees. Their faces came to mind, and gratitude welled up inside of me.

I was trained to protect, not to kill, and I would continue to live up to that for the rest of my life.

"You ready?" Ali'i asked, taking my hand as a group of people started up the path towards our home.

"Because you're here, I'm always ready," I said, and smiled at him. He had been watching the group, but his attention returned to me. I let go of his hand to take his arm, always loving the way it felt. I remembered once feeling obsessed with them, and now I simply enjoyed Ali'i and his presence.

My heart felt like it would leap out of my chest at the sight of Melika, Ua, Kona, and some little ones walking beside them.

I ran to greet my sister and Ua, as they ran towards me at the same time. Tears streamed down our cheeks as we embraced.

Life was good, and as long as I kept my sights on the right thing, it would always work out the way it should.

THE END

A NOTE FROM THE AUTHOR

Did you know that thousands of children are trafficked a year? It's a heartbreaking fact and it needs to stop. We need to protect our children, the innocent. Like Kaʻala, we can't do everything. But we can and should play a role in our communities. Maybe we can't change policy or have the media expose this atrocity, but we still have an opportunity to help.

I invite you to check out, support, and raise awareness for anti-trafficking organizations like the O.U.R. (Operation Underground Railroad). Be a modern day abolitionist in the fight against slavery. Educate yourself, know the signs, and do what you can to protect your family and community. Mahalo for your kōkua in the fight against modern day slavery. We can and must win this battle for our children, for the innocent, for the future.

Love,
Leialoha

ALSO BY LEIALOHA HUMPHERYS

Self Help

Aloha State of Mind

You Belong: Conversations on Color, Culture, & Christianity

Kaimana Island Duology

Rise of the Manō

Enchanted Hawai'i Collection

1. Lehua (A Rapunzel Retelling)

2. Haukea (A Snow White Retelling)

3. Ka'ala (Inspired by the legend of Ka'ala)

4. Kaikilani (Inspired by the legend of Kaikilani and Lonomaika'i)

5. Loke (A Sleeping Beauty Retelling)

6. Alamea (Inspired by the legend of King Hua of Hana)

$\sim$ More stories to come soon $\sim$

ACKNOWLEDGMENTS

First and foremost, all thanks and glory be to God. Sometimes we wonder why bad things happen to good people and while I don't know all the answers, I know that God knows. He loves and wants the best for us. While we can't do everything, we should all do what we can to be instruments in His hands.

Mahalo Iesu. Jesus is the Savior and Redeemer of the world. When we feel despair, hopeless, or lost, we can always turn to Him for comfort and peace. I am so grateful for that.

As always, thank you to my amazing husband, Jordan. You are my favorite person and I couldn't do this without you. Thank you for supporting and providing for our little family, helping my creativity and books come to life. I love you so much!

A huge thank you to my sister, Kamele, for beta-reading my book and giving valuable feedback, as always. I appreciate your support and enthusiasm for my work. It means so much to me.

Finally, mahalo to the rest of my fans and readers. Every review, email, and DM you send me with your kind words is deeply appreciated!

ABOUT THE AUTHOR

Originally from the Big Island of Hawaii, Leialoha Humpherys loves God, her husband (Jordan), and good food, of course! She graduated with a Bachelor's degree in English from the University of Hawaii at Hilo. Her debut novel, *Aloha State of Mind*, a self help book about creating paradise where you are, was published in 2021 and has been followed by fairy tale retellings, young adult, and epic fantasy novels set in ancient Hawaii. Leialoha loves the ocean, Hawaiian culture and folklore, creating things from her imagination, and anything with coconut. She and her husband currently live in the small town of Santaquin, Utah and have fun making cool stuff together.

If you want to stay updated on Leialoha's books and projects, sign up for her newsletter at www.naturallyaloha. com/newsletter or connect with her via social media below:

Email: leialohahumpherys@gmail.com

Website: www.naturallyaloha.com

Instagram: @ladyleialoha
YouTube: Kanani Life

Made in the USA
Las Vegas, NV
28 November 2022

60587751R00199